GREAT BRITISH HORROR VIII

SOMETHING PECULIAR

Great British Horror VIII
Something Peculiar

Edited by
Steve J Shaw

**BLACK
SHUCK
BOOKS**

First published in Great Britain in 2023 by
Black Shuck Books
Kent, UK

Set in Caslon by WHITEspace
www.white-space.uk

Cover design and interior layout © WHITEspace, 2023
Cover image courtesy of The Wellcome Collection

978-1-913038-84-7

In memory of Christopher Fowler

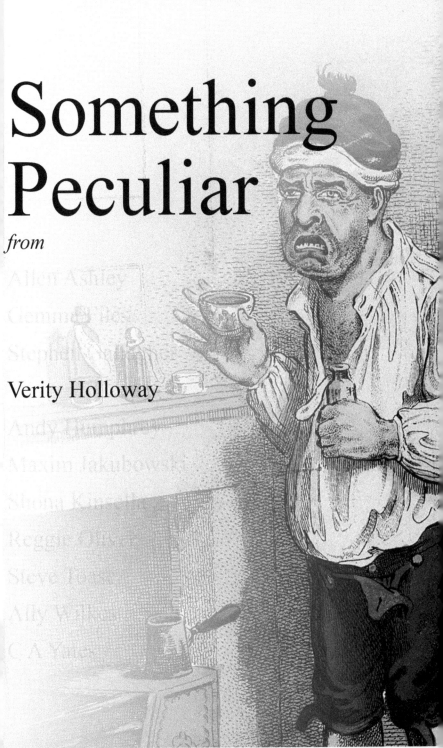

Something Peculiar

from

Verity Holloway

The Subtle Feast

"...fluency in the language of omens and portents..."

I WAS born with the cord tight around my throat, blue in the lips and silent. Midwives talk of babies who slip from the womb with the caul stretched thin over their eyes, granting them fluency in the language of omens and portents. We don't entertain such ideas where I'm from, but as the judge bowed his head for the Black Cap, my urge was to laugh. I had long known that if I, Amos Hynde, were to die, it would be at the end of a rope, by Edward's side.

Enter the world dead, leave it kicking. I turned to Edward in the dock, watched his black eyes pass over the assembled court like none of them were fit to buff his boots. Years spent by his side, tending to his peculiar wants, protecting him from them as best I could, and for what? Looking back at our time spent together, I could barely grasp it. Snatched memories stuffed into my pockets along with jewellery pilfered at gunpoint. I always had struggled to recall all but the most potent recollections.

"It's alright, Aim," Edward said as we were bundled down into the dripping cells. "It's for the best."

And the bailiffs glanced at each other so queerly.

A hare gambols across the field. Amber eyes, crackling with moon-craters, it fears nothing and knows plenty. Amos knows such fancies are superstition, but he feels a chill down his neck all the same, standing on the roadside with his collar high about his cold ears, watching these animals with their supernatural speed and their wise, desperate faces.

It's something to do, the endless walking; something other than embroidery or cheesemaking. Hares. Fields. The slate spire of Saint Peter's. Father's sheep bumbling beneath like balls of cotton. Amos is never fully here. At the dinner table, saying grace with his parents and two brothers, he feels a lightness in his bones, as if it's only the weight of the mutton and potatoes inside of him that stops him fluttering away like a piece of cheesecloth in the wind.

"We've the funds to rent a townhouse in London," Father says one evening, his smile shyly proud on his craggy face as he spoons at his stew. "Imagine that. A bolthole, a place to do business. Mary, you could travel down with us, see the latest fashions. John and Samuel can hold the fort."

London. The word touches Amos like a leech underwater. A place he's never seen, nor knows the size or shape of. London, testing his skin for an inroad. A tickling underfoot that frightens him a little, yet excites him.

He nearly feels a true emotion for the first time in months.

I was wandering the shore of the Thames when I first encountered Edward. A foggy evening, clinging cold to my bare throat. Hunger gnawed me hollow. I had no bed for the night and no coin for a meal; only my meanderings kept the blood pumping. I must have been robbed – I cannot recall. Father always warned me about the dangers of the city, how a young man with an open face is a target for all sorts of villainy. I never listened to my father. He was a business-minded man, his head stuffed with wool, and despite his gentle nature we rarely saw eye-to-eye. He had hopes for me that were impossible to meet.

And then there was Edward. A motionless shape in the fog, slender as a reed, though few things grew in the brackish filth where the barges bobbed between the drooling sewer mouths. So like pipe smoke was the night air, I couldn't tell if this stranger was staring out at the waters or back at me. This was Wapping. They hanged buccaneers here and left them to dangle; I could remember that much. If I believed in restless spirits, I would surely have mistaken him for one.

He bent down, as if noticing something near his feet. I heard the mud sucking at his boots. If he wasn't careful, he would lose them. I had heard stories of children drowning in the mud, of careless drunks found tangled in fishing nets like bloated river monsters.

I called out: "Sir, the mud is treacherous."

"Mind your business," came his answer. A voice dark and sweet, like sailors' rum.

"Can't," I said, stepping closer until my boots touched the worm-eaten slats of the jetty between us. Again, I called to him, keeping my tone light: "What's that you've found?"

His head turned, long hair flying. "A ring."

I was surprised he answered me so affably; candid and animated, like a child. "Well, then," I went on. "Can't sell it if you drown."

I saw it in the lights of a passing barge: he slipped the ring onto his finger. After a lingering look at the boats bobbing in the scum, he trudged with difficulty up the bank and faced me. We were the same age, I realised, only he was tall and well-formed where I resembled an ale cask. My mother often spoke wistfully of young brides in the village blessed by beautiful babies, implying that she herself was cursed. This young stranger, with his crinkled black hair and round, mobile eyes, was blessed in looks, alright. But he carried himself like a man condemned.

He studied my face, as if trying to place me within some dim memory. Son of a prosperous man though I am, I was dressed like any other youth seeking his way in the city. He would later tell me I reminded him of a hound; bright-eyed and eager, pleased with myself to have captured such vermin as he.

"Amos Hynde," I offered.

My hand remained at my side, but he snatched it up, pumping it with muddy enthusiasm. "Edward Rooke. When I'm hungry, I get the most morbid fancies. Supper? I know a cheap place."

You would have followed him too.

He walked me to a crooked little inn behind the boat builder's yard. We shared a bowl of gristly mutton stew there, and too much watered-down wine.

With the firelight catching in his overlong hair, he supped with one eye on the door, restless even then, before we'd begun our strange partnership. His glance flashed at me, looking me over in greedy draughts. We were equal in our shabbiness – I couldn't recall when I had last had the chance to bathe and launder my clothes – but Edward, furtive though he was, possessed a hauteur that left me in awe.

"It's a gesture of comradeship to share food," he said, chewing. "Trust and all that."

"I'm happy to be eating at all," I replied.

"Are you? I forget more often than not. I need a wife. Someone to nag me." As he used his knife to pick at a knot of gristle between his teeth, he admired the ring he found in the mud. "Glad I didn't come away empty-handed."

He held out his hand as if inviting me to kiss it. A nice little trinket – gold, with a skull carved into the band, wide and flat like an autumn gourd. A lady's mourning band, lost in the river's black silt.

"I'll keep it," he said, adding cheerfully: "I was planning to drown myself."

"I know."

And I did, that's the thing. A *thump-thump-thump* in the hollow parts of myself spoke of danger and then there Edward was, on the precipice.

He regarded me. "Amos Hynde… What brings you to the city, Aim?"

Wanderlust. Pride. I'd wanted to see real streets, the bustle of industry, like the bargemen around us now, laughing between gulps of ale. No, these were lies. I wished to become new.

"Nothing in particular," I said. "My family are in wool, up east."

"How boring."

I liked his ability to cut right to the heart of things. We smiled at each other.

He nodded at my hand, cradling my cup. "What happened there?"

My own ring finger on the right hand was little more than a stump. An old wound, well healed, and barely noticeable to myself except when I attempted to handle a quill.

When I didn't answer, Edward brought the knife to his gleaming teeth and gave it a teasing lick. "Sheep bite it off?"

John finds Amos at the millpond. The turbines spray cool droplets with every turn. Horace, the miller's donkey, gives the occasional docile haw *as he turns the millstone inside. The grass is crisp in the summer sun, and the girls of the parish have gathered in the meadow, making corn dollies for the children. When they saw Amos trudging up the lane, they laughed at the acid commentary of Hannah Catchpole, the miller's daughter, always ready with a cutting remark. Amos kept his gaze averted.*

A hare keeps him from total solitude. It sits on the far side of the pond, long paws tucked catlike, resolutely paying Amos no attention. It feels respectful, somehow, this shared disinterest, and Amos offers mutual deference by enjoying the shade in silence.

His brother, of course, has to intrude.

"Are you not making dollies?" John asks. He stands in the sunbeam, picking whiskers of corn from his coat.

"Don't make me laugh."

"Father received a letter. The house in London – the lease is his. I'll be travelling down with him to investigate the cloth markets. I'm sure he'll invite you and mother, when the place needs titivating and such…" John shields his eyes from the sun. "Is that a rabbit?"

He scoops up a stone from the pond's edge.

Amos says, "Don't."

"They eat the crops."

"They have to eat something."

John throws the stone. It lands wide, bouncing down the bank and disappearing into the pond's rim of algae with a plop. The hare is unbothered.

"It's sick, probably," John says. "They go blind."

He hurls another stone. It strikes the hare in the chest with a hollow sound.

Amos sits up. "John!"

The hare still doesn't flee. Its great ears flatten behind its skull, giving the face a gaunt, old-mannish appearance Amos finds momentarily appalling. He is struck by the sudden impression that John would stone him, too, if it were permitted. The village girls would take their turn, no doubt, giggling as pebbles pitted his cheek, specked with the black whiskers Hannah Catchpole calls his bumfluff.

Just then, there is a commotion from the mill. Horace the donkey is making a racket, and a man's cry follows, rabbit-shrill.

John gets to the mill first. He tries to shield Amos from the scene inside, but Amos sees enough from under John's arm. Catchpole the miller is bent double, pinned between the rolling millstones. His shoulder is hinged at an uncanny angle. The flour has turned to scarlet grit, trampled by Horace. Normally such a placid beast, the donkey rears with white-eyed panic, refusing to back up and release the stone from Catchpole's crushed arm.

John gives Amos a shove. "Run for the physician."

And a priest, *Amos does not add. But he runs all the same. As he takes off in the direction of the village, he notices the hare still loiters beside the pond, cleaning its whiskers.*

16

Our acquaintance was barely two weeks old when Edward and I committed the first of our robberies. "Beginner's luck?" I whispered, cramming candlesticks into a sack, but Edward was no novice housebreaker. He had watched the little house by the highway for some time and knew there was one old man inside, hard of hearing, and his sole maid was in love with the boy who sharpens the knives. She sneaked out for trysts when the master was abed and wasn't too cautious about locking the back door.

When Edward first suggested burglary – tossing the possibility at me like a plaything – I'd laughed, but he waited in quiet patience for me to come around to his will. He was accustomed to getting his own way, even then. I was incredulous enough, but penniless, and that night I'd followed him through the house's dark passages, hardly daring to breathe as the old man snored and farted in his chamber. We made off with a small fortune in silverware that night. The maid, I can only imagine, was dismissed. Later, I felt a twinge of guilt to think of it, holed up with Edward in our rented room decorated with river mud and the footprints of rats. But Edward's shining eyes as the fence handed over our ill-gotten gains banished all feelings of sympathy to the wind. Edward told me I brought him good luck. I basked in that praise as he lay twirling his hair around his finger, an undertaker's ribbon.

"Another tomorrow, then move on, I think. Bristol, perhaps. I hate the air here. You'll come, won't you, Aim?" He propped himself up on an elbow, beseeching me with his eyes, all bootblack and tragedy. "You must."

Once, I had feared my life contained no meaning. Now, it was my task to keep Edward Rooke content. This I knew in my bones.

There's a hammering at the door that wakes the whole household. John and Samuel race down the stairs in their nightshirts. Father is next, struggling into his banyan. Lastly, Amos escorts Mother to the panelled hall. Catchpole the miller was laid to rest early last week, but ever since the funeral Mother has been restless, sensitive to the rumours passing amongst the goodwives of the village. One cannot blame an animal for taking fright and causing an accident. One can, however, speculate on the cause of the shock, particularly when Catchpole – ignoring the urgings of the parish reverend – had refused to put a name to it.

John is already unlocking the door. "Someone needs help," he says, though how he can know that is a mystery to Amos. The thumping fills the hall.

Mother hangs back, fearful of robbers. "At this hour?"

Father, with poker in hand, herds John away. "Who goes there?" he calls out, and for a moment the noise ceases. "This is a private house."

The Hyndes listen out, holding their breath. Just as Father looks about to speak, the racket resumes with vigour, as if the visitor is pounding with both fists and a boot.

Samuel, the most prudent of Amos' brothers, rushes to the parlour where there is a clear view to the front door. He presses his face to the glass window there.

"They've hidden themselves," he calls to us, though this can't be true. The hammering on the door is insistent as ever. Samuel's eyes must be dim with sleep.

"Enough," says Father. Poker raised and ready, he gestures a count of three, and when he hauls open the heavy door as quick as his stiff old back will allow, the family are met with an unexpected sight.

Amos urges Mother back to the stairs. "Who is it?" she asks, her voice high with dread.

Father lowers the poker. Amos can't see past him into the dark garden; his brothers, taller than him, jostle to peer over Father's shoulder.

But the boys are laughing with relief. Father gestures with his chin. "Don't be afraid, my dear. Look at him. Bold as brass."

Around the well, Mother's daffodils sway in the night breeze. The moon is nothing more than a silvery suggestion behind the cloudbank. On the front step, where Amos kicks the mud off his boots after walking in the fields, there sits a hare.

"Go on, young lass," Father tells it, mock stern now the threat has passed. "Leave us to our rest."

The hare regards them with unblinking amber eyes. Scruffy and long-limbed, it is no different to any other creature of the hedgerows, and yet there is a cool intelligence in the pinched face that Amos is unsure how to meet. He experiences a peculiar impulse to sketch a small bow, the way one must when presented with a lady.

"Witchcraft," Mother mutters. They scoff at her, the three sons. There are Papist symbols carved about the house by former occupants: wheels and aves on beams and around the fireplaces. Protection from the advances of evil. Mother unwisely refuses to have them scrubbed away, half-believing in their efficacy despite their idolatrous origins. The hare knows nothing of these protections. It watches the Hyndes without fear, even when Father waves the poker.

Amos steps out. "Let me."

We made for Bristol the following week, having fenced the old man's silverware. We resisted the urge to spend the proceeds on sleek new clothes that might arouse suspicion, though I did pine for a pair of the beautiful riding boots I saw on every smart young man in the capital. Edward couldn't resist a knife he noticed in a pawnbroker's window. Carved into the ivory handle, the words *I bite*.

Bristol was elbow-to-elbow with people, and rich as butter. We spent the summer there, hopping from inn to inn and helping ourselves to the customers' pockets as Edward pleased. Experiencing the city with Edward was thrill enough for me: coffee houses and confectioners and tobacconists and sailors, everywhere sailors, rowdy and roving. I feared them instinctively, being small and shabby – a natural target for brawlers who didn't fancy a challenge – but Edward kept his knife close to his right hand. No one would harm us, he said. He was protected.

"I must have been five, perhaps six," he told me one night over a third mug of ale. "My mother took me to a neighbour's house. The old woman there needed help to bathe, so my mother left me in the parlour while she did her duty – always applying some poultice or other, she was. I amused myself with the neighbour's trinkets. She had a basket of fir cones for kindling, and there was an old cat who wanted nothing to do with me. But a box beside the hearth caught my eye, the sort of box a boy might find a nice little knife in, you know. I opened it. I was disappointed. Nothing interesting inside, only a black leathery thing like an old root. I was examining it when Mother caught me; gave me a good smack. 'Not for you,' she said and snapped that box shut like there was rat poison inside."

"What was it?" I asked.

Edward licked the foam from his lips. "Take the hand of a hanged man while he still swings at the crossroads. Pickle it. A woman properly trained will know how to do the rest."

I didn't hide my revulsion. "The rest of what?"

"The Hand of Glory grants invisibility to a thief. It's a sought-after talisman in our circles, Aim. My old neighbour made one for her husband and he had a great career as a pinch-purse until the palsy took him. She taught my mother the trick of it, though she never used it. Couldn't quite stomach the corpsey business. She was more about candles and pennyroyal tea."

I was a little drunk, and my thoughts spilled across the table. "Your mother dabbled in witchery?"

Edward grinned at my horror. "Dabbled? Oh no, the full *maleficium* went on in our house. Love charms, getting rid of warts, solving unwed girls' problems, all that. If she'd been born a little earlier, I'm sure the witch finders would have pricked her. She always said she did it to provide for me. I found it stifling. Silly, really. She was only being a mother, in her way. But I had to leave, Aim. You know how it is with apron strings."

I supposed I could recall my mother well enough, though now, when I put my mind to it, I could only envision the worry she wore like a shawl tight around her shoulders. I upset her, I knew I did. The very sight of me, misshapen and swarthy beside lovely John and Samuel, her strong sons.

Edward reached across the sticky inn table and squeezed my hand.

"I'm bored," he said. "What say you and I find some mischief?"

With his family crowding at his back, Amos approaches the hare with cautious steps. The wild thing stares at him, coolly perceptive, though Amos knows he is projecting his own human sensibilities onto the animal. Mother is right, though – there is something witchy about the hare. Sent, perhaps, by one of the village's lonely crones, to frighten or to warn. Who knows why witches do what they do? Boredom, perhaps, a longing for life to be more than drudgery in draughty rooms. Amos can understand that much. And yet the hare's ragged fur is enticingly soft. It feels like a gift, dropped here in the middle of the night, to cling to and snuggle like a child with a poppet.

He slowly squats, puts out his hand.

A breeze steals through the garden, and the daffodils bow in unison.

Pain tears through Amos. He clutches his burning finger to his chest, but not before he sees the white slice of bone. Blood, hot, soaks through his nightshirt, and he topples backwards into the hall. It's bitten him, far worse than he would think possible. It's as if the hare has shears for teeth.

"Unnatural thing," Father cries, and before Amos can shield his face, John is there, bringing down the iron poker onto the hare's head. Amos doesn't know whose blood is whose, only that it is hot and holy on his lips.

People reacted to Edward, I learned, as the summer grew old. He was a swaggering pouch of gunpowder. People either fell for him in an instant or drew swords. Edward was happy enough to brawl, but he viewed adoration as merely his due and kept women at arm's length. On the rare occasion he did pick a paramour, we went to her together. Edward's wiry frame with its white tigerskin scars set a fire in me that felt like pride. The girls ignored me, scrunched up in the corner like a chaperone. Few people paid me attention, eclipsed by Edward's radiance. A small price to pay to be the first to see him in the morning and the last to watch over him at night.

But Edward's power needed fuel. Any time he wasn't the centre of attention, he crumpled. Ordinary – anything but that. He had to be the most admired, the source of light in any given room. More than once I saw him reduced to bitter tears by some meaningless slight, retreating to whatever flea-ridden mattress we'd rented for hours of silent brooding. I learned the knack of coaxing him back to life with praise and cheap thrills. *That fellow isn't watching his purse,* or *I bet we could clear out that shop one night.* And it worked, by God, though I felt those little sins hot within my chest, like burning chestnuts. Risks taken too lightly. I wondered how it would feel to be branded, or to be locked in the stocks. How it would feel to see Edward treated thus.

He would drift to some new diversion. I held fast to this conviction, though it felt more like superstition with every passing day.

One muggy August night, the press gang came to town. All the single men dropped their drinks and hid. Some pretended to be married, bribing publican's widows to hang on their arms, or skipped town completely, walking all night off-road so not to be caught and dragged back to ships bound for the Caribbean. We all knew the stories: anyone slowed by drink, or without a bed for the night – or even those who had – were snatched away, marched through the street, shivering and bewildered, towards the docks. Edward knew this dance. As soon as the men appeared, stalking down the street with their cudgels, he hauled me into the inn where we shared a room, half-dragging me up into the attic, and ordered me to hide behind some linen chests.

"What about you?" I whispered.

He tossed back his hair, scraping it into a ponytail. "Score to settle."

"You know these men?"

"They're not taking us, Aim." He paused, and when he blinked I saw the salt water brimming beneath the lashes. "Not again."

I lay in the attic for what felt like all night. What if he didn't come back? What would life be worth without him?

When he returned, he had with him an unfamiliar ditty bag slung over one shoulder. A bruise shone around one eye.

"What happened?" I asked.

"We're leaving."

"You're hurt."

"Stop mithering and get a move on."

Later, miles away, holed up in a stable with a loose door, I watched him scrubbing dried blood from his knife hand, the golden skull glinting there like an oath. He slept as I kept watch, and when we rose before dawn, he said nothing of the preceding night.

"Aim, I've had a thought…" he said, picking blackberries from the hedgerow for breakfast. "Do you shoot?"

Coaches, rattling along the highway. I'd lain awake listening to them all night. I saw his thoughts and my gut turned with dread.

Two weeks pass in sweats and sleepless nights. Amos is too tired to help Mother about the house, yet too sore to rest. The smell of dinner makes his brow prickle with nausea, even the fresh knots of bread Father brings home, and when he squats over the chamber pot his urine comes dark and pungent like bad ale.

"You look like a toad," John tells him, and Samuel agrees, though he musters a degree of sympathy.

"Cast your mind to wholesome things. Think of the new London house," he suggests. "Father says you can pick the drapes."

Amos' finger throbs and oozes. The thought of loitering in a draper's shop and making choosy sounds over bolts of damask makes his guts lurch. When the sun goes down, he stands at his open window in the blessed cool and looks out over the fields, stubbly after the harvest, and he wonders what might lay beyond them, mile after dark mile through the woods and the fallow. And where are the hares tonight? Tucked up in their solitary ditches, amber eyes squeezed shut? Or do they convene like old women in the secret places of the earth, making their pacts and sowing their schemes? If Amos could start his life over, say the right words and scratch the right sigils…

A cry from behind him startles him from his reverie. Mother is calling for aid. Amos is on his side, chin wet and slack against the rush mat. He can smell his own body down here, as if he is removed from himself, delivered of it: a miasma of sweat and sweet corruption.

Robbing coaches became Edward's favourite intoxicant.

We averaged one coach a week. The papers printed pictures of our deeds, horrid cartoons depicting Edward as a fiend with a corona of hair like a halo of smoke. They ignored my existence altogether. My dumpy body didn't lend itself to the high romance of crime.

HIGHWAYMAN: Edward thrilled at the word. It was shockingly easy, running down slow, trundling coaches driven by nervous men who'd never raised a fist in anger. Edward stopped them practically singlehanded. I stood by, the wordless accomplice, watching the desolate stretch of road with my pistol held aloft as if I knew how to use it. Women wept as Edward tore away their jewellery, sometimes putting it on over his mask and gloves, preening for his captive audience. Their husbands vowed we'd hang, and Edward gave that laugh of his, lovely devil that he was, and we'd disappear into the woods like ghosts.

I had hoped it would be enough.

One night, I was foolish enough to say so.

Edward was silent the whole ride back. At our rented room, he waited for me to turn the key in the lock before crushing me face-first into the door.

"Who are you?"

He forced me to my knees. There was something slack about his face, like a coney hanging in a poacher's hut. Before I could stutter out a response, he slid the pistol's barrel over my tongue. It was cold and tasted of soot. With my eyes I pleaded with him to recognise me as his friend, his Aim.

"Tell me!" He sprayed my face with spittle.

If his finger slipped, the death would be a bad one, blowing out the back of my throat to leave me choking on my own fluid. He wouldn't, not deliberately, but when he tumbled into one of his dark moods, there was no telling what he might regret later. *I bite*, said the knife in his belt. He was honest, my Edward. Like a gut wound.

"I ought to slit you stem to stern," came his shaking voice. "See what's inside."

He drew back, wiped the spit-wet gun on his breeches. He didn't meet my eyes as he reset the hammer, twisting the skull ring around his bony finger as if it might bring him back to God's miserable earth.

"We could give this up," I said, remaining on my knees. "Take our money and go somewhere far away, buy a little farm, raise sheep. I know how. We'd be happy. And safe."

And Edward fell upon the bed, disassembled there, hair falling over his dazed eyes. "I'd be bored. And I'd turn on you for it."

You can, I thought. *If you need to. Better that way.*

I licked the gunpowder from my teeth as I watched him drift into a fitful sleep. It was my task, after all, to keep him content.

The physician is summoned as Amos sweats and tosses in his bed. It must come off, the finger. The bite is ragged, seeping hot. Nothing for it. "It will be quick," Father promises, but doses him up all the same, with brandy and poppy and a lashing of prayer.

It comes like a second bite, a hard press of cold teeth and a burn that throbs and leaps with his heartbeat. He moans and struggles, but there are hands holding him down, and John's hot breath in his ear, unconvincingly jovial: "It's just a finger. You have others."

As Amos sleeps, he dreams of his mother speaking in a low voice.

"Nineteen years old and no courses. She used to pluck her chin every day, but now she lets the hairs grow. She's well-formed enough, but her voice is like a boy's…"

The blankets shift around him like dunes, and he kicks weakly, a thumpa-thumpa *drum of danger in his ears. The air is ice-sharp against his skin, and the strange hands on his thighs drag their calluses. He feels tight, swollen, like a ram rotting in the sun.*

"When she was born, the midwives had to rub her back to life like a pup. Not a sound out of her. Could the ordeal have… damaged her somehow?"

Amos' lips draw back from his teeth. Something, stirring on the distant surface of his consciousness, is wrong.

"We may yet have to take the arm," a man says. "I'm sorry."

The stack of pamphlets fluttered in the breeze outside the printmaker's shop. Edward had overheard a tipsy man in a tavern claim the owner kept obscene French works in a hidden compartment in the back room, along with a cash box and the details of his most discerning collectors. It was a different speed to highway robbery, but the parish constables had their eyes on the roads; it was almost time to move on. Edward couldn't resist novelty. Plus, there were posters of him in the window, a masked man festooned in bracelets and diadems. I should have worried: I would know those eyes anywhere. One admiring glance could hang us both.

I leafed through the pamphlets as Edward sauntered around, hands in pockets, evaluating the premises. Religious tracts were unusual where I came from. After the civil war, my father said, people were wary of zealotry. I leafed through the pages, my eye falling upon a line by some long-dead Puritan: "A good name is a thread tied about the finger, to make us mindful of the errand we came into the world to do for our master."

Edward glanced over my shoulder. "What does your name mean, Aim?"

Something prickled in my throat. I shrugged, willing it to pass. "'Carried by God', I believe."

"Carried." He considered this. "Don't make that face. Are you surprised I can read? I learned at my mother's knee. Not much, mind you: I was ten when I ran to the Navy. Thought the life of a powder monkey was one worth living." He kicked at a stone, sent it flying. "Idiot."

He linked his arm through mine. The *thumpa-thumpa* of my heart was sweet and painful. He rarely opened himself to anyone; these crumbs of his past were a banquet to me.

"What was she like, your mother?" I asked. "When she wasn't casting spells."

Edward took a breath and blew it out through puffed cheeks. "Sad. She had a great deal of cats. I was the only one of her children who lived. It turned her brain, I think. She had a habit of wafting candles around the house, calling it 'the subtle feast', feeding the familiars and the departed, you know."

"Have you eaten today?"

"Ah." He met my eye with a grin. "My wife didn't remind me."

"Shut up, you great lobcock." As I turned my flushed face, I saw the shopkeeper at the counter watching us, his expression one of hushed concern. Time to go. I gave Edward's boot a gentle kick.

"Come on, then," he said, directing a saucy look over his shoulder. "There's nothing of value here."

When he wakes, his arm is still attached to his trunk. Both of them, when he checks. And the surgeon has spared his legs, right and left, and each cold foot, and the thatch of hair on his head, and—

Eyes open. He's out in the fields in the shadow of St Peter's. He lies on his back inside a hard furrow, and the shock brings a wave of nausea he covers his mouth to fight. A viscous wetness cools between his legs. He tries to sit up, but there's a sucking, dragging sensation in his guts that makes him fall back and cry out for his mother. Mother has gone to London without him, perhaps, or accompanied the boys to church. Damaged, she said. He remembers it plainly: damaged, damned, a worn-out dam lapping at her litter, though the pups are all silent and still. He smells an iron torrent of blood like the ewes lambing in the shed, and Amos scrambles back in revulsion, but there it is, squealing between his hot wet thighs, fur flattened with slick, its long ears pinned back as if straining to make out a threat. Its shrill defiant cry sets Amos wailing in return. He gathers the hare to his heaving chest and presses his slippery fingertips to its eyelids, pleading with them to open, to acknowledge him, to just be careful, fragile thing, to survive this time, to fight the urge to die before life has even begun—

"Time to go, sirrah," coos a voice he doesn't recognise, a woman's, rum dark and irresistible. He looks around, but he can't see another soul in the windswept field, not so much as a rook.

He turns back to the hare and smooths the rumpled fur of its brow with the stump of his ring finger. Black stitches pucker the skin, a perfect match for the creature's whiskers.

"Come," the woman tells him. "Feast."

On my insistence, we took a light supper of cold chicken and weak ale before heading out to terrorise the highway. Edward was fidgeting with excitement. He kicked me beneath the table.

"This sheep farm of yours," he said, "what would I do there?"

I looked up, trying to keep the eagerness from my eyes. He had never brought the subject up before. I shrugged; he would lose interest if I looked desperate. "Frighten off wolves," I said, and stuffed my mouth to keep from saying more.

"There's no wolves left in England," he said glumly. "Not since the old Queen died."

I paused with a strip of chicken skin at my lips. "Queen Anne died? When?"

"I don't know. Years ago. We've got a German king now. Does news not reach Suffolk?"

I scratched at my scalp. I worried about my brain sometimes. Too much sun, perhaps, sitting out by the millpond on my own. But I felt that summer optimism now, watching Edward meander towards safety, boring and ordinary, and ours. I would buy a flock at auction, and he would fix us up a neat little paddock. Perhaps my father's dull instructions would be mesmerising in my hands, showing Edward the conjurer's trick of wool, how to turn raw fleece into something bright and covetable.

"Do you think—"

He waved a chicken bone, slick with grease. "One more coach, then we move on. And you'll come, Aim, won't you? To Cornwall or Norfolk or whatever little tedious backwater—"

"Yes," I said. I could do nothing else.

It was not our last robbery, nor even the second-to-last.

I once believed my life had no purpose or direction. That nothing I did or said was of any consequence. I was a flimsy thing buffeted by winds I neither perceived nor understood. But in Edward's presence, I felt like every minute decision of mine was heavy with cosmic consequence. If I failed to amuse Edward at breakfast, he might seek out a brawl by noon. If I glanced too long at a farrier's shop, Edward would catch a mania for horse theft. That would become our life for a month or two, until his whim was quenched. If I was remiss and didn't lock away our earnings in time, Edward would lose them at cards. If I counted them carefully and put them out of his reach, he would take to his bed in a funk that was mine to fix. I cleaned his wounds and watched the highways for danger; I nursed his sore head when he'd been in his cups; I kept his coat buttoned against the wind as if he were a child, even when the buttons were flaked with the blood of the fools who stood between Edward and his wants. Love fastened me to him like shackles of lead.

It couldn't save him.

They sent a runny-nosed reverend down to the cells to comfort us in our last days. I lay in the corner on some straw, leaving the bed for Edward. The reverend sat with him, noisily clearing his sinuses every minute or so. Marvellous: Edward and I would go to the gallows with a raging cold.

"I will pray with you," said the reverend, "if you'll allow it."

Edward shook his head, eyes drifting to the slit of window up near the ceiling. We could hear the carriages in the street outside, the cries of the costermongers and the link boys cursing as they dodged mounds of dung. "Can never tell who's listening," he said.

We would die together. All at once it became real to me: the reverend's black vestments, the cobwebs draping the cell's vaulted ceiling, the piss pot we'd been left to share. My parents would hear of this. Perhaps they would see my likeness in some broadsheet and feel a tingle of recognition. I could not recall their faces now, nor even their names – perhaps they had forgotten me too. A sob escaped me, and Edward heard it. I expected to see resentment in his eyes, but he turned his face to the reverend and spoke softly.

"The rumours that I killed a recruiter in Bristol: they're true. And before that, there was a stranger in London, Wapping way – I took his purse and dabbed him when he struggled. Don't know who he was, but his death is on me. A year or two prior, I fled the Navy the moment we made port. They'd flogged all the obedience out of me; this is what's left. Might as well hang me for all of it."

I knew none of this. My mouth dried up as I considered how to comfort him. "You were surviving…" I began, but he waved me silent.

"I could have survived on a tedious little sheep farm. I just didn't fancy it." He rubbed at his face. We had no washing facilities, and the cell's dirt had crept all over him, dulling his skin like a treasure hidden in the muck of the street. He sighed. "I've been alone my whole life. Even when I was small, I fought like a cat when my mother tried to hold me—"

I wanted to speak, to reassure him, but the reverend cut in with a verse:

"When I was a child, I spoke as a child, I understood as a child, I thought as a child: but when I became a man, I put away childish things."

Edward held out his hand, showed the reverend the ring on his slender finger, the golden skull cheerful as ever. "I found it in the mud on the foreshore after I killed that stranger. I meant to wash off the blood, perhaps drown myself – I don't know. But I read the name engraved inside and… well, I was fanciful. As a boy, did you ever dream up a playmate?"

This, too, I did not know. Some rare part of Edward kept hidden from me.

He sucked in a breath. "I ran away to sea at ten. A moment's impulse I'd regret all my life. When I finally took the chance to desert, I journeyed home only to find a new family occupied our house. Mother had died long ago. They'd even turned her cats out onto the street." He wet his cracked lips. "She promised me she'd always protect me and watch over me, but she couldn't, not in the end, not when I finally wanted it. I hated her for being so unlike other mothers. No respectable woman talks to spirits in the mirror. They don't sell acorns to ward away lightning strikes."

He paused, having exhausted himself with the truth. The reverend wisely kept silent.

"More than that," Edward went on, "I hated myself for running away, for needing excitement. And the guilt only made the impulse worse. The thieving and the gambling and the fighting, it kept me alive. And Aim—"

The reverend nodded. "They told me you speak of an accomplice."

He gave a wan smiled. "My accomplice."

"Edward—" I started, but he ignored me.

He twisted off the ring with difficulty. I'd never seen him without it; a vertiginous feeling, like watching him walk away without a backward glance. He turned it in his fingers for a moment before handing it to the reverend. "Take it. Sell it, maybe. Alms for the poor, to weigh against my soul."

The reverend did so with a great sniff, and held it up to the window to better examine the engraving inside.

"Aimee Hynde, obt 1713 Æt 19," he said. "Someone's tragedy, almost twenty years past." The street outside was quiet. The costermongers and the carriages had paused their racket, stopped dead like my breath.

Edward rubbed at the groove on his ring finger. "Someone's tragedy. But for a while, my friend."

My heart *thumpa-thumpa*'d in my ears. I scrambled to my feet, sending straw flying. "Edw—"

The hangman's trap swung open beneath me, sending me plummeting into a dark, forgetful chamber.

I am in my bed, swaddled in woollen blankets. The fever has passed. I look down at the ball of bandages that is my hand and wonder at it. I can feel my whole finger still, though I know it is the physician's possession now, taken with him to be burned or displayed in a jar of alcohol. I kick off my sweaty bedspreads and shuffle to the edge of the bed, setting my feet down on the cool floorboards, heavenly after my ordeal. No one is watching me through the night. They must all be abed, I tell myself, and gingerly stand to see if they have left me a pitcher of water. After the fever, I am parched.

I turn too fast, almost succumbing to dizziness. The room is small all of a sudden, or perhaps I am tall now, long-legged and strong like my brothers. The smell of cooking and washing and rank close quarters living threatens to turn my stomach. A string of drying clothes bisects the room: women's things, much mended and brown with age. I do not know this place, its mean sooty windows, nor its tallow candles trailing black threads of smoke.

To my surprise, there's a woman on the bed, hunched over a kitchen pan. She's whispering to herself, strange words in a foreign tongue, and I smell the Popery on her as strong as the mould spreading over the walls. In her fist is a ribbon of crinkled black hair. She lays it in the pan with care. I hear a rattling beneath the bed, a struggling bundle of claws, and before I can open my dry mouth to confront the woman, she reaches down and drags a dark something out into the candlelight, bound in twine like a cut of beef. A knife follows, and I hear a high whine escape from my own lips as I realise what I am about to witness.

The woman passes the blade through the hare's throat, soothing it through its death throes, and guides the fount of blood into the pan as best she can. Filigree words roll off her tongue. I recognise the names of the apostles jumbled in with nonsense such as a drunk might mutter at the moon. She is a handsome woman, not some malevolent crone. I see cats in the room's dark corners, six of them, watching me with shining eyes.

"Go to him," she says, when the pan is almost full.

"What is this?" I choke.

She cannot hear me. "Tend to him."

"Who are you?"

With a gasp, she looks up. She stares at me, wide-eyed, not mad but full of sober intent. I am an intruder in her lonely little home, but she views me not with surprise, but gratification.

In the pan of blood and hair, I see my face. Lips blue as frost on a millpond. And my eyes: moon-cracked amber.

"Edward," she chants, her gaze meeting mine. "Edward."

I know no one by that name.

Her eyes brim with tears. The house is empty, I realise. Just this woman and her cats and the girls who come to her for pennyroyal tea. The churchyard holds her husband and her babies, and now she fears the sea may take the only thing she has left.

She holds the pan aloft, bids me drink. My mouth aches for moisture and I drink with gratitude. It is, I dimly recall someone telling me, a gesture of comradeship.

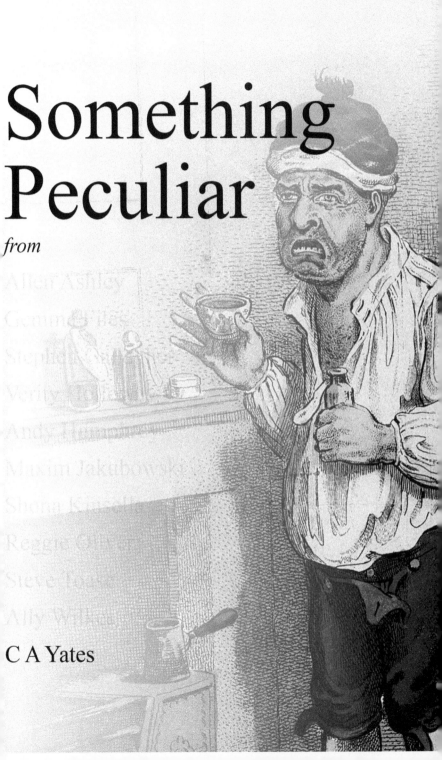

Something
Peculiar

from

C A Yates

The Ripe Fruit
in the Garden

"...that old courtesan chartreuse..."

THE PLANTS in the glass-paned backyard temple strain towards the falling droplets, bobbing their sweet emerald heads in thanks as the woman, Ivy, tilts the watering can above them. They seem to bask in the life-giving liquid that spills forth, indeed it is as though they sing back to her, and she smiles with a gladdened heart. *All things bright and beautiful, all creatures great and small...* The glasshouse and the garden that surrounds it are her home, far more so than the house of bricks and mortar she inherited from Father. Ivy has lived there all her life, in the tiny box room with only a single bed and a broken chest of drawers, but it has never been home nor homely, not even once Father died – laying on the floor in a puddle of stinking ochre piss, crying for help with one breath, cursing his daughter with the next. Ivy had finally, irrevocably been done with Father, and she had sat in her glasshouse and sung to her plants, to *Him* and them who had given her the strength to do what had to be done, while Father, with his broken hip and evil temper to the last, had died alone on his bedroom floor. *All things wise and wonderful, the Lord God made them all.*

Father's death had taken the best part of two days and Ivy's only regret is that it had still been a better one than he'd deserved. Of course, she would never say such a thing out loud, and it's not as if anyone has ever bothered to ask her about him anyway. They tend to avoid the subject, always have. Plenty of "good" people knew how cruelly Father had treated her, but no one had ever done anything about it. Not the vicar, Reverend Thomas, with his big red drunkard's nose, always poking it in where it doesn't belong but only when it serves him, of course. Not Mrs Jenkins from number five, who used to bring cakes to share with Father every Thursday afternoon – Ivy never got one – and left her knickers sometimes too. Not even Miss Childs, Ivy's primary school teacher, who Father said wore too much lipstick and deserved what she got, whatever that meant, but for whom Ivy had written stories, thinly veiled pleas for help, or so she'd thought. Miss Childs had left the school suddenly one day never to return. Bitterly, Ivy had come to the conclusion that while people say all you have to do is reach out to get help, in truth not many actually want to do anything *to* help. Certainly not old Mr Reith who used to live on the corner, and Mr Reith had hated Father nearly as much as Father had hated him, but not even half as much as Ivy had hated them both. He'd once told her she should cave her dear Pa's head in with a shovel given the opportunity. She had been eight years old and terrified of the old goat, but could still remember the way he'd laughed down at her, the snarled whiskers hanging from his nose caked with dried snot, false teeth barely holding onto his ancient puckered gums. He had been a disgusting old man and no one had missed him after he had done the decent thing and died, choking on his own tongue, pissing in his trousers on his bathroom floor, head cracked and oozing. Almost exactly like Father, except Ivy hadn't had to push that disgusting old man out of anything. Not by herself. *Each little flow'r that opens, each little bird that sings.*

Ivy had been wrong. She had thought herself all alone, but after she had waited so patiently and prayed so hard, and the time had finally been at hand to deal with her situation, someone *had* helped her, had told her quite clearly what to do. He – King of Kings, The Creator, The Main Man, Lord of the Green – had come to her in a vision, and his disciples had finally shown themselves. She had left Father where he had fallen, once she'd got him right to the edge of the bed and then let go, and Nature had taken its course. Nature was God's hand, after all, and Nature had known what was best for Father… even if it *had* taken an awfully long time to do something about him.

Still, what's done is done and what's lost is lost and what's gone is only gone forever if no one remembers you but, then, who wants to remember a nasty old man like Father? Ivy is free to sing to her good green plants unmolested, and don't they just sing right back, and she is happy for the first time in her life. She has built a small altar in the glasshouse, not just because it's her favourite place, although it is, but it is where He comes to her, where she knows He listens best. There is power in the glasshouse, in the whole garden really, and that she knows for sure. Reverend Thomas says you are supposed to worship God in the church and because church numbers are falling the devout should be as supportive as they claim to be, but the vicar has grabbed Ivy's bottom with his big sweaty hands too many times for her to put any stock in the things he says, and so she'd stubbornly made the altar and there she worships, three times a day, morning, noon, and night. She adorns it with the best offerings from the garden: the brightest red tomatoes against the deepest velvet-dark purple of the kale. Sometimes she even offers Him bright bluebells pulled up from the nearby woods, even though she knows it is Not Allowed, but God doesn't mind, God appreciates her efforts and, besides, they are God's creation. God is good and He loves us every one. And of all those things He has created, the birds and fishes, the flowers, the meat sacks, and the seashells, God loves those that are green the best. *He made their glowing colours, He made their tiny wings.*

Which is probably why Ivy's dreams are replete with it, every frame, every image soaked in viridescence, night after night. As she walks in the dream world He has created just for her, she bathes and dances in every shade – pea, sage, olive, apple, even that old courtesan chartreuse – and every tone, always green. It is the essence of everything, the fuse that sparks life and consumes it once it has been extinguished. The throbbing heart of Being. This is why He loves it so. Everything in Ivy's dreams is heavy with fecundity, but the weight of it is a pleasure to gladly bear; an eau de Nil burden. She becomes the Ivy she is meant to be in those dreams; the one that screams to be free of the colourless blouse always buttoned up to her neck, swamped by the tatty over-washed cardigan, obscured by the heavy black-framed spectacles she hates and does not really need. Father's insistence, of course, and she has no idea why she hasn't yet rid herself of the habit of wearing them. Another item she will add to the list.

All that is forgotten in her slumber, however, as she tumbles through the glorious patchwork of green like Alice down her rabbit hole but, unlike Alice, she never hits the bottom. Instead, she carries on plunging through the Green Lord's rich brown earth, her arms spreading like the white roots of a freshly planted fig tree, lush with promise even in their unfurling infancy, ever reaching, pullulating, benignly anchoring her below even as her legs sprout above the dirt, yielding soft leaves, replete with chlorophyll, and crowned with nascent flowers, undecided and still green, but like stars against the rich malachite sky above.

Every night Ivy dreams, and every morning she wakes filled with greater resolve and ever more love for her Lord and Saviour. *The sunset and the morning that brightens up the sky.* How could she not? His love surrounds her, is made manifest in every shrub, every flower, every tree, and every bud she sows. The glasshouse grows thick with plants of as many varieties as she has space for, vegetables fill the trenches she digs in the garden, and beans climb the trellis she has raised. The work is hard, she will not deny it, but the work is shared by the other women, her sisters now, who also believe it is His will and she could not have shirked it even if she wanted to. This is her purpose, their purpose. It is a special place, her garden, it has been foretold, and she watches it grow and flourish. As it does, her barren life too becomes fruitful. In the mirror, something she has never thought to bother with much before, she sees the verdant wealth the Lord has bestowed upon her garden bloom in her too. Her cheeks glow pink, her hair falls in lustrous waves to her shoulders and, for the first time in her life, she feels like a woman from head to toe. At night, when the weather is fine, and sometimes even not, she goes down to her glasshouse, no need of a light as she knows every nook and cranny, every step and crack, and she lays down amongst her plants and learns her body, makes it her own at last. It has been hidden for so long but, now she is free, it is hers to do with as she pleases. Each night and day passes in the midst of her green sanctuary, and every one is better than the last.

Rain had taken a savage hold of May this year, *the cold wind in the winter, the pleasant summer sun,* but now the garden is lusher than ever. Ivy's always hated being wet and cold, which was why Father often used to lock her out of the house for days at a time as a punishment for whatever something and nothing she was supposed to have done. Some punishment! She had taken shelter in the broken down old glasshouse her long departed mother had had erected and promised herself she would repay it for the protection it afforded her, as the woman she had barely known had not. It had taken years, the work necessarily quiet and small at first, but once Father had been confined to his room and then his bed, it had all become so much easier. These days she does not need to worry about the rain or, indeed, Father. She knows it now for what it is – a sacred gift from the Lord, Her Lord – and she glories to see it do His work. *He made them every one.*

One afternoon, she is sitting in the glasshouse; she has taken to dragging a deck chair in there so she can read amongst her plants in comfort. Relaxed and comfortable in her happy place, the soporific patter against the panes quickly lulls her eyes to heaviness, and then her mind to doze, the book falling unheeded to the floor. She settles deeper into the chair and, as always, her verdurous surroundings go with her. She skips through the forests of her dream-mind, running her hands across every illusory leaf and sprig, marvelling at the rainbow of colours flickering around her, all manner of flora trying to compete for her attention, but the greenery beneath always glows brightest. *The tall trees in the greenwood, the meadows where we play.* She sees Him waiting for her in the dark green shadows, He is always waiting, and she runs to Him, throwing herself into His arms and laughing as He nuzzles His green beard into her neck, His mouth as hot as ever on her skin, His godly hands touching her everywhere and oh, she wonders, has anyone ever felt so much joy as this? Has anyone felt so at peace? Whether it is here in this ethereal dream space with her heavenly Beloved or in the garden she has cultivated in the mundane world with the others, has anyone ever been so blessed?

She knows there will be changes, nothing stays the same, and she has felt them within herself as surely as the sun rises in the morning. It is almost as though by claiming her peace she has challenged the Lord to give her something more to contend with, some sacred task to complete. There are moments when she doubts, how can she not? It is inexplicable, ineffable. It's just a dream, she has been telling herself, but her certainty has been growing stronger for days. It started as a fluttering deep down in her womb, a place she has barely ever thought of in all her years. Her dream-self marvels at the knowledge that comes to her in an instant, even as her lover takes her body as his own, and she knows it must be true. Surely, she is with child. The Lord's child. Praise be. She must tell the others.

The rushes by the water, to gather every day.

In the aftermath of their lovemaking, when her lover has left her to tend to His other creations, an almighty dread comes upon Ivy. Shadows fall all around her, darkening the dream-garden, all colour but one seeping away as though sharing in her fear and running from it. What is left is a green as dank as the vegetal detritus that lays in wait beneath the surface of a lake, greedily seizing men where it can and dragging them down into the deeps, choking and gasping as they go, never to be seen again. It stinks and it is cold; so very cold, and so very wrong.

"Ivy." Someone calls her name, someone deep within the fetid swamp, someone mired in it, someone she hadn't realised was there. "Ivy." The voice calls again, but Ivy cannot see who it is. She backs away, not wanting to be found, not wanting to see what lies within that ghastly slough. *The purple headed mountain, the river running by.*

"Ivy!"

The shock of someone shouting in real life pitches Ivy from her dream and she wakes, heart thumping like it is going to jump right out of her chest. She opens her eyes to see Reverend Thomas standing in the doorway, his eyes glued to where her skirt has ridden up her thighs. It was him who had called to her, that much is obvious. Anger fills her. He has sullied something precious. She wants to go back to her dream, to go back to her revelation and the peace that had filled her so completely, but this man has taken it from her with his greedy intrusion, his assumption. This man.

Ivy sees red.

Blood red.

It comes over her in a flash, the vibrant scarlet of a Don Juan rose slashing across her vision, spleen swelling with carmine waves that spill over and rush through her, overwhelming every sense, commanding every muscle, spreading through her body, jumping from nerve ending to nerve ending, to meet the bright crimson of the wrath that pulses hot at her very core. She is aflame with it, incandescent with righteousness.

Thrusting herself up from the chair, she stands, her legs shaking beneath her, still held by the gossamer fear of the dream and the surging anger that moves her so fiercely. She reaches for the man, and blinding heat suffuses her arms, gripping her flesh with merciless power. Her hands flex, her mouth opening and closing in gasping rings of useless breath, and she begins to scream silently, all her energy focussed on her outstretched limbs as they twist and pulsate, stretching, muscle and pale skin seeming to rip only to reknit, reshape into something stronger for the task at hand. It is agony but the change is glorious. Redeeming. Empowering. No child within her, she realises that now; the life force she felt inside, so powerful, so fierce, is something else and it has her in its grasp and will not let go. A child was not what she needed. This is. Now she is fire and fury and she will smite.

She wants to grab the nearest thing she can find, to test her strengthening limbs: there is a heavy metal trowel on her workbench, old fashioned but sturdier for that. It's within easy reach, just a half step and she wants to grab it, but she cannot, not yet. The light in the glasshouse has darkened, as though shadows loom outside, but the rain is long gone, the sky clear blue and the sun strong.

"What on earth has gotten into you, Ivy?" He is all incredulity, this devout man of the cloth who was enjoying a glimpse up her skirt just a moment ago.

"*Ivy, Ivy, Ivy*, will you shut your bloody mouth, you nauseating old prick?" The words surprise them both, but it is the vicar who takes a very sensible step back. Ivy has never so much as raised her voice in his presence before, let alone used an obscenity. Besides that, if she could see herself she would understand his fear. She would have thought herself magnificent in her ferocity. Lips peeled back from her teeth, her eyes flashing with madness, her small frame divinely, exquisitely bolstered; she is a Fury of myth, an avenging angel, her rage exploding forth, consuming all in her path like a swell of seething amber magma, every step she takes an aggression.

The old priest's eyes widen – *the rich man in his castle, the poor man at his gate* – and for every step Ivy takes towards him, he takes one back. His fear is palpable; a heavy brown scent on the air, like cooked meat, and Ivy throws her head back and howls. She will rip the coward's throat out and drink down his hypocrite blood. She will eat him and shit him out and use it to fertilise her garden. She will not waste a drop, she will not…

The priest slaps her so hard her ears ring. Ivy staggers and everything flares for a long moment, bells and whistles cacophonous in her suddenly bright white head. For an instant it is as though she is seeing herself through someone else's eyes, someone who is on her side but so angry, more angry than she could ever be, despite everything, someone who holds fast to their temper when she cannot, and together they must find balance… and then they are gone again and she is bereft. Despite the anger, there had been warmth, affection beneath, and it had called to Ivy's heart. As Ivy opens her eyes, she blinks once, twice, and the viridian wealth around her floods in, shimmering and sparkling like the great city of Oz when Dorothy first sets eyes on it. One deep breath in, one deep breath out. Ivy steadies herself and then she knows, is fuelled by epiphany. *Why.* This is *why.* This is why her garden grew. This is why she has been chosen.

Retribution. Rebalance.

These are the words that ring inside her head as though someone has screamed them. This man, this sinner, this hypocrite has been brought before her this day for a reason. Her Lord, praise His name most high, has entrusted her with His punishment. She can feel the power course through her veins. She is His vessel and she knows exactly what to do. *God made them, high and lowly, and ordered their estate.*

And then she sees the women.

Four familiar figures, beloved faces now that once were all but strangers to her, despite living in the same street for so many years. They have been called to her, to this place. One is Earth, One is Air, One is Fire, One is Water, and she, Ivy, is Spirit. They are one together beneath the cerulean sky, and the time has come once more to make sacrifice. The garden must be tended, the plants must be fed.

"Ivy, I don't…" The priest stops short as he takes a look behind him to where she is looking. He sees the women, who have formed a semi circle, blocking any escape. They all see him have the thought that they are just women, that he, a big man and strong, could easily get past them, but Ivy has already shifted towards him, her limbs quick with adrenaline and divine intervention, and she thrusts the trowel into his side as hard as she can, using every ounce of God-given strength she has. They all cry out, one in agony, the others in ecstasy. The Reverend clasps his hand to his wounded side and opens his mouth, closes it, then opens it again, seems about to say something, staggers backwards, half a step forwards, and then takes an enormous breath in and reaches for his chest, blood smearing up and across his shirt. He clutches at his heart, his eyes bulging, and there is a moment of absolute stillness. Nothing moves, nothing makes a sound, there is only the perfect calm of the in-between… and then he gasps, half retch, half accusation, and he slowly sinks to the ground, almost tumbling in on himself, but grabbing Ivy by the arm as he goes, taking her with him. They are both breathing hard, staring into each other's eyes. She scrabbles at his grip on her, surprisingly strong considering he is having some sort of attack – she'd say his heart if she thought he had one – trying to prise his fingers from around – in – her arm. Finally she breaks his grip and pushes him onto his back away from her. He resists, but his strength is waning, it is little more than a cursory protest, and she scrambles on top of him, pulling the trowel free. Blood gushes out, a rich fountain of colour, loaded with that luscious coppery smell. For a moment, one heartbeat, two, three, she isn't sure what to do. She tries to remember the song, where to place her hands on his constricted chest, but all she can hear is the beat of the earth beneath them, the beat of the life force within her, the gasping breaths of the man under her fading fast, and she knows this ending, his ending, is the right thing. She is praying, and her sisters' voices join with hers, the words a jumble of holy litany made dark by the erratic rise and fall of the reverend's chest and a steady flow of blood flowing from his wound.

He gave us eyes to see them and lips that we might tell.

"The Lord is our shepherd, yours and mine, isn't that right, Vicar? We shall not want. And neither will you. He maketh us to lie down in green pastures," Ivy grits out the words as she bears down on him, pushing at his wound not to stem the bleeding but to encourage it, to help him on his way. Smite, smite, smite. "We admonish you, sinner, in His name and in ours. Yea, though we walk through the valley of the shadow of death, we will fear no evil for thou art with us. Pray for us sinners now and at the hour of our death – Father, I said say it with us – forever and ever and ever."

The Reverend tries to throw her from him, the wild desperation in his eyes a final resistance, but it is an agony his failing body cannot aid. For she is possessed by the power of Her Lord, by His fecund majesty, and she stays atop the large man, holding steady as he struggles to cling on to his miserable, misused life, sweat pouring from her as much as him until, at last, they still as one. The heart within the body beneath her beats no more. Ivy shudders with sudden weakness as her Lord's strength leaves her, her task done, and she lets the trowel go, unaware she'd been digging it into him, her arms shaking as the strength of her fury begins to recede. She should have been no match for him and yet he sank like the Hesperus, wrecked on her rocks by the sins of arrogance and indecency, betrayed by his wicked heart. She is the vessel, the tool of the Redeemer, and she truly hopes, as his very last breath soughs forth, rattling from his chest, that he has repented, for surely he will find peace and forgiveness beyond this life, as it has been promised.

"Amen." Ivy sits for a moment, her mind as blank as the priest beneath her is unmoving. As her heart rate eases and the fierce waters of her anger begin to ebb, she looks to her sisters. They know what to do, have performed this duty before, although this is the first in the garden, and it is about time. She gets to her feet and they form a circle around the big body of the old reverend. They reach for each other and join hands, gripping hard. They are bound. Earth, Air, Fire, Water, and Spirit. They can feel the earth pulsing beneath their feet, once, twice, and then on and on. They move with it, eyes closing, chins lifting as their heads fall back, mouths open in rapture. The power is rising, coming up from the depths of the soil, through the roots they have planted, along every branch, drenching every petal. They feel the spirits of long ago and the more recently departed. For the first time, they feel Ivy's mother, buried within the concrete foundations of the glasshouse. Ivy cries out, knows who was seeing through her before, knows where that anger had come from.

'Mum?' She cannot believe she did not know, even in death her Father had somehow hidden his darkest deed. How could her Lord have kept this from her? She wants to trust Him, wants to understand His purpose, but she cannot stem her mounting fury, quickening the beat of the earth as she struggles to make sense of it. The ground shakes and the women tighten their grip on each other even as they look to one another for reassurance, for explanation. Ivy's eyes are closed, her thoughts within as the beat intensifies, the shaking becomes deeper... And then she sees again through her mother's eyes, her memories, and her anger. It is as though she and her mother are reunited in what is at once a moment and an eternity. She can hear her, feel her within her, around her, her spirit ferocious, determined that this be done. Ivy sees the punch that ended her mother's life, her father's fist, and finally she has her answer. It tenses her gut, spears her mind's eye. This man knew, he knew where her mother was, he knew what Father had done to her, with her, had known what Ivy had been allowed to believe all this time, that she had been deserted, unwanted. He is the last piece of the puzzle. All the women feel it. Some have suspected, but none had known. The Lord of the Green had been waiting for him to come to them, to make proper sacrifice, untainted by coercion. He needed the reverend to step into the garden, into His holy place, so few are left to Him these days, of his own free will. He had to present himself so that the forfeit could at last be made, the price be paid.

The power moves through them all as his dead body still drip, drip, drips blood between them, leaves blowing from branches, petals whipping from flowers in a whirlwind of divine justice, and the earth beneath their feet cracks gently open, zigzagging between them in five directions. They avoid the fissures as best they can without breaking their grip on each other, keeping steady on their feet, determined to see this to the end. It must be done. Light flares up from the break in the ground, flooding the glasshouse, but it does not blind the women, it is not harsh. This light is not for scourging, it is the light of passage, and the reverend, almost entirely exsanguinated now, begins to sink into the waiting ground, skin shredding, muscle blending, bone splitting, organs seeping as he goes, becoming one, being consumed. Nothing is wasted. Nothing remains. What comes next is for his soul to bear.

How great is the Almighty Who has made all things well.

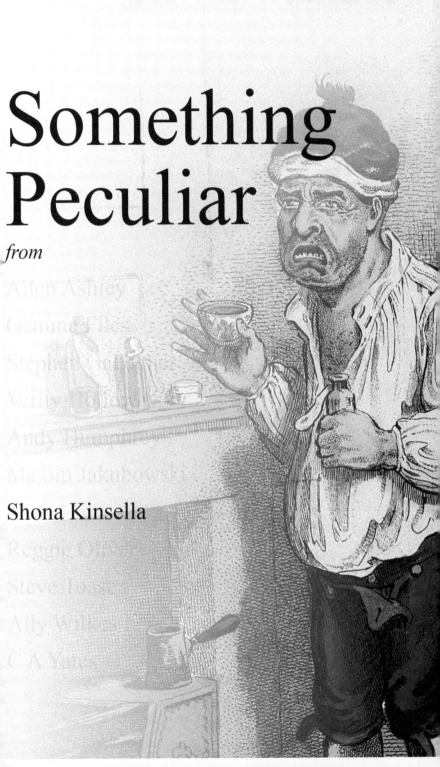

Something Peculiar

from

Shona Kinsella

Professor Flotsam's Cabinet of Peculiarities

"…what is grief but love unspent…"

Burak wrinkled his nose in disgust; the air swam with smoke and sweat and the sour tang of days-old fish. He hated it when they had to set up near the docks – the canvas would smell like fish for days after they had moved on, and the wagon he shared with Thomas wouldn't be much better. Not that any part of London smelled good. It suited Abaye, though, to be close to the water. Otherwise, her scales would dry out, become dull and lifeless. Burak didn't know how she could stand to swim in the Thames; he had never thought it possible for water to be so filthy.

The tent flap at the front of the big top opened, allowing smog and damp chill into the interior.

'Are you ready, my friends? Showtime is almost upon us!' John Smythe – also known as Professor Flotsam – strode into the tent, the peacock feather in his hat bouncing jauntily. 'They've been lining up outside for the last hour.'

Burak stretched and lifted another screen; there was a strict order to what the clientele saw and when. The professor had spent a lot of time working out exactly the best way to use his 'peculiarities' to create the delicate balance of disgust and fascination which would bring the normies crowding in here night after night.

Burak and Samson moved the last of the silk screens into place, creating a maze inside the giant tent, through which the crowds would be led in small groups by one of the professor's glamorous assistants in their scandalously revealing outfits.

'It's all about titillation,' the professor had said, more than once. 'Feed all of their appetites and they'll pay with blood if they have to.'

The low murmur of voices from outside was beginning to take on an impatient edge. Burak took one last look around, making sure everything was ready. Gas lamps hung from wires crisscrossing the roof space of the tent, casting a warm, flickering glow over the space, but carefully positioned to leave shadows in the right places. To the right of the entrance, Umberto and Lucian, the Amazing Acrobatic Midget Twins, were warming up with some simple tumbles. On the left, Eloise the Wolf Girl was curled up on a pile of sackcloth, the hair that covered her skin brushed to a fine sheen. She wore a pretty lemon day dress, with a hole cut in the back for her stubby little tail to stick out.

Burak walked quickly through the maze to his own area, passing several of the other performers on the way. Almost as soon as he was in position, he heard the tent flap being opened and the professor launching into his spiel.

'Welcome! Welcome to Professor Flotsam's Cabinet of Peculiarities! I have gathered together the most interesting, the most talented, and the most bizarre people from all across the world and brought them here for your delectation. But I must warn you, we do not offer refunds to those who faint.'

There was some nervous laughter at this. There always was. Burak stretched and popped his joints as he listened, preparing for the performance he would give somewhere between ten and twenty times this evening, depending on how busy it was. It was their third night in London, on this tour, so things might start to slow down a bit. But then last week in Bristol they'd been at full capacity every night.

Burak peered around the screen in front of his area, so that he could see Abaye. She lay in a copper bathtub, her legs sticking out over the end. She flicked the fins which took the place of her feet at him in a wave, and he grinned at her. The iridescent scales which covered her from the breasts down dazzled against the darkness of her skin and the thick, black hair which tumbled down her back. She was always careful to keep her mouth closed whenever there were customers in – the double-row of wickedly pointed teeth would likely frighten more than a few.

Burak took a few steps to the side and peered round the screen in the other direction. Thomas was already in position, his back turned to Burak, elaborate tattoos on display. The sounds of the first group making their way through the maze drew closer, and Burak slipped off his robe and climbed on top of the reinforced glass cube which took centre stage in his area. His skin was lightly oiled, preventing him from sticking to the glass, but it meant he had to move carefully so as not to slide across the top of the cube. He eased himself into the lotus position and closed his eyes, waiting for the first group to reach him.

By the time the last of the normies had passed through the tent for the night, Burak was ready for food and then bed, but just as he was helping Abaye out of the bathtub and into the elaborate leg braces which allowed her to walk, the professor called him over.

'Will you make it to the water alright?' he asked Abaye in a low voice.

'It will not be a problem,' she said, patting his shoulder. Her voice was low and melodic. 'I hope you are not delayed too long from your own meal.'

'Let us hope.' Burak turned and hurried to where the professor stood with one of the glamourous assistants. 'How may I be of service?'

'Keep him waiting for a while and then bring him to my wagon,' the professor said to the assistant.

'Yes, boss.' She gave him a saucy wink and walked off.

Smythe turned to Burak. 'Will you join me in my wagon for a meal, Burak?'

Burak bowed his head. 'Of course.'

'Splendid!' The professor slapped Burak's back jovially, then strode through the tent towards the rear exit.

Burak followed, catching sight of Thomas and waving to let him know that he would be dining alone tonight.

Outside, smog filled the open spaces, making everything hazy and indistinct. The shifting currents of air made eddies in the haze, revealing some wagons and concealing others. It deadened sound and made their footsteps sound oddly muffled on the hard-packed earth. Smythe led the way to a wide wagon, painted deep blue with gold trim. In the dark, it looked black and seemed to loom out of the shifting smog. Burak felt a chill of foreboding. He shook himself, pushing it away. This was a night like any other, and he had joined the professor for a meal many times in the past.

As soon as they were inside, the professor lit an oil lamp and then went to the stove, stirring the embers and adding some more wood. He spoke over his shoulder as he worked. 'There's a man, says he has a business proposition for me. I was hoping you would oblige me by using your… other talents this evening.'

'Of course,' Burak answered. 'Do you have any idea what this man plans to propose?'

Smythe straightened and lifted a frying pan, placing it on top of the stove. 'Not in the slightest.'

'And yet you agreed to meet with him? That's not like you.'

'Pass the bread,' Smythe said, gesturing to the cupboard behind Burak. 'I have heard of this man before. His name is Charles Fortitude, an explorer and trader. Recently returned from New Guinea, if I recall correctly.' He took the bread that Burak handed to him and cut two slices, adding them to the frying pan alongside some bacon.

'Perhaps he has found another wonder for us,' Burak said, leaning against the wooden wall of the wagon. He was tired and his body ached. The contortions he put it through night after night were not so very difficult, but the cool, damp climate worked its way into his joints. He would feel no relief until summer arrived – and then only briefly, in this miserably chilled country.

The professor took two plates from a shelf beside the stove and set them out on the small table, then added cutlery and two glasses, into which he poured generous measures of brandy.

'You distrust this man?' Burak asked, watching as Smythe plated up the bread and bacon and cracked two eggs into the frying pan.

The professor gave him a wry smile. 'I distrust most men.' He gestured to the table. 'Please, take a seat.'

They ate together in companionable silence. Burak had been with the professor for years now, almost since the very beginning. Only Samson had served longer, being one of the first acts the Cabinet opened with. People came and went in this business, but Burak knew he was a lifer; he would carry on with his act for as long as his body allowed, and when he could no longer twist and bend himself into the shapes he could now, he would take over some of the domestic tasks involved in caring for a travelling troupe such as theirs, if Smythe would keep him on.

Finishing his food, Burak pushed his plate away and took a mouthful of brandy. The alcohol warmed him all the way down to his toes. That, a full belly, and the heat coming from the stove, combined to make him sleepy and he supressed a yawn.

Voices approached, followed by a sharp rap at the door.

'Enter!' Smythe called, waving to Burak to stay in his chair.

The assistant – Burak couldn't remember her name, there were many and they never stuck around for long – opened the door and ushered a large man into the wagon.

Well over six feet tall, and almost as broad across the shoulders, his looming figure suddenly made the previously cosy space feel crowded.

The professor stood and offered his hand. 'Mr Fortitude, a pleasure to meet you. I am John Smythe, also known as Professor Flotsam.'

Fortitude took the professor's hand in his bear-like paw and shook it firmly. 'Delighted. I've been hearing about your show for some years now, but we never seem to be in the capital at the same time.'

'Please, take a seat.' The professor indicated one of the chairs at the small table.

Fortitude eyed it doubtfully. 'I think I'll stand, thank you.'

Burak thought that a wise choice. The spindly chairs did not look strong enough to bear a man of Fortitude's proportions.

Smythe shrugged and sat, taking his pipe from a shelf and beginning to fill it with tobacco from a tin in his pocket. 'Amelia tells me you have a business proposition to discuss?'

Fortitude looked questioningly at Burak.

The professor waved a hand in dismissal. 'My financial advisor.'

Burak sat forward, his hands on the table, fingers laced together. He breathed deeply and sank into a light trance state. He was still fully aware of everything going on around him and could respond, if necessary, but he had expanded his senses. In this state, he could hear the pounding hearts of both other men in the wagon, the bellows-like sound of their chests pulling in air. More importantly, he could sense their intentions, feel their emotions, to some small extent. There had long been tales of men who could read another's thoughts, and that, sadly, was beyond Burak's abilities, but this smaller talent also came in useful from time-to-time.

'You may be aware of my recent return from New Guinea?' Fortitude began.

The professor nodded and lit his pipe. 'Of course.'

'There was a village we visited during our time there, one of crudely-built huts and native peasants, largely ignored by settlers and outsiders.'

He paused, and Burak had the sense that he was waiting for some sign of approval from the professor. This was a man who wanted to impress people.

The professor waved his pipe. 'Go on.'

Fortitude frowned but continued. 'We found the villagers living in fear of a local legend; the beast-man of the jungle. There had been sightings of a strange creature, neither fully man nor beast, and those who entered the jungle alone often did not return. Superstitious poppycock, we thought at first.' He leaned back against the cabinets behind him, folding his arms over his chest.

Burak could feel Fortitude's confidence as he fully engaged with the story. This was the truth – or at least, he believed it to be true.

'While we were there, one of the natives went into the jungle to collect vines – they use them for all sorts of things in the village, quite ingenious really. Anyway, this man headed out one morning, just after dawn, and one of my men, Mateo, decided to go with him, see what he could learn about the terrain there before we moved on. The rest of us stayed in the village. We were helping them dig a new well after the old one had dried up. It was back-breaking work, and the weather there is so hot and humid that such tasks take twice as much out of you as they ought to. So it's no wonder really that none of us noticed they hadn't returned until twilight.'

The professor handed Fortitude a glass of brandy. The explorer swirled the liquid around in the glass, sniffed it but did not drink from it.

'By the time we had noticed they were missing, we were already losing the light. My team wanted to go out searching for them straight away, but the natives convinced us that it would be foolish to attempt the jungle at night.

At this point we were concerned, but not overly so. They were both capable men, and there were many reasons that their return might be delayed. So we hunkered down for the night and waited.

'When dawn came, we were ready. Half of my team remained in the village, the other half came out with me and one of our local guides, an English lad who had grown up there when his father was posted to the governor's office on the island. The villagers had told us roughly which direction they would have been likely to go and what signs to look for; the natives have ways of marking their path as they go so that they don't get lost. It's easy to get turned around in the jungle, lose your sense of direction. So we set off, following their tracks, and calling out to them every so often.'

Fortitude sipped the brandy. His heart rate had increased, his breathing grew shallower. He was anxious. Perhaps even frightened. Burak's own skin came out in goosebumps in response. The professor was rapt, completely engaged in the tale.

'We walked for hours, the heat of the jungle pressing down on us. We passed many places where they could have harvested the vines they came out looking for, yet the trail continued. We came to the point when our guide wanted to turn back, lest we lose the daylight and become lost ourselves. We argued about it – the last thing I wanted to do was leave Mateo out there for another night – but eventually I saw the wisdom of it when my second-in-command pointed out that it was better to lose one man than six.

'I can't help but wonder if things would have turned out differently if I had insisted on pushing on that day.

'We returned to the village, arriving with the last light of dusk. We began collecting camping supplies. I intended to go back out there the next day and not return until I had found Mateo. In the end that was not necessary.'

He paused then, a haunted look passing over his face. Burak could taste his regret, the salty tang of tears he refused to shed. Fortitude swallowed the rest of the brandy in one, steeling himself to continue.

'It felt like I had only been asleep for minutes when the shouting woke me, but the fire in our hut had burned down to embers, so it must have been longer. We rushed outside in our underclothes, guns in hand. Torches burned around the perimeter of the village – supposedly a deterrent to predators from the jungle. There was enough light for us to see a group of villagers huddling around something, just on the edge of the village. That's where the shouting was coming from. We hurried over, thinking maybe one of the more dangerous animals had found its way in… I wish to God that was all it had been. I pushed through the crowd, gun ready to take down whatever the threat was.

'It was Mateo's head.'

The professor gasped, though Burak could feel that he was not truly surprised. Smythe stood and refilled Fortitude's brandy glass. The explorer gave him a grateful look and swallowed it one.

'What on earth had happened to the poor chap?' the professor asked.

'This was no clean cut like one would see from an axe, nor even the multiple blows that might be expected from a sword or machete. It was ragged and distorted, the skin stretched, tendons and veins hanging from the bottom. It looked as if it his head had been ripped from his body by brute force. I've never seen anything like it. While we were still all standing around, staring at it in shock, the native Mateo had gone out with came stumbling out of the jungle, his arms wrapped around his torso. He was babbling something about the beast-man. One of my men grabbed him, shook him, demanding to know what had happened. The poor man let go of his torso and his guts fell out. He had been holding them in, hoping he could make it back to the village, to warn everyone. He died before we could get much sense out of him.

'The next morning, my team headed out into the jungle, determined to deal with this "beast-man" once and for all. Some of the men from the village joined us, carrying the machetes they used for cutting through vines, and some with poison darts and blowguns. None of their weapons could match our rifles, of course, but every little helps. We were able to follow the trail of blood left the night before, which made the going much faster than it had been the previous day.

After a while, we came upon a clearing, but not a natural one. Plants had been cut and trampled and there were signs of great violence. In the middle of it all lay the strangest creature. The size and shape of a man, he was heavily muscled beneath a thick, dark pelt. He had the head of a man but the snout of a boar, with wickedly sharp tusks. His hands and feet bore claws as large and as deadly-looking as a tiger's. This could be nothing but the man-beast the villagers had spoken of. He was covered in wounds. From what I could tell from a distance they were largely superficial but there must have been twenty or more.

'I raised my rifle to shoot him, but one of the village elders pushed the barrel of the gun down and pointed at their hunters. I wanted to be the one to kill this creature, for what it had done to Mateo, but over the years, the villagers had suffered far more at his hands. I chose to give them the kill. Two of them shot it with their poison darts. The creature flinched and whined but did not make any move to defend itself.

'Some of the villagers lashed it to a long pole and carried it back to the village to show that their hunt had been successful. I negotiated with the elder to be allowed to bring the body back to Britain with me, knowing how much the queen enjoys an oddity. It was only after we had left the village that we discovered the beast wasn't dead. Instead of killing it, the poison had acted as a sort of sedative. By that point, with it safely captive, it felt unsporting to kill the thing. So we acquired more of the poison and kept it sedated until we could lock it up on the ship.'

'And your men went along with this?' the professor asked. 'Weren't they worried about suffering the same fate as Mateo?'

Fortitude scoffed. 'My men are no cowards,' he said. 'Besides, they figured out that bringing such a creature home could bring us all a very nice windfall indeed.'

Smythe laid his pipe down and sat back, lacing his hands over his belly. 'Am I to understand that this is where I come in?'

Fortitude smiled and opened his hands. 'You are a man with a keen eye for opportunity, or so it is said.'

Burak sensed Fortitude's energy change. He was preparing to haggle, and he wasn't above a little deception if necessary. The professor's energy sharpened; he too was a keen haggler, and he lived for finding new oddities. Although he maintained his casual pose and was outwardly calm, Burak knew he would be almost salivating over the prospect of acquiring this 'beast-man'.

'The creature you have described sounds extremely dangerous. I'm not sure it is suitable for an entertainment establishment such as my own,' Smythe said, his voice mild.

'I would of course provide you with a regular supply of the sedative.' Fortitude's smile turned wolfish. 'For a reasonable fee, of course.'

'Of course.'

The professor glanced at Burak who gave an infinitesimal shrug. The explorer was definitely keen to offload this creature, but there had been no lies so far. There was a tinge of fear underlying everything he said, but that was hardly surprising given the story he had shared.

'I have to give this some thought,' the professor said. 'Not to mention inspecting the creature. I have the safety of my other performers to consider.'

Fortitude straightened and placed his brandy glass on the table. Burak knew he was about to play what he thought of as his trump card.

'You must of course be sure of your decision. But, if you are not interested in the creature, I am sure P.T. Barnum will be.'

Smythe shot to his feet. 'Barnum? He's in London?'

Burak felt the alarm radiating from the professor.

'His ship is due to dock in two days. The queen has granted him another audience. I would think he would be most pleased to present the creature to her, never exhibited anywhere before.'

Burak knew that Fortitude had won then. He could feel the eagerness rolling off Smythe in waves, tinged with the faintest trace of greed.

'When can I inspect the creature?' the professor asked.

'Does noon tomorrow suit?'

'Where?'

'My warehouse at the other end of the docks. That's where we're keeping him for the moment. Do you know where it is?'

'I'll find it,' the professor answered. 'May I offer you another drink?'

Fortitude shook his head. 'I thank you, but I should return to my men.'

'Until tomorrow then.'

The two of them shook hands and Fortitude left. Burak released his trance and sat back in his chair, suddenly exhausted. The professor poured him a generous measure of brandy and put the glass in his hand.

'Are you well?' he asked. 'You look pale.'

'Just tired,' Burak said. 'It has been a long day.' His eyes felt gritty, and he longed to close them.

'Did you get anything from him? Is the beast real?'

Burak sipped at his drink. 'It's real, or at least he believes it to be so. He felt genuine fear when he told his story of the jungle, and he mourned for Mateo.'

Smythe drummed his fingers on the table, swigging from his own glass. 'We can't compete with Barnum financially. Why would Fortitude offer the creature to us first, if Barnum will be here so soon? Surely it would be more profitable to wait a few more days and offer it to him? Or hold an auction to drive up the price?'

'Perhaps you could ask him tomorrow.'

Burak strode through the docks at Smythe's side the next day, though his head pounded with every step. Men called to each other, gulls squawked, carts clanked, and crates crashed against each other, none of it helping the sick thudding behind his eyes and at the base of his skull. Even the weak London sunlight seemed to be attacking him, making him squint. These headaches were not uncommon after the use of his gifts, but this one felt especially vicious.

By the time they reached Fortitude's warehouse, he was grateful just to step inside the cool, dim interior. Fortitude himself met them at the door and led them past shelves stacked with riches brought back from his various expeditions, alongside piles of supplies for wherever he was off to next. The echoey space was filled with an expectant hush. There was more going on here than met the eye.

'I assume you wish to see the beast first,' Fortitude said over his shoulder as he walked. 'Then we can retire to my office for tea and negotiation.'

The professor laughed. 'You seem very sure that there will be something to negotiate.'

Fortitude glanced over his shoulder and smirked. 'I would be very surprised if there is not.'

They rounded the end of a row of shelves and entered a large, mostly empty space at the rear of the warehouse. In the centre of this space was a large cage, like something used to transport wild animals. Two men stood on watch at either side of the cage, one with a rifle held at his side, the other with what looked like a blow gun. Burak frowned. Even without dropping into the trance state, he could taste the metallic tang of fear. These men were taking no chances with the creature.

Inside the cage, half of the floor was covered by something which looked like a mattress of sorts, piled with blankets. There was a ripe, animal smell in the air. A shape on the mattress moved, rolled over, and Burak got his first proper look at the 'beast-man'. His thick pelt was matted and dirty, and it covered him from head to toe, thicker and bristly on the top of his head. He was hunched in on himself, his head pulled forward, as if the weight of it was more than his neck could bear. From the back, his head was the shape of any other man's, but from the front, he resembled nothing so much as a wild boar, bearing as he did a snout and wickedly sharp tusks. His eyes were small and positioned on either side of his snout.

Looking upon this creature, Burak had some of the same sense of fascination and disgust that he knew the normies felt every night as they passed through the cabinet, but there was pity mixed in there too. Something about this creature just felt so unutterably sad.

The professor moved closer to the cage and Burak felt Fortitude stiffen beside him. Both guards tensed, their weapons held ready. These men really were frightened of this creature.

Smythe crouched down on his haunches, peering into the cage. 'Extraordinary,' he said, in a tone full of wonder. 'I've never seen anything like it.' He glanced to the other side of the cage, where there were two metal bowls, one filled with water, the other containing smears of something unknown. 'What have you been feeding him?'

'Stew, mostly.' Fortitude's voice was calm, but his body was still tense and ready for action. 'Some porridge, some vegetable scraps. He hasn't turned his nose up at anything, but we don't have the first idea what an appropriate diet is for a creature such as this.'

The professor straightened with a groan. 'Shall we go to your office, then?'

Fortitude led the way to a spacious office, with a wide, high window, which let in enough daylight that the gas lamps around the room remained unlit. At one end of the room was a large desk, while at the other was a small grouping of leather armchairs around a walnut coffee table, inlaid with ivory and mother-of-pearl. Maps and nautical charts were tacked to the walls, with pins and notations all over them.

'Please, take a seat,' Fortitude said, gesturing to the armchairs. 'I'll go and arrange for some tea to be brought in. Unless you would prefer something stronger?'

The professor smiled. 'It's a little early in the day for me. Tea will be fine, thank you.' He sat in one of the armchairs and crossed his legs. Burak followed suit.

As soon as Fortitude had left the room, the professor leaned over and spoke in a low voice. 'What an extraordinary find. This creature is worth a substantial amount of money. Most likely more than we can comfortably spend. So I must wonder again why Fortitude came to us.'

Burak nodded. 'Also, why these men are all so scared of it. Certainly the story he told of the jungle was awful, but these are hardened explorers, many of them military trained. I think we must ask more questions before agreeing to anything.'

'The tea will be here in a few moments,' Fortitude said, striding back into the room.

Burak sat back in his seat and rubbed his temples. Though his headache had eased somewhat since coming inside, he knew from experience that it would linger for the remainder of the day.

Fortitude sat on the edge of one of the armchairs, his bulk making the chair look small. 'So, what do you think?'

Smythe rubbed his chin thoughtfully and sighed before answering. 'I cannot lie, I am deeply intrigued by this creature you have discovered. He is fascinating and would no doubt make a fine addition to my cabinet – *if* he can be controlled. But I am not without doubts.'

'Please, share them. Let me address your concerns.' Fortitude leaned forward, all outward signs showing earnest interest.

Sighing, Burak settled himself into the trance state, the thudding in his head receding, along with all other physical discomforts. Fortitude's emotions came into sharp relief; he was very anxious.

'I have to wonder why you came to me with this proposal,' Smythe said, still sitting back in the armchair, in control as always. 'If Barnum is to be in London so soon, it seems more sensible for you to wait and take your creature to him. You must know that I do not command the same resources that he does. I simply cannot pay as much as he can.'

'There are a few reasons,' Fortitude said, but stopped as a young man came into the office bearing a silver tray with a tea pot and delicate cups-and-saucers set upon it. The explorer leaned back in his chair and waited while the young man served everyone. 'Thank you, George, that will be all.'

When the assistant left and they had all dutifully sipped at the tea, Fortitude resumed.

'Firstly, you are an Englishman, and Barnum is not. Prejudiced though it may be, I prefer to do business with my countrymen where possible. There are practical reasons in this case too; it will be much easier to maintain a supply of the sedative to you, here in England, than it will be to ship this to America on a regular basis.' Fortitude scratched absently at his stubble. 'In addition to that, when I first arrived back in London with the creature, I reached out to my contacts before deciding on the best way forward. Your name came up time and again as an honourable man who treats his... oddities well.'

Burak could feel the professor's confusion.

'Why would you care for the wellbeing of a creature which killed one of your men?'

Fortitude sat back, crossing one leg over the other. 'Honestly? I don't. It will mean nothing to me if the creature dies. But someone who does not take good care of the beast is less likely to maintain the appropriate sedation schedule. Should that result in harm to others or, God forbid, more deaths, then their blood would be at least in part on my conscience, as I chose to allow the beast to live. So you see the trust I am placing in you.'

The professor pinched his lips between thumb and forefinger, a gesture he made when he was thinking deeply. Burak drank some of his tea, although the trance state made it seem far away and unimportant. It would seem suspicious if he sat completely still though. He had discovered over the years that people were not comfortable with stillness. With silence.

'Why are your men so scared of it?' Smythe asked, staring at Fortitude intently.

Fortitude shrugged. 'You heard of what happened in the jungle. It is only natural that they would have a healthy fear of the thing.'

He was lying. Or at least not telling the whole story. Burak could feel the deceit running beneath the words, and the explorer's own guilt over it. He cleared his throat, the signal to the professor that Fortitude was attempting to deceive him.

'I don't believe you're telling me everything.' Smythe stood. 'Burak, I don't believe we shall be doing business here today after all. Come, I know a pleasant enough tearoom nearby, we can stop for lunch on the way back.'

Burak stood. 'A pleasure to meet you, Mr Fortitude. Good luck on your next expedition.'

Fortitude sighed heavily. 'Please. Sit. I'll tell you the rest. Then you can decide.'

Burak gave Smythe the merest nod; Fortitude was resigned to telling the truth. They both sat back down and Burak reached for his tea.

'There was an... incident on the ship.' Fortitude rubbed his eyes. Suddenly he looked weary beyond measure. 'We were keeping the beast in the cargo hold. We have a couple of cells there – when you're at sea for a long time, tempers can fray. Sometimes you need to give men some time to cool down and regain their senses. That thing was locked up in one of them, sedated. There was no reason to think he was a danger. I still can't figure out how…'

He got to his feet and crossed to a sideboard against the far wall. He lifted a decanter full of amber liquid and poured some into a glass. 'Whisky. Are you sure you won't join me? Either of you?'

Smythe shook his head.

'I will,' Burak said, surprising himself as much as the professor. He wouldn't normally indulge during the day, but he sensed that Fortitude would relax a little if he wasn't drinking alone, and the alcohol might even help the headache, which would only be worse when they left here.

Fortitude brought the drinks over and handed one to Burak, but he didn't go back to his seat. Instead, he began to pace between his chair and the sideboard, his movements jerky, all signs of the self-assured explorer gone.

'We posted a guard to keep watch over the creature. It took us some time to figure out the best schedule for the sedative, and besides, we didn't know enough about it to be sure of what it was capable of. We couldn't take any chances that it would get out of its cell. On the fourth day after we left the island, it somehow managed to kill the guard, although it did not get out of the cell, and his body was found at the other side of the hold. We could only assume that he had gotten too close to the bars and the creature had reached through – his chest was cut down to the bone and a wound in his back had pierced the kidney. We think he must have stumbled across the cargo hold, trying to get to help.' He took a deep swallow of whisky.

'The worst of it is, none of us heard a thing. He must have called for help, the attack itself must have created some noise, but we were completely unaware of it until the next man went down to relieve him. The creature was sitting peacefully in the back corner of the cell, watching everything but responding to nothing. None of it made any sense.'

Smythe leaned forward until he was perched on the edge of the chair. 'Why didn't you kill it at that time?'

'There was discussion about it,' Fortitude said. 'Some of the men wanted to toss the thing over the side and leave it for the sharks. Others argued that to get rid of it then, for there to be no payout at the end of it all, would mean that Mateo had died for nothing. Before anything could be decided, we ran into a tropical storm which lasted for three days and three nights. It almost sank us more than once. By the time we came through that...' He shrugged.

Burak finished the whisky in his glass. He knew the explorer was still holding something back. 'What else?' he asked in a low voice. 'What are you still not saying?'

Fortitude shook his head. 'Some of the men think we've been cursed. The rest of the voyage home was plagued by bad luck and they blame the creature. I don't believe in such things, it was nothing but ordinary bad luck, the kind which happens at some point in every expedition. But some of the men do, and that's why they're so scared of it.'

Smythe looked at Burak, who nodded. After that, there was just the haggling.

When Professor Flotsam's Cabinet of Peculiarities moved on from London, the Beast-Man of New Guinea was travelling with them. He had his own wagon, albeit one which locked only from the outside, and he was no longer kept under armed guard, although several of the long-term performers now carried blow guns, just in case. The sedative was administered on a day-to-day basis by adding it to his food, rather than shooting at him. The beast had shown no sign of violence or aggression, but the professor was handling him with caution.

When they stopped at the end of the day, pulling up the wagons and making camp for the night, Burak volunteered to take food to the beast. He wanted a chance to study the creature more closely.

Making sure he had a blow gun ready, just in case, he took a bowl of mutton and potatoes over to the beast's wagon. The professor had arranged for some adaptations – there was a hatch made in the door for sliding food through, and the upper part of the wagon was made from steel bars, topped by a reinforced wood roof. There were removable shutters for the sides, which could be taken off to allow light in, or closed to protect against inclement weather.

Burak pushed the food through the hatch in the door and then removed the shutters on one side of the wagon to give the creature some light and fresh air. He climbed onto a small, portable platform to look inside and was surprised to the see the creature standing just on the other side of the bars, gazing out at him. This was the closest he had been to it while it was awake, and he was struck by how still it was. How self-contained. Being close to it felt almost peaceful. After hearing the story of the death on the ship, the professor had been careful to make sure the bars on the wagon were close enough together that the creature could not reach through it, so Burak felt no fear in being so close.

He and the creature stared at each other, both curious. It took a step forward, moving into the light, and Burak gasped. *Its eyes! They're almost human.* As he watched, the beast titled its head to one side and mewled, a desolate sound which made the hairs on Burak's arms stand on end. Waves of grief and loss rolled off the creature, battering against Burak, even though he was not actively using his gift. He staggered backwards, stumbling at the top of the steps up to the platform and tumbling down to land on his back on the grass.

He lay there for a moment, winded and disoriented, before Abaye appeared at his side. She moved as if to bend down to help him, but he waved her off; the braces she wore on her legs made such movements difficult for her.

'Are you well?' she asked. 'Did the creature harm you?'

'I'm fine,' Burak said, getting to his feet with a groan. 'I was harmed by nothing but my own clumsiness.'

'He is fascinating, is he not?' Abaye said, looking towards the bars, where the beast was looking out, the side of his face pressed against the bars, straining to see.

Burak looked back at the creature. 'He is fascinating indeed. I think there is more to his story than we are yet aware of.'

Abaye was staring up at the beast almost wistfully. 'There is something almost beautiful about him, beneath the fur and tusks. Something gentle. I wish I could talk with him somehow.'

She shook herself and looked back at Burak, as if waking up. The setting sun reflected on her scales, making her even more dazzling than usual, and Burak felt an ache in his chest. She looked at the creature in a way she had never looked at him, and never would.

'There is definitely some intelligence there,' he said, looking over her shoulder towards the professor's wagon. 'It is possible we may learn some effective means of communication with him, when trust has been established. If you'll excuse me, I must speak with the professor.'

'I will speak with you soon, my friend.' Abaye turned back to the beast before she had finished speaking.

Burak gave her a sad smile then hurried away, towards Smythe's wagon. *My friend.* He would always be her friend, though he had longed to be more, since the moment they first met. He had just reached the professor's domicile and was raising his hand to knock when a scream split the evening air behind him. He whirled, his heart thrumming in his throat.

Abaye was floating in the air beside the beast's wagon, her hair pulled up straight from her head as if she were being lifted by it. The beast was throwing himself against the bars, trying to get to her. Burak staggered back towards her on legs made weak by fear. He heard the wagon door open behind him, the professor rushing out.

'What in the Lord's name is going on?' Smythe bellowed.

Burak could not answer, could do nothing but watch as Abaye was slammed against the bars of the beast's wagon by some invisible force. Purple blood flowed down her face from a wound on her scalp, and her screaming was reduced to whimpers. A terrible tearing sound filled the air and Burak could only look on, helpless, as Abaye's skin split from breastbone to lower belly, her intestines slithering out. She let out a choking scream and then her head was viciously yanked to one side, breaking her neck. Her lifeless body fell to the earth, and Burak threw himself to the ground at her side.

All around him people were screaming, crying, retching. Burak's shock had triggered his gift; grief, anger, fear – all of it beat against him, a maelstrom of emotions.

'Abaye, Abaye,' he wept, cupping her face in his hands, willing a spark to appear in those lifeless eyes. 'My friend. My love.' His tears mingled with her blood, running over the smooth planes of her face.

'She's gone, Burak,' Smythe said, pulling him to his feet. 'She's gone.'

Burak stood trembling beside the professor, his mind refusing to process all that had happened. He had been speaking with her only moments before, how could she possibly be dead?

'Kill the beast!' someone cried from behind them.

'It killed Abaye!'

'Kill it! Kill it!'

'No,' Burak croaked, his voice lost in the chaos. 'It wasn't the beast.'

Something soared through the air and smashed against the side of the wagon. The shouts increased, more items were thrown, the crowd turning into a mob.

'Enough!' the professor shouted.

No one listened.

'STOP IT!' Burak roared, his voice breaking with the volume.

The crowd froze, shocked at the outburst from the ordinarily softspoken contortionist.

'Just stop,' he said again, at a normal volume. His throat ached from the shouting. It felt as though something had torn inside. 'It wasn't the beast. He couldn't reach her.'

All Burak could feel from the beast was grief. Loss. Shame. There was not a hint of aggression or violence in its mood.

'Then what was it?' someone shouted.

'I don't know.' Burak looked from face to face, seeing fear, anger, loss everywhere he turned.

Smythe straightened his spine and rolled his shoulders, pulling himself up to reassert his position as boss. He turned in a circle, making eye contact with as many of the performers as he could. 'What has happened here is both a tragedy and an outrage and it will not go unanswered. But for justice to be served, we must first understand the cause so that we may see the right person punished.'

There were mutterings and sobs, but the mood of impending violence had broken.

'Someone must fetch a policeman,' called a voice from the back.

'No!' Burak's heart started to race again. 'There must be no police. We all know the indignities which would be heaped upon poor Abaye's body if ever the scientists got a hold of her. Not to mention some of the other performers here, who manage to go unnoticed because no one looks too closely at us.'

'Burak is right,' Smythe said. 'We will give Abaye a decent burial, but we cannot allow her body to be examined. Now, who will help me prepare a grave?'

'I will.' Samson stepped forward from where he had been lingering in the shadows.

'And I,' Thomas said.

'I will.' Burak's voice cracked, and the tears began to flow freely again. He bent and hoisted her body into his arms, cradling her close to him, heedless of the gore.

'I'll help you with her.' Amelia, the bearded lady, stepped up to his side. 'We'll get her all cleaned up and ready. Put flowers in her hair.'

Burak sniffed and nodded, following Amelia as she led him away.

In the small hours of the morning, when Abaye had been laid to rest, the beast had been heavily sedated, and the site had been cleaned up, all evidence of what had happened here hidden, Burak sat in Smythe's wagon, staring blankly at the flames in the small stove. The professor kept topping up his glass with brandy, and he had been sipping at it steadily for a while now, but he was yet to feel any effects from the alcohol. He felt numb. Swaddled. His grief a filter between him and the rest of the world, through which nothing could really penetrate.

'What happened, Burak?' the professor said, breaking the silence. 'I couldn't see what... how was she in the air?'

Burak looked at Smythe. It took a monumental effort to make himself speak. 'I don't know. It looked like she had been lifted by her hair, but I couldn't see anything above her.'

'And you're sure it wasn't the beast?'

Burak scrubbed a hand over his face. 'I'm sure. He was trying to stop it. I could feel his panic. They... they felt something for each other, Abaye and the beast. There was some sort of pull between them.'

Flames popped and crackled in the stove. Rain started drumming on the roof of the wagon. *At least that will wash away any blood we missed.*

Smythe topped up the glasses again. 'I'm sorry. I know you and she were close.'

'She was my best friend,' Burak said simply. 'I loved her.'

'It seems likely that whatever happened here, is also what happened to Fortitude's men. The beast may not be causing it, but it is clearly linked to him somehow.' The professor paused and sipped from his drink. 'It may be that killing the beast is the best way to stop whatever this is.'

'No.' Burak shook his head. 'The creature is innocent in all this. Would you really make him pay with his life for something which he tried to stop?'

Smythe sighed heavily. 'No. I suppose not.'

'Besides, we don't even know for sure that such action would prevent any more violence.'

Silence fell between them again as they sipped their drinks and listened to the rain and the fire. The camp around them was quiet, its people in mourning.

Eventually Smythe said, 'Do you think Fortitude's men were right? Is there a curse?'

'I do not know,' Burak said, finishing his drink and standing to leave. 'But I think we must find out soon.'

The Cabinet was expected in Margate, and if they failed to perform, they would soon fail to eat, so they continued with their journey. The performers all stayed as far away from the beast as possible, approaching the wagon only when necessary. Burak could not help but pity the creature, although resentment towards it curdled his stomach. An irrational part of him blamed the beast for Abaye's death, even though he knew it had fought to reach her, to protect her. The professor had written to an occultist he knew, seeking advice, and hoped an answer would be waiting for them in Kent.

Instead, when they arrived, they found the occultist himself waiting for them.

'I got straight on the first train, old chap,' he said, shaking Smythe's hand vigorously. 'I simply had to see what you've discovered.'

'I didn't discover it, so much as acquire it,' Smythe said, leading the way across the fairground where they always set up in Margate.

On the edge of the town, and close to the sea, the fairground had been a perfect location for Abaye. Burak swallowed past the lump that settled in his throat as he walked across the muddy field, carrying food for the creature, the professor and the occultist close on his heels.

'Burak, this is William Haversham, the man I told you about,' Smythe said, catching Burak by the elbow. 'William, this is Burak, our contortionist, and my friend. In addition to his flexibility, Burak has the gift of being able to touch the emotions and intentions of others. He knows more about the creature than anyone else here for that very reason.'

The occultist turned his gaze upon Burak, his face lighting up with curiosity, and held out his hand. 'How very interesting! A pleasure to meet you, Mr Burak.'

Burak shook his hand and gave him a tight smile. 'Just Burak, Mr Haversham.'

'Then you must call me William! Now, where is this "beast-man" you wrote of?' he asked, turning back to Smythe.

Burak led the way to the beast's wagon, pushing the food through the hatch in the door while the professor removed one of the side shutters, allowing Haversham to see inside.

'Good lord!' the occultist exclaimed upon seeing the creature. 'I would not have believed it coming from anyone but you, but I knew you would neither lie nor be easily duped. What in God's name is that thing?' This last was muttered as he peered between the bars.

Daylight was fading, and on the other side of the camp Burak could hear some of the others building a bonfire and preparing to spend an evening together in food and relaxation before the work of the week began in earnest the next day. He longed to be with them; laughing with Thomas, watching for Abaye to return from her hunt in the briny water of the bay below them. He would give anything to have those simple days returned.

'I have a room at an inn along the road a little,' Haversham was saying. 'My trunk is there, with as many of my instruments as I could pack. I will bring them along tomorrow and carry out an examination, if that suits you?'

'Of course,' Smythe said. 'As long as you don't mind us setting up around you. The show opens tomorrow night.'

Haversham flapped his hand. 'Of course, of course. It is one of the great tragedies of this age that one must continue to make a living, regardless of the wonders in which one is caught up.' Tearing his gaze away from the wagon, he turned to the professor and Burak. 'Would you gentlemen care to join me for a meal at the inn? I would be most honoured to buy you dinner and hear the details of your adventures so far.'

The occultist was back at the camp bright and early the next morning, unpacking a baffling array of instruments from an enormous trunk. Burak caught sight of him now and again over the course of the day, seemingly measuring things which could not be seen with the naked eye. There was no time to chat though. The big-top had to be be set up, with all the props and lamps and screens carefully positioned within.

Burak's heart felt like it was breaking all over again when he saw the empty space where Abaye's bath should have been. Sobs wracked his body and he collapsed onto his glass cube, shaking with each breath. Amelia appeared beside him and wrapped her arms around his shoulders, holding him to her bosom and making shushing noises until he was able to get himself back under control.

'Thank you,' he said, looking at her with eyes which were puffy and sore.

'Why don't you go and get some rest before the show starts?' she said gently. 'We can finish set-up without you. There's not much left to do.'

Burak didn't want to shirk his duties, but she was right – they could manage without him. And he could hardly greet the public looking like this. He stood and kissed her cheek. 'I'll be back soon.'

The inside of the wagon he shared with Thomas was dark and quiet. He didn't bother lighting a lamp, just lay on his bunk, an arm over his eyes. The weight of his grief bore down on him, pressing his limbs into the thin mattress. *Why didn't I discourage the professor from acquiring that creature? I had my doubts all along. If I had just told him that Fortitude was lying, maybe none of this would have happened.* With such thoughts echoing in his mind, he drifted into a fitful sleep.

He awoke to screaming and chaos.

For a moment he did not know where he was. Shadows danced across the walls and smoke filled the air. Screams sounded from outside and he struggled to his feet, groggy and weighed down by confusion and grief. He staggered to the door and opened it upon a scene out of a nightmare.

Over the roofs of the nearby wagons, he could see flames leaping into the air. People were running every which way, many of them blood spattered or cradling injuries. Burak stumbled down the steps, missing the last one and going to his knees on the muddy ground before pulling himself upright. Heart pounding, mouth filled with the taste of smoke and ash, he hurried in the direction most of the screaming seemed to be coming from.

Towards the beast's wagon. Of course.

Burak had no idea how long he had been asleep, but it was dark and there were normies in amongst the performers, some of them forming a bucket chain to bring water to the fire, others running around in a panic. He emerged from between two wagons and stopped, his mouth hanging open until he started coughing and doubled over. The next row of wagons was entirely aflame.

Thank the gods this happened during set up, most of the wagons will have been empty.

He turned to join the bucket chain trying to control the fire, but then heard a choking scream which made his legs turn to water. Giving the blazing row of wagons a wide berth, he staggered on, heading for the source of all of this.

The creature's wagon was intact, a soul-rending howling coming from inside. Haversham, the occultist, was cowering against the side, arms held above his head. His brass and wood instruments were scattered around him in a wide circle, broken into countless pieces, some of them twisted or crushed in ways that defied human action. Just like the bodies which lay discarded in the same manner.

As Burak watched, an invisible force lifted broken pieces of instruments, along with a severed arm, and hurled them at the beast's wagon. The items bounced off an invisible barrier which shimmered at the point of impact. The beast howled again, and the wagon shook on its wheels. Burak forced himself to move forward, wanting nothing more than to turn and run in the opposite direction from whatever was happening here.

I'm at least partly responsible for all of this. I have an obligation to try and stop anyone else getting hurt.

Haversham had spotted him and was shouting something, but Burak couldn't make out what it was over the roaring of the fire and the howling of the beast, all against the backdrop of screams and shouts from those who hadn't yet run away. The wind began to pick up, adding its voice to the cacophony. It pulled at Burak, making his clothing flap around him, stinging his face with pieces of grit and embers. He put an arm up to protect his face, his eyes streaming with tears as he pressed forward.

Something heavy hit him between the shoulder blades, driving him to his knees. Debris filled the air, pieces of various sizes battering off him, but nothing penetrated the area around Haversham and the beast. Burak put his head down and crawled towards that area of stillness, every foot of progress hard won. At the back of his mind, he wondered if he would be able to cross the barrier, or if it would repel him as effectively as it did the missiles which had been flung at it. Perhaps this whole attempt would be wasted. But if anyone could offer some insight into the madness which had overtaken the camp, surely it was Haversham. He had to at least try to reach the occultist.

He knew when he reached the barrier; all of his hair stood on end and a cold flush raced down his body, from the crown of his head to the tips of his toes. He passed through and as soon as he did, the noise dropped. He rolled over, gasping, and lay on his back for a moment.

'Burak! I wasn't sure you would get through!' Haversham crawled to Burak's side and helped him up. 'What are we going to do?'

'What happened?' Burak demanded, clinging to the occultist. Blood flowed down his leg from a wound acquired when he was hit just before passing all the way through the barrier. 'I was asleep and I woke up to…' He gestured to the madness surrounding them.

The beast howled and the torment in the sound chilled Burak to the marrow.

'I found something,' Haversham said, panting. 'I think the "beast-man" used to be a man. There's some sort of demonic presence attached to him, but it's like nothing I've ever seen or heard of. Something from the nation he came from no doubt. As soon as it knew I was aware of it, it attacked. It couldn't harm me, because of the standard protections I weave around myself when I'm working, so it grabbed the nearest person and ripped them to pieces, right in front of me. I started a binding immediately, of course, but it managed to kill several more people while I did the rite.' He drew in a shaky breath and scrubbed his eyes. 'I managed to bind it from direct harm. That's why it's throwing things and starting fires now.'

'How do we get rid of it?' Burak asked.

Haversham shook his head. 'I have no idea. I told you, I've never come across anything like this before.'

Burak stared out at the devastation surrounding their small, safe space. It suddenly occurred to him that he hadn't seen Smythe, which seemed very out of character for the man. 'What about the professor? Have you seen him?'

Haversham paled and pointed a shaking arm towards a nearby heap of debris. 'He came running while I was doing the binding. It had him when the spell took effect. It dropped him and then bombarded him with my instruments and anything else that was lying around. He hasn't moved since.'

No! The professor can't be dead. We need him. I need him! The wound in Burak's leg throbbed in time with his racing heart. There had to be a way to end this, if only they could see it.

The creature in the wagon behind them let out a cry of desolate horror, the pain it was feeling crashing over Burak. He staggered and sat down hard, his head swimming. The barrier that protected them from the demon did nothing to prevent the smoke reaching them and Burak coughed until he saw spots. He slipped into the trance state without meaning to, all of his lines of control blurred by the extremity of the circumstances.

The camp was filled with fear and anger and pain, and it all battered at Burak. He retched, and then howled to the sky, pouring all of his grief into that sound.

Then he felt it. A tug. Something pulling at the emotions swirling around him.

It was the demon-thing. It was feeding on all of the negative feelings that filled this space. Suddenly, he understood. Whatever this thing was, it caused terror wherever it went and then fed on the pain it caused. It was attached to the beast-man because he was so full of pain, enough to sustain it between larger meals.

Burak grabbed Haversham's arm. 'It feeds on pain,' he gasped. 'Pain and anger and grief and fear. We're feeding it!'

'I've heard of beings like that!' Haversham ran his hands through his hair, making it stand up even more than it already was. 'Demons and monsters which thrive on the destruction they bring.'

'So how do we stop it?' Burak leaned on the occultist's arm and pulled himself to his feet again. He swayed for a moment, dizzy from the smoke and the tide of emotions pulling at him from every direction.

'If I recall correctly, positive feelings – love, hope, joy – all are anathema to it. They will act like a poison to it, driving it away.'

Burak looked around the devastated campsite. Fire still burned, bodies lay scattered on the open ground, the people he could see were all injured. He could feel no positive emotions here at all. How could anyone feel hope or joy when surrounded by the destruction of their home and grieving the deaths of their loved ones.

But what is grief but love unspent? I grieve for Abaye because I loved her and now all of that love is still inside me with nowhere left to go.

He closed his eyes and searched within himself. He reached for memories of Abaye. At first, all he saw was her lifeless body lying on the ground like a discarded toy, and rage rose up inside him, curdling his stomach and making him clench his fists and his jaw, but he pushed past that, forced that memory aside. Instead, he saw her laughing as she splashed water at him when he reached to help her from the bathtub, remembered long nights sitting by a campfire sharing secrets, saw the flickering flames reflected in her scales.

There it was. Love. He sank into it, at the same time opening himself up and pushing all of that emotion into the sky, towards the demon-thing which raged on the other side of Haversham's barrier. He felt it weaken, felt the pain his love caused.

'It's working!' He turned his tear-streaked face to Haversham. 'I know what to do. But I'm not enough. Not on my own.'

'What can I do?' Haversham asked. 'How can I help?'

'I don't... I need more...'

The thing outside the barrier picked up a whole wagon and threw it into the fire, which had been finally starting to fade. Screams went up from the people who were still in the area, the fear they felt pressing against the love which Burak was pouring out, revitalising the demon.

'I need you to find as many people as you can and tell them to focus all of their thoughts on the people they love. To think of the happiest times they can remember. It's going to take all of us to defeat this thing.'

'We have to go together,' Haversham said. 'Otherwise the barrier will move with me and you'll be left exposed.'

Burak shook his head. 'I can't do all that and focus on channelling the energy at the same time. Besides, we don't want it to figure out what you're up to. Let it think I'm the threat.'

Haversham grabbed his arm and shook him. 'You don't understand – you won't be protected. It can't directly harm you because of the binding, but you saw it throw that wagon.'

'I know.' Burak said, patting Haversham's hand. His concentration was faltering, and he could feel the demon getting stronger again already. 'I understand.'

'You'll die.' A barrage of debris hit the barrier again at his words.

'I know. But I think I can hold out long enough to take it with me.'

'I cannot in good conscience—' Haversham began, but Burak held up a hand and cut him off.

'If we do nothing, everyone here will die. This way, at least there is a chance. Please.'

Haversham swallowed hard and then shook Burak's hand firmly. 'You have my deepest admiration, sir.'

Burak briefly considered crawling under the beast-man's wagon in the hope that it offered some protection, but then he remembered the thing throwing a wagon into the fire and dismissed the thought. Instead, he settled himself on the ground in the lotus position and trained his thoughts on Abaye once more.

Haversham squeezed his shoulder and then moved away. As he went, Burak felt the occultist forcing his own emotions towards love and peace, and he added those feelings to his own as he projected everything skyward once more. As well as Abaye, he remembered Smythe and many nights on the road, sharing a meal and a brandy, interviewing performers to determine if they would be a good fit. He remembered days of setting up and maintenance with many of the others, moments of friendship and fun, and he allowed all of it to flow through him and towards the real beast which beset their camp.

The moment that the barrier no longer protected him, Burak felt the wind batter him, bits of metal and wood bouncing off of him, embers alighting on his arms, but Burak had spent years training himself to ignore physical discomforts. It would take more than this to break his concentration.

Haversham did as he had been asked, and Burak could feel the change in the group energy with each person the occultist spoke to. Each added their strength to his. The demon was weakening, he could feel the pain it suffered with each new bond of love added to the stream that Burak kept up. It grew desperate, hitting him with more and more items, shrieking in an uncontrollable rage.

Something heavy hit Burak, knocking him onto his back. At first, he thought it wasn't that bad, but then he realised he couldn't get up. His body was no longer responding to his command. That invisible monster above him roared in triumph and, for a moment, Burak's conviction wavered and he was filled with fear. There was no pain, but he couldn't get a deep breath. Something inside his body was broken. His vision started to cloud and he felt the fear returning to the camp, but then Abaye appeared at his side, smiling and holding her hand out to him.

The surge of love within him was enough to light up the world. The demon was blasted away, dissipated by the force of his adoration. The wind dropped, the debris still flying around fell to the ground, and the last thing Burak saw was Haversham dropping to his knees on the grass at his side.

'You did it, man! You saved us all.'

Abaye stood and started to walk away, and Burak followed.

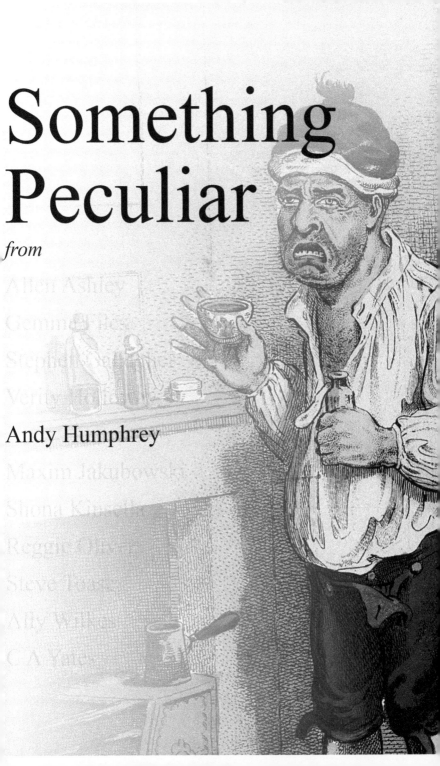

Something Peculiar

from

Andy Humphrey

Hide and Seek

"…do you like games…"

Hide

DANNY WAS looking forward to the Findus crispy pancakes and chips that he was having for tea, when the woman sat next to him on the bench next to the swings.

She sat close to him, and he was already pressed hard up against the chipped wooden arm on the right hand side of the bench. Her leg touched his. Strictly speaking it was the cloth of her skirt and the grey polyester of his school trousers that touched, but he didn't like it much and there was nowhere for him to go.

She looked at him, *right* at him, and he looked back. He didn't feel as though he had a choice.

"Well, that's rude," she said. There was a large black bag in her lap and her hands were folded around it.

"What?" Danny said.

"I'm forty two. That's not old. Not old at all."

"I didn't say anything." But he had *thought* it; that she was old. Very old, even older than his mum. Probably. It was hard to tell these days.

"It's not her fault," the woman said. "It's the drink. Well, I suppose that *is* her fault. Technically. I mean, I assume there's no-one pouring the stuff down her throat through a funnel, but… your dad." She shook her head. Her hair, which was dark and short and neat, didn't move.

"I'm sorry, Danny, but… your dad. I mean, who can blame her? A little vodka. Lots of gin. Who can blame her, Danny?"

He couldn't stop looking at her. He blinked back tears. "Who are you?"

She sat back suddenly. "Oh. Well, that's me being rude, isn't it? I haven't even introduced myself." She didn't say anything else though. She just stared at the swings opposite. Her clothes were grey and plain. *She could be a teacher*, Danny thought. *Or a librarian.* He looked around, but the park remained resolutely empty. It was why he liked coming here.

"I've got to go."

"Of course you have. Findus crispy pancakes and chips. Maybe a piece of Viennetta for afters. You'll get a bit more than your sister, but I suppose that's only fair. Growing boy and all that."

"Mum said I shouldn't speak to strangers."

"But we're not strangers, Danny. We're the firmest of friends. Always have been, always will be."

"I'm scared."

The woman huffed out a tiny sigh and stared straight ahead again, past the swings and towards the row of trees that shielded the houses beyond. It was winter and the branches were bare. "How old are you?"

"Nine."

"Don't lie, Danny. You're eight."

"I'm almost nine."

"It's three months until your birthday. A quarter of a year. Facts matter. Don't lie, it demeans us both."

He'd never heard the word *demeans* before and didn't know what it meant, but he was a bit angry now, as well as scared. "Why ask me then, if you already know? Sounds like you think you know everything."

Her mouth twisted into something that might have been a smile. "Do you like games, Danny?"

"I need to get home. Mum will worry."

"Well, we both know that's not true." Danny pulled his school bag onto his lap and tried to stand. He was wedged between the woman and the arm of the bench. "What about hide and seek? Do you like hide and seek?"

"That's for kids. It's stupid."

"It can be fun."

"Okay," he said slowly. He turned his head away. Perhaps if he wasn't looking at her she wouldn't be able to read his thoughts. "You go and hide. I'll count to a hundred."

The woman gave a dry chuckle. "Very clever. But, no. You hide. I'll find you."

"I don't want you to find me." He looked back at her. The skin on her face and hands was very white. He thought of milk and then, unbidden, of bone.

"Perhaps I won't find you."

"But you know everything."

"I don't know *everything*. And I don't cheat. I never cheat."

"I don't want to play." He was close to tears again. He didn't want to cry. He hated crying.

She gave another sigh, a longer, deeper one. "Oh, Danny. Don't be a disappointment."

"Okay." He shifted a little and his knee scraped against the woman's leg. "But you're the grown up. A hundred isn't enough, I need more of a chance. I'll go and hide, but you have to count to a *million*."

"Wow. That's a big number. Do you know how long it would take me to count to a million?" He shook his head. "Eleven days. How far could you get in eleven days? Where would you hide? You could fly to the moon."

"I don't think I could."

"No. Perhaps not. Anyway, a million… it isn't enough. Let's make it a billion."

"A billion?"

"Do you know how long that will take, Danny? Of course you don't. Thirty one years. It will take me thirty one years to count to a billion. Then I'm going to come and look for you."

"This is silly."

"I agree," she said, "Very silly. Still… here we are. Do we have a deal?"

"A deal?"

"Don't worry, a nod will do. I'm not going to touch you." He realised that he was trying to shrink away from her. "Not yet."

Something chilly skittered along the length of his spine. He nodded. She inched away from him, allowing him to stand. He did so gratefully, clutching his bag to his chest. His legs felt distant and weak. "You won't cheat?" he said.

"I never cheat." She brought her hands up until they covered her face. Her nails were bitten to the quick. "Hide," she said. She started to count. She was slow and methodical.

When she reached nine, Danny ran.

"You usually love the old crispy pancakes," his mum said later, as he sat at the kitchen table and manoeuvred a couple of peas listlessly around his plate.

"I'm not hungry," Danny said.

"Can I have his chips?" Ruth said. His sister sat opposite him. She was a couple of years younger than Danny and she had a floppy blonde fringe and a pouty mouth that often hung open as she ate.

"Give him a chance, Ruthy." His mum was loitering behind him and he felt the palm of her hand, rough and cold, as she pressed it against his forehead. "You're not warm. Could be going down with something, though. Loads of bugs, aren't there? At that bloody school."

"Bugs," his sister said, with a wet giggle. She was kicking her feet rhythmically against a table leg. It didn't seem to bother his mother, but it drove Danny mad. She had a chip speared on her fork. She bit it in half and chewed noisily.

His mum didn't smell of drink yet. Which was good. It was early, Danny supposed, but it wasn't *too* early, and often enough over the last month or so he'd come home to find her face down on her bed or on the settee in the living room. On those occasions he'd pour his sister and himself a bowl of cereal. It was fine. They both liked Coco Pops. Still… Ruth kept asking where Daddy was and why Mummy was sleeping during the day and why she smelled funny sometimes; he couldn't answer these questions and increasingly he thought that it was unfair that he was being asked them at all.

"I'm not ill," Danny said. "Something happened. At the park."

His mother went still and quiet and then she yanked a chair from under the table and sat on it. She nudged up close to Danny and put a hand on his arm. "What happened? Who was it, Danny? What did he do?"

She was too close and it made Danny think of the woman in the park. Even though this was his mum, he didn't like that her face was so near to his; he could see the lines on her forehead and the red threads that laced the whites of her eyes. He could smell her breath.

"It wasn't a he," Danny said.

"What?"

"It was a lady."

"Okay, Danny." Her voice was getting a little higher now, a little thinner as her patience ran down. "What did the *lady* do?"

Danny hesitated. His sister was staring at them, blue eyes wide open. She'd stopped kicking at the table leg. That was something at least. He wished he hadn't started this, but it was too late now. He told them what had happened in the park. He said it quickly, barely drawing breath. When he'd finished it was quiet in the kitchen for a moment and then his sister gave a shrill laugh and his mum said, "Do you seriously expect me to believe that?"

"It's what happened. I can't help it."

"You can't help it?" Danny stared at his plate. His mum's voice was becoming small and mean. This usually happened after she'd been drinking, not before. "I haven't got time for this."

"Danny's going mad," Ruth said, matter-of-factly. Then, "Can I have some ice-cream?"

"I know you like your stories, Danny, I know you like your books…" She shook her head slowly. Danny saw her eyes flick up towards the cupboard that contained her gin and vodka. "No harm in that, I thought. Bit *too* much like your dad for my liking, but still…"

"It's not my fault."

His mum stood quickly and pushed the chair back in place with a squeal. "Are you seriously telling me that if we go over to the park now we'll find an old woman sitting on a bench with her hand over her eyes counting to a billion?"

Yes, Danny thought, *that's exactly what we'll find*. But he knew how it sounded. He knew how this was going. He was losing, had already lost. He should never have said anything. "I've got a headache," he said.

"Of course you have," his mum said. She grabbed a glass from the draining board, then went over to the cupboard and pulled a bottle down, cradling it to her as she made her way out of the door. "I'm going upstairs. Do your homework, both of you."

"Danny's mad," Ruth said again.

He looked at her, then back at his plate of cold food. He never ate another Findus crispy pancake. He never went to the park again, either.

Seek

Two years after his mother's funeral, on a sweaty husk of an evening at the end of a stinking hot summer, Danny pulls his sister from a squat in a sink estate at the edge of Norwich city centre.

"Fuck's sake," Ruth says, sliding from his damp grasp, twirling away from him towards the pavement and the hot, empty street.

It's like a dance, Danny thinks, as she pirouettes and faces him again. Her sleeveless t-shirt is grubby, bunched at the waist, where it hangs over the beltline of her tiny pink shorts. Her arms and legs are thin and underdeveloped. She still has her floppy fringe; sweat-heavy, it droops down to her eyebrows. She's twenty-one years old, but she could be forty or fifteen depending on how the light catches her.

"How many times? Stop white-knighting me."

"I don't know what that means."

"You *do*!" She's hunched forward, rocking on the balls of her feet. Her indignation is so cartoonishly palpable that Danny almost laughs. He doesn't, though, and it's probably just as well. "Stop fucking saving me. It's really annoying."

"I'm not saving you."

"Jesus!" She shakes herself, and moisture sprays from her hair and face. *She looks like an animal*, Danny thinks. Wasted and wretched and lost. "My friends are in there." She points at the terraced house behind Danny and he instinctively turns to look at it; boarded windows, a scabby plywood front door that hangs half-open. Music, something dull and percussive, filters distantly from somewhere. There's no other sign of life. The house's occupants had scuttled into shadowy corners when he'd gone in after his sister. *Like insects*, he thought. Cockroaches. "What will they think?"

"They're not your friends."

"Danny! Fuck!" She puts her hands to her face and gives another petulant, wringing quiver and then starts to cry. *Of course she does*, Danny thinks. She's silent at first, but soon the sobs become shrill and braying and start to draw the attention of some other occupants of this wretched street. A man shouts from a window; *if someone doesn't shut her up, I will.*

Danny steps towards her; he's grown big and strong, physically at least, and he towers over his sister. He tells her to shush and her sobs subside a little. He stretches his arms out towards her and she steps into them, as she always does. *It's just a dance*, he thinks. He feels her heat, pulsing against him. Her skin and bone meld into his ample flesh. Although he can smell her and her breath is urgent and irregular against his throat, for a moment he is unsure if she is actually there at all.

He thinks, unbidden and for the first time in years, of a cold, pale woman, sat on a park bench, counting and counting.

Two days after their mother's death from alcoholism, aged forty-four, Danny found Ruth in a surprisingly up market apartment in a gentrified area of Glasgow. There was no response from his sister when he told her of their mother's passing; she remained hunched forward on a faux-leather sofa, rolling a joint. She didn't want to go back to Norwich. He didn't entirely blame her for that, but he was damned if he was going to the funeral on his own. She lasted to the end of the service, which was something, he supposed. Then she disappeared again.

When he's thirty Danny is dragged to a cabin in an Estonian forest as part of a stag weekend. The groom is a colleague, rather than a friend – Danny has spent his life assiduously avoiding any meaningful friendships – but he's also the boss's son, and it's made clear that it would be bad form not to attend.

The lodge has wooden walls and stone floors, and the head of an enormous wild boar is hung above an open fireplace. It's a Sunday in October and the bulk of the party are roaming the surrounding woods, accompanied by dogs and a pair of supremely indifferent local guides. They are hunting for elk and deer; the echoes of occasional, desultory gunshots drift across the still morning. Danny has avoided the hunting trip, citing a savage migraine and braving the derision of his heavily hung-over companions.

He is left in the company of Gordon, a mild, inoffensive man who seems as out of place this weekend as Danny himself.

"What was your excuse?" Gordon says, pouring himself a cup of strong, bitter coffee and joining Danny at the vast oak table that dominates the kitchen area.

"I've got a migraine."

"Nice one." Gordon places a hand on his own chest and mimics a weak cough. "Asthma attack."

"I've got no idea why I'm here."

"Me either. It's hard to say no to the old man, though, right?"

"I suppose." Another gunshot sounds, closer this time, followed by a peal of laughter. "Perhaps they're hunting each other and not the deer."

"One can only hope. Still, strippers later. Something to look forward to."

"Strippers? Out here?"

"Yeah. They bus them in, apparently. All part of the service."

"Jesus Christ."

"What? Not your thing?"

"No. Not at all. It's so…" Danny searches for a word, and then it comes, along with a memory, or a part of one. "…demeaning."

"Demeaning? Okay. Hey, what's up? You've gone white. You seen a ghost or something?"

"I don't believe in ghosts." Danny drains his cup. There's a grandfather clock in the corner of the room, its ticking low and sonorous. He thinks of a woman, counting.

Gordon shifts in his seat. "You're hard work, Dan, I'm beginning to wish I'd gone hunting."

"Sorry."

"Just kidding. You're not that bad. How's Ruth?"

Danny's head snaps up. "Ruth?"

"Your sister."

"How do you know Ruth?"

Gordon waits a moment, then speaks carefully. "You brought her to the Christmas do? A couple of years ago. We sat at the same table. Remember?"

Danny remembers. It had been during a good spell, six months or so, Ruth in her old room, meals together. She even put on a little weight and laughed a couple of times. "Of course. Sorry."

"She's seemed like a nice girl, I just wondered…"

"I don't know how she is, Gordon. She disappeared again, that Christmas Eve. I haven't seen her since."

"I'm sorry, man."

"I've hunted for her. I mean, I always do. But… this time, it's as though she really doesn't want to be found."

"She is an adult, I suppose."

"Yes," Danny says slowly. "She is an adult. You know, maybe she'll be one of the strippers that they send in later. That would be quite the break, wouldn't it?"

"Fucking hell," Gordon says.

A few weeks shy of his fortieth birthday, Danny's company send him to Japan to attend a conference. It's held in a hotel in Sendai, a large city to the north of Tokyo. The conference lasts for a week but his boss tells him to stay for two. He supposes it suits his colleagues that he is away for a while, preferably in a different continent. He is aware that he has become an unwelcome presence in the office – a sour, unapproachable fixture, welded to his corner seat, rarely vacating it, even for lunch. He often works weekends too, and he supposes that his colleagues must feel that they never have a break from him. He doesn't get much time away from them, either, but that doesn't bother him as he can barely recall any of their names.

The conference is tedious and mostly peripheral to Danny's work. He endures the sessions that he has to attend and retires to his room or the restaurant's bar when his obligations are over. He speaks no Japanese but finds that pointing and gesturing are perfectly adequate when one's needs extend only as far as something to eat and drink. The hotel staff are scrupulously polite, but not overly attentive, which is the perfect combination as far as Danny is concerned.

He settles in a corner booth, nursing a glass of ginger ale with lime and lots of ice. He can see the street through the window opposite; it's busy, but not intimidatingly so. It's early evening and humid outside, but the air-conditioning, which mumbles unobtrusively in the background, keeps the bar pleasantly cool. He has a well-worn book in front of him – a collection of Robert Aikman's short stories. He's read them before and will do so again. He likes M R James too, and Le Fanu and Machen and Lovecraft. He finds that if a writer is still alive, he probably won't enjoy their work.

He's preparing to read when a woman sweeps into the booth and takes the seat opposite him. He doesn't look up. He knows who it is.

"Fancy seeing you here," the woman says. Danny keeps his head down. He scrunches his eyes shut. Perhaps if he can't see her, this won't be actually happening at all. "Hello? Bit rude, after all this time. You could at least look at me."

Her voice is exactly the same. Danny feels as though he's eight years old again. Ruth and his mum are waiting at home. His tea will be on the table soon. "I don't need to look at you."

"He can speak. That's something, I suppose." He feels her breath on his face as she sighs. "Oh, Danny. What ever happened to that sweet little boy?"

He raises his head slowly until their eyes meet. She looks exactly the same as that day on the park bench. He is not remotely surprised. "What do you mean?"

A waiter materialises at the table. The woman orders something, in what seems to Danny to be flawless Japanese. The man bows and glides away again. Turning back to Danny, she says, "You were my favourite."

"Favourite?"

"Now look at you."

He glances down at himself, inadvertently. "What's wrong with me?"

"Have you never heard of salad, Danny?"

"I have a sedentary job. And I'm big-boned. My metabolism…" His voice is sliding into a whine, so he pauses. "It's none of your business what size I am."

She adjusts her hands so that the palms are facing him. "Your poor heart, is all I'm saying."

"At least I have a heart."

"Good one," she intones. "Burn, as the young people say."

"You're a fraud." Danny feels a slow, ponderous anger growing in him.

"I beg your pardon?"

"I went past that park bench several times. You were never there. This is some kind of cheap trick."

She sighs. "It's lies again, is it? You never entered that park again. And if you had, perhaps you would have seen me, perhaps you wouldn't. But this is no trick."

"Nothing but riddles. You were there, but you weren't there."

"Not everything is literal, Danny. Linear."

"Schrodinger's witch," he says, tossing back the remainder of his ginger ale. It burns like raw spirit.

"I'm not a witch."

"What are you, then? What would you call yourself?"

"I'm not a witch," she says again, and then the waiter is there, with more ginger ale for Danny and a large glass of a colourless liquid for the woman.

"Hit a nerve, have I?"

She curls her fingers around the glass. The nails are blunt and ragged. "You have no imagination. The things you could ask me. The things I could tell you."

"Such as?"

Her head comes up; unlined features, eyes like stone. "How your father died."

"My father's dead?"

"You know that he is."

"I really don't…"

"You do now."

And he does. It was over a decade ago. The date is a live, fluorescent thing, crawling across his brain. It was an overdose. Of course it was. On the floor of a tenement, a slum. A needle jutting from a skinny, pale arm. So utterly predictable. He outlived Danny's mother, though, where's the justice in that? The images fade. The imprint remains. "How can I trust… that?" His voice is not entirely steady.

"I think you know that you can." Her voice is softer now, and no longer taunting. She raises her glass and tilts it towards Danny. "A toast. To your father."

"I'm not drinking a toast to him."

"Your mother, then?"

"My mother?"

"I can tell you her thoughts before she died, if you like?"

"No. Christ, no. Please don't…"

"Okay, okay. But… she did love you. She did care. She just couldn't cope. That's all. Not her fault."

"Not her fault," Danny says mechanically.

"Not really. But not yours, either. Although I know you think it is."

"You don't have to be a witch to work that out."

Her smile is surprisingly gentle. "No. I suppose not. But, as I said, I'm not a witch."

"What the fuck are you, then?"

"Maybe I'm your fairy godmother, Danny. Did you ever think of that?"

"No. I really didn't." He starts to raise his glass, then stops. "You haven't spiked this, have you?"

"You know better than that."

He finds that he does. He drinks. "If you're my fairy godmother," he says, looking into her face, "Tell me where Ruth is."

"At last," she says, her eyes finally coming alive. "A decent question."

She stretches a hand out towards his face. He expects her touch to be shocking, but it isn't. The woman's palm, warm and smooth, presses against his cheek.

Ten days later Danny stands at the edge of a drive that leads to a pleasant semi-detached on the outskirts of Edinburgh. It is a soft evening. The day sheds its light gently. It is diffuse, amber-coloured; Danny feels it falling, gathering on his arms and face.

The drive is neatly shingled and curves artfully towards a timbered porch. The house itself has an exposed brick frontage and is impeccably maintained. Danny does not know what to think. This is not what he was expecting. He anticipated the usual; a slum, a squat. Lives on fire.

As Danny hesitates, the door at the front of the porch opens inwards. His sister folds her arms and leans against the frame. Her head tilts to one side as she looks at him. The sound of a child's laughter drifts from the open door, followed by a man's voice, warm and kind.

She seems more substantial, Danny thinks. She appears to glow. It could be the residual light from the house's interior, he supposes. Or the particular way in which this day runs down. He isn't sure. He doesn't care.

He clears his throat and feels the crunch of the gravel beneath his feet as he steps onto the drive.

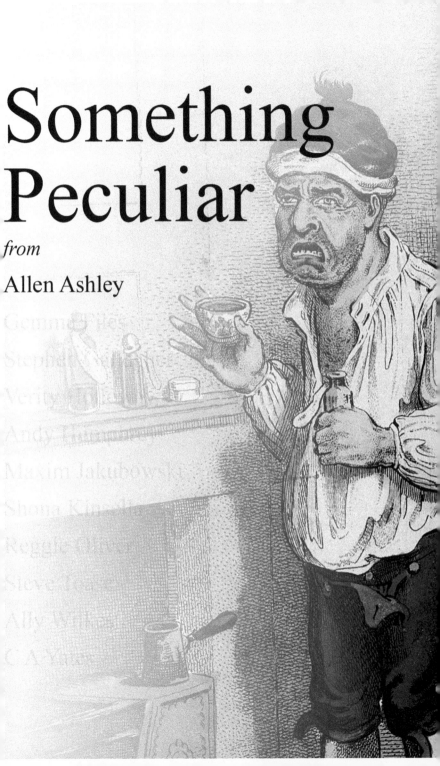

Something Peculiar

from

Allen Ashley

Lightbulb Moments

"…don't open that box…"

HEY, HOWIE, come and check this out. Something weird is going on."

Howie paused the novel on his Kindle. Honestly, Jack was a good-looking guy, and bright in so many ways, but on occasion he was dumb as a parking fine.

"I give you one job to do in the house and—"

"Shh, Howie. Listen to this lightbulb… Well?"

"It's hissing. It's defective. I told you not to go to the discount hardware shop."

"No, man, it's singing. Come on, take a look at it."

"And get purple flashes for five minutes? You must be joking, Jack."

"I'll turn it off. Wait 'til it cools down."

It was a standard bulb: thin curved glass encasing electric filaments, copper coloured metal screwing thread.

Howie kept the font size large on his devices, but now he reached into a pocket and extracted reading glasses.

"It's… a person," he whispered. "Trapped inside, bent over like they're praying. A Halloween trick?"

"In July?"

"Well, Studley's is known for keeping out of date stock."

"I think he's alive," Jack whispered.

After a few beats: "So do I."

❖

"What's he doing now?"

"Nothing, Jack."

"Is he dead?"

"Nah, he moved his arm a bit."

"I think he needs to be plugged in to keep alive."

"That's the maddest suggestion, Jack."

"This is the maddest situation, Howie. We've got a mini person stuck inside a lightbulb. He could be real; he could be some AI construct. He could even be a trapped soul."

"Souls don't turn up in table lamps."

"Are you sure of that? I was brought up Catholic before I came out. We got saints and angels and spirits in every vessel you can think of."

The tiny, trapped figure appeared to be oblivious to their conversation. He was lightly bearded and clothed in an off-white one-piece garment. A visitor from the future?

"Old Watts will be round for the rent later," said Jack. "Can you check the shoebox for cash? And I'm going to plug our little friend back in. I'll take full responsibility if… anything goes wrong. OK?"

Howie was in a reverie, wondering what it would be like to be as small as the character he'd nicknamed Eddie – short for Edison, of course – when the doorbell rang. He heard Jack admit their landlord Mr Watts. Some sort of tax dodge, no doubt. Nobody else he knew paid weekly in cash, but their rent was a few percentage points lower to compensate.

"Old school," Watts would mutter. ("Old fill in your own cuss word," Jack had later commented.)

"Nice to see you boys keeping the place neat and tidy," said Watts. He sniffed. "And no jerk chicken or curry. Good. But what's that high-pitched whistling noise?"

"Must have left my phone on Spotify," Howie answered.

"I thought you types all liked disco and *YMCA*."

"Everybody likes *YMCA*," said Jack, miming the actions.

Watts strode over to the corner table and put his ear, but crucially not his eyes, close to the lamp.

"I know you guys ain't rich," he offered, "but you'd do well not to use any substandard products around the house. You catch?"

"Sure thing, Mr Watts," said Howie. "Only the best Chinese imports for us, straight off the container ships."

"Did he see it? I mean him, I mean Eddie?"

"I don't know, Jack. Watts is a hard one to read. Let's get some food on."

"And what about our lightbulb man?"

"I need to sleep on it. Let's just treat things as normal for now – keep the lamp on until bedtime."

But Howie didn't sleep well. As Jack tossed and turned under the duvet, Howie was pushed to the edge of the bed and felt increasingly cramped. At some time around 4am he tiptoed to the bathroom then, on his way back, stopped off at the lounge. He switched on his phone to get the torch function going and shone it just past the lamp. Even half-asleep, he appreciated the irony of using a light to examine a lightbulb. The figure – Eddie, oh god, now they'd named him they were surely responsible for his welfare – was slumped and somnolent. How could something so small be causing such a brain ache? Then again, viruses were microscopic and look at the damage they'd inflicted over the past few years…

At breakfast, Jack said, "I didn't get offered a shift today. I'm going to stay home, keep an eye on… things."

"It's like we've finally got the pet we always promised ourselves," Howie laughed.

At work, he spent most of the day in a tiny cubicle tied to a screen and a phone line. He had hoped that, post-Covid, he would be working from home, or at least hybrid, but Mrs Osram was old school and had insisted that they all be back in the office as soon as was practical. Howie had once overheard her say, "I like to keep all my staff where I can see them." Howie noted that, in this nest of cubicles, Mrs O could discern occupation but not individuality.

The security lights on the walk back from the station only sprung into life as you approached them, and they still felt new and troubling. Jack had moaned several times about the route becoming "A paradise for muggers" who would simply wait motionless in the gloom. "Save the planet – over my dead body." But Jack could look after himself and had proved it several times. Howie wished his partner were beside him on the pavement right now.

Howie let himself into the apartment. He could hear the rhythmic chirr of an old inkjet printer.

"Idea of mine," said Jack. "Print a message in a tiny font which will seem big for Eddie. Get him to have one hand for yes and two for no."

They propped the page against a pair of wineglasses. Waited. Either lit or dim, the man in the lightbulb didn't respond. Surely the glass of his enclosure was transparent, not opaque.

"Run it through Google Translate," Howie said. "Try French. Maybe Italian or Spanish as well."

To no avail. Jack thought he discerned a shrug from the tiny figure, but Howie was blinking away after-images at that moment so couldn't confirm. "Poor Eddie," said Jack. "What do we do now?"

"I'm tired and hungry. Let's order a pizza and watch TV like a normal couple."

Jack didn't have a shift assigned for the next day, either. He was going to stay at home, do a little research, be there for a couple of home deliveries. Howie hid his annoyance but on the way home stopped off at Studley's discount hardware shop, asked the clerk about old-style lightbulbs.

She pushed a lock of pink hair back behind her ear and said, "I think they was faulty or we 'ad some complaints an' all. They's ready to go back to the depot."

"Could you have a look out back for me, please? I've got this Edwardian lamp…"

"Edwardian? Wassat – a new make?"

"No, it's a time period in history. Like *Downton Abbey*. You know, antique stuff."

Eventually, she returned with a medium-sized box. Bare lightbulbs sat in loose straw like protected eggs. A couple of them were shaded red or green.

"I'll take the lot," said Howie. "How much?"

"Dunno, there's no barcode. Offer me something."

He refused the extra surcharge of a large carrier bag. The weather was dry and not too breezy, he could carry the package safely home, holding it between chest and hip height throughout, like a precious treasure. Like Jesus in the manger or Moses in his wicker basket.

"I'm convinced Eddie is a soul," said Jack, when he got home. "God, what have you got there?"

"Maybe a load of junk. Or maybe a few more spirits in limbo."

Crammed in together with only a smattering of straw packaging for ballast, some bulbs were shaded amber or red, one green, others plain. A few were cracked – mishandled or simply unfortunate. Shards sharp and finger-piercing produced exclamations of surprise and pain, drops of blood from pricked fingers as if in sacrifice.

At last, they were sorted into empty and occupied. Six new souls, two of them appearing to be female. All somnolent.

"So what now?" asked Howie.

"We plug them in. In turn, if necessary."

"This is getting too weird, Jack. I think I want to step away from this spooky religious stuff."

"We can't. We've got a moral responsibility here. Where's your sense of curiosity?"

"Dead, like the proverbial cat. Look, you do what you feel you need to do, I'm not sure I want any part in it."

❖

The cold and empty other half of the bed. The lack of company, comfort… Then that noise, like some awful experimental vocal symphony by a crazed avant-garde composer… Morning. At last and too soon.

"I feel like death," said Howie, "but you look even worse. Try to get some rest today."

"I'm fine. Buzzing, in fact. One of the, uh, characters in the new lightbulbs I think just might be my old high school teacher, Mr Ligetti. I could try the printout on him, he spoke English and Italian and Russian."

"I vaguely remember him. But these… characters in the bulbs are just one inch high. Mr Ligetti was probably five foot six."

"You think our souls are as big as our bodies? That's so sweet." Jack reached his hand towards Howie's face. For a moment there was the unexpected fear of being struck. But the touch was gentle. Jack added, "I meant to say, I've got a sort of secret project going on in the utility room. A birthday surprise for you. No peeping."

"I told you not to spend anything on me this year, money's too tight."

Walking to the station, Howie dreamed of the double espresso that he'd prepare as soon as he got to the office. He was worried about Jack, who tended to have these obsessions from time to time. It had been pottery a year ago, basket-weaving before that.

Howie refused to delve too deeply into the lightbulb mystery. He accepted that he might seem soft, more a musicals man than a horror movie fan. Aged fourteen, a group of his friends had experimented with a Ouija board.

He and Jack had come out of it alright, but their friend Liam had gone somewhat off the rails soon after.

Focus. Don't open that box. Compartmentalise. Get on the train.

Tiredness and the burden of being the sole breadwinner was grinding Howie down. He felt slightly distanced from the real world, as if he were just going through the motions. Yeah sure, motions of commuting and fulfilling his job description as his bright-eyed partner stayed at home all day checking on his menagerie of "souls", or else spent time in the closed-off utility room attending to his secret construction.

Mrs Osram called Howie into her office shortly after lunch. Old school as ever, she'd asked him to print out his updated customer figures. The machine had whirred and fizzed as Howie waited over it. Now, as Howie handed over the pages, they both received an electric shock.

"Sorry, some sort of static build-up," said Howie.

She was cradling her fingers beneath her armpit. "Too much nylon in your clothing. Or a mineral and vitamin deficiency. Did you know that? Saw it on Google."

Howie shook his head, but not too hard for fear of further live charges.

It was odd. He and Jack had argued last night and Jack had pushed him a couple of times. There had been a little jolt of electricity then, and not in a passionate way. The spark had made Jack retreat, mumbling.

Mrs Osram was still pontificating. "We're not s'posed to talk about someone's skin colour these days, but you look a bit peaky, Howie. Are you sure you're not coming down with something?"

He gave his bravest, brightest smile. "A cup of coffee and a cereal bar from my desk will do the trick."

Later, on the train home, he found a seat with surprising ease. He tried to read the showbiz gossip in the free newspaper but the carriage lights seemed to be operating at low power, giving everywhere a tinge of yellow.

❖

When Howie arrived home from work he noticed a few packages stored in the lounge and a chair blocking access to the utility room.

"What gives, Jack?" he asked.

"I'm working on a surprise out the back."

"I'll need to wash a couple of shirts soon."

"Leave them with me, I've not got assignments for tomorrow."

"What are these purchases?"

"We had some cash in the joint account. I got a deal on lamps. I'm going to hook up the other bulbs that have occupants."

"This is getting weirder by the minute, Jack."

"Come and have a look at Edison. He's positively glowing."

The figure's arms stretched upwards in supplication or adoration; a soul shining brightly in the glow. All very neat and uplifting but so far removed from this world and its everyday concerns.

Howie blinked away after-images, said, "Did you pop to Tesco and get anything for dinner?"

"Nah, been busy. Had to stay in for the delivery." Jack's tone was calm, but his eyes flashed with hints of the anger that had been evident once before, when he'd beaten off two boneheads who'd accosted them on the way back from a club. "Might need an extension lead," Jack added. "Gonna set up an array."

"No concerns about the energy price rises, then."

"F'sake, Howie, it's just a few table lamps. Live a little."

Howie took himself off to the bathroom on the pretext of having a shave. Live a little? Those little creatures or animatronics or fakeries, were they living a little in some bizarre way? He wished he'd never mentioned the strange phenomenon, had quietly unscrewed the bulb and put it out for the trash. But now he was complicit in this Pandora's Box business. When and how would it all end?

"Edison's dead," Jack announced. "But it's OK, everyone else is shining brightly in their spectral light."

Howie hung up his coat, following his partner into the living room where the lamps glowed like yellow-white ghostly floodlights. *Occupied* floodlights. Jack handed him the dead lightbulb. It was dull to the touch, the surface slightly clouded but revealing a tiny, curled-up corpse within.

"What do you want me to do with this?" Howie asked.

"Maybe we should bury him?"

"We don't have a garden. And the plant pots on the balcony are too small."

"I was thinking the park. At the weekend."

"OK. In the shell or out of it?"

"I think it's more respectful not to break the container, Howie. Then again, we could... find out stuff if we open the bulb."

"I get the feeling you want me to make the decision. And to do the deed."

"Yeah, spot on. Just give me a synopsis. When you can."

The bedroom curtains didn't close properly anymore, so Howie's sleep was disturbed by the combination of a nearby streetlight and a full moon, as well as Jack's snoring and somnolent elbowing and duvet-stealing antics.

Howie was in no mood for work that morning but somebody had to go out and earn a crust. He found Edison's expired lightbulb resting next to the microwave. He wrapped it in a torn jiffy bag and buried it in his holdall, intending to dispose of it later.

Whenever Mrs Osram was busy fussing over her other employees, he'd been researching on Google, Bing and other engines about people or spirits in lightbulbs. He'd picked up a few esoteric sect practices, and several musical and literary references to souls in goldfish bowls, but nothing specific to the curious phenomenon that was obsessing Jack. Howie tried to project his thoughts into a time, maybe two or three weeks from now, when life might return to normal and the whole episode would become a weird *do you remember when* shared memory.

There were two slightly dried-up Pritt sticks in the stationery cupboard. He pocketed them. Ensconced in the gender-neutral toilet, he peeled the bubble-wrap inner layer away from the manila outer envelope. Carefully now. A little glue, press lightly against the glass then pull away. Not too fast now, don't want any cuts from the fractured shell.

The tiny body certainly looked human enough and the anatomical details beneath the white shift covering were convincing. The body was held in place by a couple of wire filaments. He gently relaxed these, lifted the... figure? Corpse?

It had the softness of flesh yet could have been plastic also. Or maybe something like Play-Doh, which he'd loved as a kid. A soul, though? The essence and immanence of a person?

The broken bulb and torn envelope could go in the bin that was designed for women's sanitary products. But the figure...?

Howie tore off some streaks of toilet paper, wrapped them around the minute body, flushed the cistern three times in quick succession. Let the sewers and the sea deal with disposal.

Howie had another couple of moments at work where he received electric shocks. Maybe he should change his suit material to non-conductive cotton. At another point, he thought he could discern a yellowish glow around his fingers, but decided it was to do with the brightness settings on his PC monitor.

As he readied the key just outside his apartment, he heard some choral singing. No actual lyrics, more like a choir holding a top C, or maybe a semitone or two below it.

All the lamps were on in the living room, their shades removed so that the ecstatic souls were visible inside the bulbs. And in front of them, naked as a newborn and with his arms raised in spiritual supplication, was Jack. Normally, coming home and finding your boyfriend bare-arsed by the sofa would have been the opening gambit for some fun and games, but today... Jack hadn't noticed him. Howie sidled into the kitchen, wondering whether he dared flick the kettle switch to make a coffee or herbal tea.

What the actual heck. And now there was a bolt on the door leading to the utility room. His literary heroine Alice wouldn't have hesitated and neither did Howie – he quickly loosened the lock.

Where the washing machine had once stood solo, now there were piles of boxes and assorted wooden and metal panels, and what looked like an overlarge visor or a plastic windscreen for a small car. A business card advertised the carpentry and fixing services of a local handyman. Was Jack seeing someone else or was the odd job man genuine?

The sounds from the lounge had ceased. Howie wondered when, even if, he should clear the air with his partner.

The ritual seemed to be over. Howie waited a while before leaving the kitchen, thinking how Jack had fervently rejected his religious upbringing all those years ago when they'd first realised their true natures. But did that stuff ever truly leave you? Maybe this bizarre belief was filling some sort of void for his usually cynical boyfriend.

Jack was now wearing a white T-shirt and some grey jogging bottoms. The lights still burned, unshaded. Jack's features had a glow. Not like he'd been under a sun lamp, more like he'd necked some of those dodgy pills they'd briefly become fixated upon back in their Ibiza days.

"Oh, hi, Howie," he breezed, "didn't hear you come in. I've had a productive day. Things seem clearer."

"Elaborate."

"Well, look, I'm hungry. What about I check the dates on stuff in the fridge and cook up a Jack's Mixture of whatever's expiring?"

Howie sought a corner of the sofa where the lamp array was mostly behind him. He didn't dare turn the lights off, worried that Jack's currently bright temperament could be extinguished at any moment. Or turn violent like a newly reborn crusader of righteousness.

The TV stayed off. Jack kept up an inane commentary about a charity project one of his work colleagues had instigated. Colleagues? When had he last gone into the office, or even logged onto his work email?

Howie pleaded a headache – it wasn't hard in the oppressive brightness – and retired to bed early. The moonlight through the curtain crack seemed mild by comparison. He lay awake waiting for Jack. The distant traffic blended into a hiss like an expiring bulb. He stayed on his side of the bed. He remained alone.

After a working day characterised by silent, solitary devotion to the demands of the screen, Howie stopped off at the corner shop to pick up a few household essentials. Three times contactless, two with a PIN, his card still refused to work. He had a little cash ready for the rent so used that instead.

"Maybe got corrupted," the shopkeeper said. "Put it next to a magnet or something."

Howie shook his head. He hadn't even touched a magnet since a school science project back when he was six or seven.

Jack opened the front door, bright-eyed. "I've freed them all," he announced.

"You've done what?"

"I've smashed the bulbs and let the souls free. They thanked me for the gift of light and life then they went off in search of paradise."

More like they scurried away to the skirting board like vermin in search of a bolthole. Howie tried to disguise his tired sigh. And now there would be tiny shards all over the floor, ready to inflict a nasty cut at any moment.

Hoping he could hide the sarcasm, he said, "Is this the end of all our troubles, Jack?"

"Their troubles are over, yes. Ours too? Not just yet but soon. we will also find paradise."

"I'm not really finished with this world yet."

"Trust me, Howie. Everything is almost ready. Stay out of the utility room for now, everything's finely balanced."

Howie excused himself to prepare some food. He ached to try the bolted and locked door, maybe even force it if he could summon some energy, but he let it be. Later, they watched an American comedy series on TV, and it was almost as if things were back to normal. The zealous glow in Jack's eyes dimmed but didn't wholly disappear.

Lying in bed, Howie wondered how you could know someone for so long, even sharing some of the growing up years, and yet still not really know them at all.

"Come on, Howie, my gift for you – for us – is ready. Come to the utility room. It's revelation day, my love."

"It looks like a metal and Perspex box. Something you might sleep in on a spaceship. What the—"

"It's our escape. From work, from Old Watts, everything. It's our salvation."

"I can't deal with any more of this, Jack. I'm… oh no, you just reminded me it's rent night. Stay out here or in the kitchen or something, let me deal with Old Watts by myself."

Howie tried the biscuit tin, the teapot, even below the lining of the cutlery drawer. But he was still thirty quid short.

Their landlord sniffed, surveying the untenanted lamps and the unfashionable wallpaper that he had no intention of replacing any time soon.

"Just another indication of what's wrong with this country," he stated, adding, "I knew I shouldn't have trusted your sort."

"What do you mean 'our sort'?" said Howie. "Do you want to elaborate on that?"

Watts shuffled from one foot to another. "Just make sure I get paid the extra next time. Final warning."

As the front door slammed, Jack reappeared from the kitchen. "No point picking a fight or making a complaint," he said, "we wouldn't be believed. 'Our sort' never are."

"You've changed your tune. I thought you'd slap him one. But I've bitten my tongue so hard it's nearly in pieces."

"I thought he'd never go. Just forget him now. Come on, I was showing you what I've been working on. All right, I got in a craftsman to help me but, look, this metal bit unscrews here and if you get inside carefully—"

"You paid a craftsman to make this *thing*? No wonder we couldn't pay our full rent. You've known me long enough, Jack, to know I'm not into theatre or role play."

His partner laughed. "This will be a good hideaway whenever the landlord comes calling."

"You're mad. Next thing, you'll be wanting to plug it in or something. I'm going out, Jack. Getting away from this madhouse. Don't wait up."

Howie found the next hour no less stressful, spending most of it on the phone to his bank's customer helpline. Eventually they rebooted his card with just enough credit for a long vodka or three.

Jack was asleep in their bed when Howie returned. This nocturnal vision of their normal life felt rare and precious. Howie brushed his teeth, stripped down, slid under the duvet, and felt his partner turn comfortably in his sleep to offer a cuddlesome arm.

Howie woke in an unfamiliar space and position. If he could just turn a little, see things, touch the sides.

Suddenly everything was bright and vibrant. He felt the buzz, the light, the immanence. His lips formed a beatific smile. He did not speak but these were his words:

"I am turned on. I am ecstatic. I am not the keeper of the flame for I am the flame itself."

When the burst finished, he relaxed his outstreched arms, turned enough so that he noticed the cracks in the outer casing starting to spread like the filaments of spiderwebs. Slowly but inexorably breaking up his happy home.

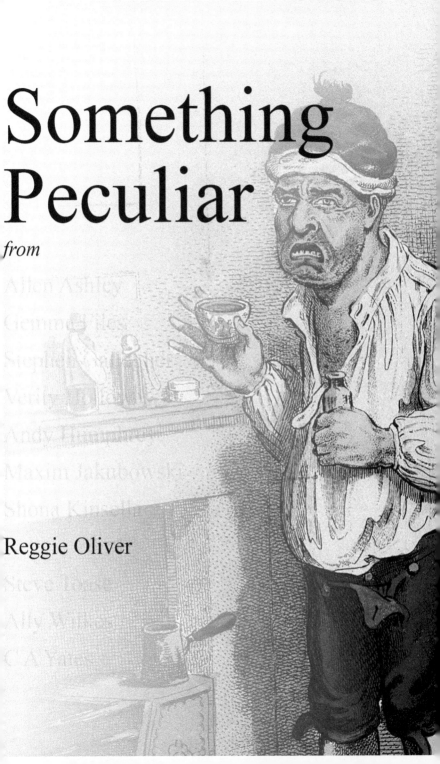

Something
Peculiar

from

Reggie Oliver

Fell Creatures

"…arise, ye unlearn'd emigrants of hell…"

THE RICH are different," Hemingway once said to F. Scott Fitzgerald. "Yes," replied Scott Fitzgerald tartly, "they have more money." Or so the story goes.

My own view on the matter is undecided. Are the very rich just ordinary people with more to spend, or does extreme wealth warp their characters in a peculiar way? I have known very few such people in my life, but I did know one couple who made me ponder the question.

After I had retired from teaching, my wife and I went to live permanently at the little cottage we had bought in Norfolk. It was situated at the end of a lane next to an old 18th century farmhouse, called Strellbrigg Hall.

The Hall was a pleasant enough old building of mellowed brick, but no architectural gem. It was large, rambling, and, when I first knew it, rather run down. All the land which it had once possessed had been sold off long ago, though it still had a substantial garden at the back leading down to a stream, which also passed along the bottom of my land.

It was owned by a man called Roger Mason-Fell who, some years ago now, decided to sell the property. He had inherited the Hall from distant cousins, but had found it hard to maintain and ruinously expensive to heat. In addition, Roger's children had fled the nest, as had his wife shortly after their departure. I was a widower by then, and Roger and I would commiserate with each other occasionally over a drink or two.

Nobody seemed to want to buy the place, despite Roger's dropping the price several times; then, one May evening, he came round to my cottage bearing a bottle of Champagne. He had managed to sell the Hall.

I always felt a little awkward when Roger came for a drink because of his height. He must have been at least six foot six, and my cottage, though otherwise the pleasantest of homes, had been built for agricultural labourers, not giants. Roger occupied the entire space vertically between the floor and ceiling, and. even then, he was forced to stoop because of the oak beams. I was never entirely at my ease with him in my house until he had sat down, nor was he. Roger was retired from the insurance business which had bored him, and was generally rather a melancholy man, but this evening he was in high spirits.

"They didn't quibble about the price, bless 'em," he said, referring to the purchasers. "Must have shedloads of cash. Money no object. Youngish couple, in their thirties. They're probably going to do terrible things to it, put a jacuzzi and a sauna in the stable yard or whatever, but that will be your problem not mine."

"It won't worry me," I said, "as long as they keep the noise down. How did they make their money?"

"Their name, appropriately enough, is Argent. She is Lady Celia, daughter of an earl, I believe, and she is one of these posh 'events organisers'. Her husband, Piers Argent, is in the city. He tells me he deals in futures."

"That phrase has always puzzled me. How can you deal in something that doesn't yet exist?"

"You were a history teacher, weren't you? You dealt in the past. That equally does not exist."

"On the contrary. The past is the only thing that does. In any case, I didn't deal in the past, but you could say I dwelt on it."

"However that may be, you are going to dwell next to some very rich people who will possibly make the next six months of your life a misery by turning an old farmhouse into a gin palace."

"Oh, surely they have more taste than that. Do they have children?"

"Three, I believe, all infants, but they are well kitted out with nannies. So the Hall will once more echo to the sound of childish cries." There was a note of wistfulness in his voice.

"Won't you miss the place?"

"Me? Good God, no! I always hated it really. Too many rooms, too many draughts. I'm sure the Hall was one of the reasons Madge left me after the kids had gone. I might even be able to get her back if I find somewhere decent to live."

My late wife, the kindest of women, used to say she found Madge "tricky", and "tricky" was the worst adjective she would ever apply to anyone she knew well. I also had never warmed to Madge, and it amazed me that Roger would want her back, but then there is a mystery at the heart of every marriage, even one's own.

"But hasn't the Hall been in your family for ages?"

"Oh, yonks! But it belonged to another branch, a family called Fell. And I am only a Mason-Fell. My grandmother was a Fell, you see, and insisted on attaching her name to my grandpa's when she married. The last Fell who owned this place died without making a will, and I, being next of kin, believe it or not, was the lucky or unlucky beneficiary." He paused and took a long draught of his champagne. "The Fells were an odd lot, but they must have had strong genes. You have noticed my excessive inches?"

"Hard not to."

"Well, the Fells, male and female, were all extremely tall. Some even taller than me. Grotesquely so in some cases. They were also very long lived. My Gran – rather a horrible old woman incidentally – managed to pass the hundred mark. So there's that to look forward to." Roger stared at the fire; his habitual melancholy had returned. I refilled his glass and we discussed cricket scores.

A week later, a removal van arrived, and Roger was gone. Shortly afterwards I myself went away for some months to stay with my married daughter in Canada, so it was a considerable time before I had any contact with the new people at the Hall.

The first person from Strellbrigg Hall that I met was not a member of the Argent family. One autumn day my doorbell rang and on the doorstep was an elegant, blonde, slightly-built woman in her mid-thirties. She introduced herself as Nicola Waley-Ruthven, and described herself as the Argents' "stylist". This meant, apparently, that she was supervising the renovation and interior decoration of the Hall, the hiring of builders, the sourcing of furniture and fabrics, the garden design, in fact everything that most people usually want to do for themselves when they buy a new home. But, I suppose, if you are wealthy enough, you might want to spare yourself the trouble of creating your own style.

She wanted to ask me if I wouldn't mind if a couple of trees, in the Hall's garden but adjacent to my land, were cut down. I had no objections. Then she said: "The family aren't here at the moment, but I usually have a drink around 6.30. Why don't you pop round and I can show you what we've done to the place?"

The walk to the Hall from my cottage was little more than a hundred yards or so. The main front door was covered in scaffolding because they were adding a mock Georgian portico to it, so I went to the side door, as I had always done when Roger lived there, and rang the bell. Nicola opened the door to me and we entered by a short passage into the kitchen. It was the room at the Hall I knew best because Roger and I often used to share a bottle of wine there after we had both been made single, sometimes even a scratch meal.

It had been transformed. The floor of grey York paving stones had become marble, white, waxed, and spotless. The handsome great deal table in the middle of the room had been replaced by an "island" topped with highly polished granite, and fitted with dishwashers, freezers, and cabinets all painted a tasteful matt dove grey, also the colour of the walls which, in Roger's day, had been a nicotine-stained cream colour. Even the Aga which, apart from an arthritic door, used to be perfectly serviceable, had been replaced with a newer, bigger, more gleaming version. Above it hung a row of shiny copper pans, like the chef's domain in a Michelin starred restaurant. It was still recognisably a spacious farmhouse kitchen, but now it belonged to the genus approved by *Homes and Gardens* and *World of Interiors*.

I complimented Nicola with a decent amount of sincerity on her refurbishment. She smiled and opened a bottle of expensive claret. I had detected an awkwardness, even a touch of fear, when she first came to the door, but she was now almost at her ease. We took the wine and glasses through the dining room and into the sitting room. There the changes were even more radical.

The bulbous chintz sofas and motheaten armchairs of Roger's occupancy were gone. The old elm boards had been sanded, polished, and covered with expensive rugs. The furniture was white and well-upholstered. Swags of cream satin were bunched extravagantly over the windows, masking the tops of equally lavish curtains. I was able to appreciate for the first time the handsome proportions of the room with its high ceiling, more suited to a Georgian manor than a mere farm house.

Nicola directed my attention to the wallpaper which, she told me, was "from an original 18th century design." Its pallid floral filigree delicacy was pleasant enough, if you like that sort of thing, but hard to hang a decent picture on. Nicola was particularly proud of the effect because, she said, the patterns were in exact correspondence with the period of the house. The date 1743 was carved on the lintel of the front door.

Yes, it was all very correct and pleasing, if, for my taste, a little lacking in character. Nicola was obviously a gifted and sensitive interior decorator and I told her so. She smiled with relief. Again, I was conscious of a certain nervousness and lack of self-assurance behind the façade of confident expertise.

We sat down on one of the wide white sofas – I was careful with my glass of red wine – and we talked.

"Of course, it hasn't been easy," was her opening remark.

"Really?" I said. "In what way?"

I thought she was about to take me into her confidence, but she hesitated, and instead decided to give me a brief resumé of her life so far. She and Lady Celia Argent, whom she called "Seals", had been best friends, or "besties" as she liked to call it, at Benenden. She had been married "which didn't work out" and had then joined her friend's firm, doing the décor for weddings and other "events". Then she had branched out "with Seals's approval" into interior design. "I found I had a bit of a flair for that sort of thing," she said. "Of course, I do a lot of research as well before tackling a property like this." Once more I was conscious that nerves and uncertainty were taking over. "Actually," she said. "I wonder… this is a bit of a cheek. I heard you taught history."

"I did. Who told you?"

"Oh, I… Anyway, history… old things… you know a bit about that sort of thing."

"A bit. Yes."

"Well the thing is, when your friend vacated the Hall, he actually left quite a lot of stuff behind."

"Really? You mean furniture?"

"Oh, yes obviously. And we got rid of that. But no. I mean, rather weird, possibly valuable things. They were in some of the rooms upstairs and in the attic, and I don't even know if Mr Mason-Fell knew about some of them."

"Haven't you got in touch with Roger about these things?"

"Well, yes, I tried to. But he's dead."

"Good God! What happened? He was perfectly well when I last saw him." The shock was considerable. I was also invaded by a strong sense of guilt; I should have kept in touch.

"Some sort of fall. It was all a bit strange. I spoke to his wife. Midge or something?"

"Madge."

"Right. I didn't get very far with her."

"Ah, yes. Madge is… can be… tricky."

"Tricky is not the word."

"Perhaps not."

"Well, I wasn't able to explain about this stuff to her, but I thought you might…?"

"You want *me* to talk to Madge?"

"Oh, grief, no! I just want you to take a look at some things and tell me what you think."

"I am not an expert valuer or anything."

"Oh, no. Just… I've put it in a room upstairs. The whole house isn't done yet, of course."

We went upstairs. Most of the rooms had been "done" and I admired the bland perfection of their new decor. I had never been in this part of the house and noted its spacious proportions and high ceilings. Nicola led me to a room at the end of the house.

This was unreformed and I was immediately struck by the difference. It was still handsomely shaped but it was bleak by comparison with the other rooms in the house and even exuded a slightly damp odour. It contained an assortment of objects which had clearly been left behind by Roger. On a table in the middle of the room was a tall, square shouldered object covered in a dust sheet.

"I rather want you to look at this," said Nicola removing the dust sheet. As she did so I noticed that she shivered slightly and kept her eyes on me rather than the thing she was uncovering.

It was a doll's house, an early one at that, almost certainly eighteenth century. It had been well made by a skilled craftsman in wood and meticulously painted. It did not at all resemble the Hall, but rather a typical Georgian town house with a red brick front and a pillared portico in the middle sheltering a front door painted dark green. There were a few scuffs and scratches and the bright red paint representing the bricks was a little faded, but otherwise it was in remarkable condition.

I had admired it wholeheartedly for about half a minute before something about it made me a little uneasy. It was the proportions of the building. Though two round *oeil de boeuf* dormer windows in the gabled roof suggested garrets, the doll's house had two main floors, a ground and a first, but it was disconcertingly tall. The four sash windows and the door were too high and narrow to look graceful; there was something almost grotesque about it. It was as if the elegance of Georgian architecture were being consciously mocked.

The whole of the façade swung open on a single hinge. "May I open it?" I asked, almost hoping that Nicola would refuse me, but she said: "Yeah, yeah! Go ahead," backing away to one corner of the room as she did so. I opened the door.

It consisted of four chambers, a dining room and a kitchen on the ground floor, a drawing room and a bedroom on the first. (As in most doll's houses, there were no stairs.) All the rooms were furnished with exquisitely made miniature items: pictures, chairs, tables, plates and cutlery; even, in the drawing room, a glass fronted bookcase full of tiny volumes. All belonged to the mid eighteenth century and all, despite their almost pristine condition, looked as if they had been made in that period. I was astonished.

"Amazing!" I said.

"Isn't it?" said Nicola, but I noticed that she was looking at me and not the doll's house.

Nevertheless, richly fascinating though I found it all, I was subject to the same unease as I had felt about the façade of the house. The proportions were not right; everything was elongated. The chairs were too tall; the legs of the tables too long; the brightly painted plaster apples that stood on a pewter plate in the dining room were conical rather than fat and round. On the kitchen table lay the model of a plucked fowl with a grotesquely extended neck so that the beaked head hung limply over the edge. The legs too were long and thin, suggesting not so much a chicken or even a goose, as a heron, perhaps, or a crane.

Of the four rooms, the drawing room was the most elaborately furnished and decorated. Before the fireplace in which red tinted foil had been placed to simulate a fire, a table had been set, complete with white cloth, cups, saucers and a china teapot. Around it on miniature chairs in the Chippendale style sat a family of dolls, a man, a woman, and three children, two girls and a boy.

They also belonged to the eighteenth century and were made of wood. Their faces were painted in a severe, stylised way, utterly unlike the cherubic sweetness of Victorian porcelain dolls. Their black eyes stared at me with a kind of vacant malevolence, their little beaky noses, the only concession offered by the doll-maker to carved facial features, jutted aggressively. I was astonished at the preservation and quality of their costumes. They were dressed in stiff embroidered silks which, though their colours were somewhat faded, seemed otherwise in perfect condition. The lace at their necks and sleeves was of the finest quality.

The doll children, as so often in that period, were represented as small adults, with no concessions made to the chubbiness of infancy. They had narrow oval faces and thin shapely bodies, but what differentiated them and their parents from the normal run of dolls was the length of their legs. The white silk stockings and the little black buckled shoes that encased their tiny feet only enhanced what seemed almost a deformity. Their arms, of normal and proportionate length, looked stubby by comparison. There they sat, all five of them, their long thin legs sprawled out, collectively encompassing almost the entire width of the elegant miniature drawing room.

There was one other doll in the house, and she was on the ground floor in the kitchen. I had not noticed her at first because she was, by contrast with the others, small, almost dwarfish in stature. She wore a brown dress of some coarse sacking material with a white apron and mob cap, evidently intended to represent a kitchen maid of some sort. She was propped up against the kitchen range, as if in an attitude of exhaustion. Above the range was a row of tiny copper pans, like a miniature version of the ones I had seen in the kitchen downstairs. I had an irresistible urge to touch the pans to see if they were separate items or all stuck together. They were indeed all tiny individual copper pans and, when I fingered them, they clinked together, sounding like the chimes of a minute clock.

"What do you think?"

I had been so absorbed by the spectacle that Nicola's question startled me. I was unable to form a coherent opinion. All I could say was: "Well! Extraordinary!"

"I mean, do you think it's worth anything?"

"Yes... Possibly unique... Maybe it should go in a museum. But would the Argents want to sell it?"

"Oh, I should think so, don't you? I mean, their kids wouldn't want it, would they? It's too valuable to play with. And there are these other things."

By this time I was rather anxious to escape and drink my claret in the nice bland sitting room, but Nicola had other ideas. She went over to a corner and uncovered a stack of pictures in dull gilt frames. Again without looking at them she ranged them against the wall for my inspection.

They were all family portraits from the eighteenth to the early part of the nineteenth century. The subjects, male and female, faced the viewer full on, with very little in the way of "pose" about them. The portraits were the work of country journeyman painters of the kind who also depicted livestock for proud farmers, those representations of prize pigs, sheep, and giant cattle in profile, beloved by some modern collectors. The paintings were flat and stiff in execution, and I suppose they might have had a certain primitive charm were it not for the obvious charmlessness of their subjects.

These men and women looked moderately prosperous, soberly dressed but severe in aspect. Though the artists had depicted them only down to the waist, you could tell from their narrow shoulders and preternaturally long heads that they were tall people. There was a strong family resemblance in the dark, closely-set eyes, the wide thin mouths, the general angularity of feature, all of which reminded me vaguely of Roger, now mysteriously deceased.

"These must be Fells," I said.

"What?"

I explained about the Fell family who had owned the Hall.

"Oh, right," said Nicola, obviously uninterested. "Do you think they might be worth anything?"

"I doubt it very much." Just then I felt a slight prickling at the back of my skull. It came and went swiftly, but I became anxious to leave this room and return to the modern comforts of the rest of the house.

"Then I found these old books," said Nicola, pointing to a box of ancient leather-bound volumes. "I wonder if you might—"

"Let's take them downstairs and have a look at them there, shall we?"

"Oh. Okay." I bent down to pick up the box. "Here, no! Let me!" And she took it herself. I sometimes forget that, in the eyes of others, I am old.

The relief when we reached the sitting room again, for me at least, was palpable. I wasted a little time drinking and complimenting Nicola on her decorating skills, before she called a halt to this.

"Could we have a look at these books? I just want to know if I should chuck, or if they're worth anything."

The idea of "chucking" any book is anathema to me, besides Nicola's insistent preoccupation with monetary value was beginning to irk, so I began look through the books rather briskly. They were in good calf bindings of the period. Nearly all of them were collections of eighteenth-century sermons by Wesley, Blair, Sherlock and the like. I told her that these were not likely to fetch much money in spite of the bindings. Nicola hesitated and then said: "Actually, these might do for the library. Seals and Piers want the house to have a library."

"Really? And are they specially interested in old sermons?" Nicola looked shocked.

"Good grief, no!" Then she saw that I was smiling, and she smiled too. "No, but they'd like a room full of nice old books. It's an image thing really. These look quite smart. You know, to have on your shelves. I suppose you disapprove."

"I do rather."

"Well, maybe I do too. A bit. But don't tell them I said so." She was not joking.

"My lips are sealed."

There was one book among this sober collection that was bound with scarlet leather with extravagant gold tooling on the spine and boards. It stood out among the demure but rich volumes of smooth brown calf skin with a minimal use of gilt on the titles.

"This looks interesting," I said. I opened the book at the title page. It read:

A TREATISE OF HUMAN FLIGHT
By means of the Transmutations of the Four Elements
By The Reverend Ezekiel Fell
Doctor of Divinity, Rector of Strellbrigg in the County of Norfolk
Sublimi feriam sidera vertice
Hor. Odes I, 1.

The quotation from Horace, translated, meant "with head uplifted I shall strike the stars." The date at the bottom of the page was 1798, and the work was published "by private subscription"; in other words, no reputable bookseller had considered it worth printing. On the opposite page was an engraved portrait in an oval frame of Dr Fell in gown and bands. The long head, narrow shoulders, gaunt features and close-set eyes were immediately recognisable as family traits.

There was an "epistle dedicatory" in heroic couplets to "The Prince of Aire", whoever that might be, which seemed to be routine stuff apart perhaps from the opening triple rhyme:

> *Arise, ye unlearn'd emigrants of Hell*
> *And to these words with trembling hearken well,*
> *My wits are as my name and nature, Fell!*

After this preliminary flourish the rest of the book was in prose. I glanced through the densely printed pages. They were as littered with occult references and classical allusion as Burton's *Anatomy of Melancholy*, but even a cursory glance told me this was the work of someone deranged. It was a wild mixture of alchemy, astrology, bizarre interpretations of obscure biblical texts, and primitive scientific theory. The text was interrupted by strange sigils and geometrical diagrams. Its aspirations were grand to the point of egomania.

A typical passage ran as follows:

"Through the commingling, by means of *Galvanic Energy*, of human seminal fluid with that of swans or similar large avians and then inserting the amalgam into the *Venereal Portions* of some fertile woman of the labouring classes, it will be possible to engender a race of intelligent winged creatures who may serve to take messages through the air with astonishing swiftness or, as *volucrine* cavalry, to inflict a sudden and terrible reckoning upon our enemies.

Additional advantages may be obtained, for it is oft reported that the excrement of swans is a sovereign cure for the ague and a *prophylaxis* against the debilities of old age."

An engraving followed, depicting Leda and a decidedly amorous swan coupling inside a giant alchemical glass vessel.

After that, I closed the book and handed it back.

"It's totally insane," I said, and again I felt that pricking at the back of my neck.

"Oh... Right... But do you think it could be valuable?"

"Possibly. I'm sure it must be pretty rare." I think I let my irritation with her question show, because she dropped the subject after that. In spite of this, we parted on good terms, and I sensed that she was rather reluctant to let me go home.

In the months following I would see Nicola occasionally as I passed by the Hall on my afternoon walks. We would wave or exchange a few friendly words. She seemed a little reticent and nervous. Once I invited her for a drink at my cottage and she came. She pronounced the interior "sweet" and was charmingly complimentary when I explained that whatever sweetness it possessed was the work of my late wife. Still, I detected the same disguised nervousness as before. She told me that the Argents were at their London house (the fashionable part of Clapham) and asked me if I knew someone local who might act as "housekeeper" to the Hall; that is, come in two or three times a week, clean and generally look after the place. I suggested a few names but Nicola told me she had tried them and they had all, for various reasons, refused the task. She seemed more distressed by this state of affairs than I thought it warranted, but perhaps I had underestimated the obligation she was under to her friend "Seals".

It was not until late into the following Spring that I finally met the Argents. I saw them first across the fence in my garden while I was scything nettles. Nicola was with them and their three young children were some distance away with a nanny in attendance.

Celia Argent, at Nicola's prompting, waved at me and came towards me, closely followed by her husband Piers.

"Hi!" said Celia. "We meet at last! I've heard so much about you."

She was a beauty, like Nicola a blonde, but half a head taller than her, and exuding a kind of patrician confidence that cannot, in my experience, be faked. Her husband was equally tall and good-looking but lacking his wife's special glamour. He gave the impression, even when he seemed to be attending to you, of having half a mind on other things, but he was pleasant enough. Celia beckoned over her children, Rosamund, Marcus, and Isabella – seven, six, and four respectively – who were solemnly introduced to me. We shook hands over the fence. They looked as if they had inherited their mother's blonde good looks, but not, as yet, her poise and assurance. Marcus pointed at my scythe and asked, fearfully, what it was. I told him it was for cutting nettles.

"Does it kill the nettles?" he asked.

"Yes, it does."

He looked troubled by this, and I rather regretted the baldness of my answer.

"Marcus is the sensitive one," said Celia. "Come on you kids, go back to Magdalena." And they ran off towards their nanny. "You must come over to dinner one night."

"That would be delightful," I said.

I thought no more about it, but roughly a week later, I received an invitation to dinner the following Saturday evening at Strellbrigg Hall. The note, from Celia, read that "Nik" (presumably Nicola) would be there, as would "a couple of friends" whom she would like me to meet.

I was met first by Celia and Nicola in the kitchen. Celia greeted me effusively while Nicola, who was chopping vegetables, waved shyly. As I was taken through to the sitting room Celia told me that I was to meet "Paul and Reiner". "I think you'll like Paul. And Reiner is a scream. You mustn't mind him; he can be a bit outrageous." Thus prepared, I was introduced to Paul, a dapper, bald man in a velvet jacket, about my age, and Reiner, in his thirties, tall gaunt and bespectacled. He spoke good English with an Austrian accent.

"So," said Reiner after we had shaken hands, "You are the old schoolmaster I hear so much about. Did you used to beat your little schoolboys a very great deal?"

I replied that happily even I was not old enough to have been obliged to do that. Reiner seemed disappointed.

"You'll have to excuse Reiner," said Celia. "I warned you he could be outrageous."

"Always, I am being told that I am 'outrageous'," said Reiner with a complacent smile. "But I only ask the simple innocent question."

At that moment Piers entered the room and the conversation became general, so I was spared any more of Reiner's outrageousness. I noticed, though, that when Nicola finally came into the drawing room from her labours in the kitchen, she studiously avoided being too close to Reiner. When their eyes happened to meet, she would turn away.

It was an enjoyable dinner; the food and wine were excellent. I gathered from the talk that Paul was some kind of art dealer and an old friend of Celia's family, while Reiner belonged to Piers's world of finance. He and Piers would occasionally exchange brief, cryptic remarks about trades and futures and stock options, at which Celia would rap the table with her knuckles and say: "Come on, you two, no shop here!" Then both would laugh, cease to talk high finance, and talk instead of shooting, about which both Reiner and Piers seemed almost as enthusiastic.

Piers asked me if there were any good shoots in our part of Norfolk. I said I wasn't sure, but pheasants regularly came into my garden in search of food and, presumably, refuge. They were almost certainly escapees from a nearby estate which had bred them for shooting.

Reiner said: "Perhaps we will come into your garden one day, Mr Schoolmaster, to kill some birds!" There was laughter and I summoned up a smile, even though Reiner's remark contained a suggestion of threat.

Towards the end of dinner, Celia, who was seated at the head of the table to my right, turned to me and said; "You know we have a lot to thank you and Paul for." I looked enquiringly at her. "The book!"

"Ah, yes, the book!" said Paul. "The Reverend Ezekiel's *Treatise of Human Flight*. It was, as you spotted, a considerable rarity. And the binding was choice. I managed to get it into a specialist sale at Christies and it went for over six thousand."

"Of which *we* saw barely five," said Piers, "after commission and what-have-yous. Bloody ridiculous!"

"That, Piers dear," said Paul. "is the wicked way of the world with which you are not exactly unacquainted."

Celia said: "Paul's also had a look at the doll's house. You think it's quite a find, don't you Paul?"

"I do."

"So, how much, Paul," said Piers. "Twenty... Thirty thou...?"

"Quite possibly. Even more perhaps. It's exceptionally unusual and the condition is superb."

"I should like to see this famous dolls' house again," said Reiner. "Let us take a look at it after dinner. And our schoolmaster can give us a lesson about it, no?"

At that moment, a welcome distraction came in the form of Magdalena ("She's from Albania," Celia had informed me.) bringing in the children to say good night to their parents and their guests.

After this had been done and they were gone, I asked: "Wouldn't the children like the antique doll's house to play with?"

Celia looked shocked. "God, no! As a matter of fact they absolutely hate it. Especially Marcus; he won't go near the thing."

"That boy is too soft," said Reiner. "You spoil him."

"He's only six!" said Nicola. I think they were the first words she had spoken to Reiner all evening.

Reiner stared at her, apparently delighted by her outburst. "Let me tell you something, little Nikki, when I was only six, I— Well, I will not say; I do not want to shock our schoolmaster here."

When coffee was over, Celia led us into a room I had not seen before, newly painted white. It was lined with bookshelves, which were empty apart from the row of handsomely leather-bound sermons that I had seen before. "This is going to be our library," said Celia.

In the middle of the room was a table, and on it was the doll's house. In these stark and incomplete surroundings, it seemed even more angular and unsettling. I noticed that the little servant doll in the kitchen was no longer slumped against the kitchen range, but had fallen to the floor. The rest were in their accustomed places.

"Yes, this is quite exceptional. This should be in a museum, you know, Celia," said Paul.

"How much would they give for it?" said Piers.

Paul turned and stared at Piers without a word. I noticed that Reiner had edged close to Nicola and had begun to run a finger down her back. Nicola flinched. I came up behind Reiner and, as if accidentally, pulled his arm away from her. He turned on me a look of concentrated rage.

"I would say 1750s, wouldn't you, Paul?" I said, hardly thinking of what I was saying, merely to fill the awkward space of silence. "The dolls look like figures out of a painting by Arthur Devis."

"Who sometimes used dolls as models for his portraits," said Paul. "Yes. This must be one of the earliest dolls houses I've ever seen."

"You must sell at auction," said Reiner, shaking off my hold while Nicola moved to a safe distance. "But I think you should keep these." He reached into the little drawing room and pulled out the two adult dolls.

"Oh, why?" said Celia.

Reiner presented them to Celia with a flourish. "Because they are like you, Celia and Piers. So beautiful, so elegant."

"Oh, Reiner! You are sweet!"

"Not such bloody long legs, though," muttered Piers. Celia turned to me.

"By the way," she said. "Have you seen the portraits?"

"I have indeed. Nicola showed them to me when I came here for a drink."

"No, but you haven't seen them since they've been done."

"Done?"

"Yes. Reiner gave them a sort makeover and presented them back to us as a gift. Wasn't that sweet of him? They're an absolute scream. Come on, let me show you."

"I don't think our schoolmaster will approve," said Reiner.

"Oh, come on! Of course he will. They're an absolute hoot. Come on!"

She took me by the hand and led me towards a passage which looked out on one side onto the old stable yard. There, ranged along the wall, were the severe, primitive portraits of Fell family members that Nicola had shown me.

They had been cleaned and varnished, so that what colour they possessed now glowed, but what was most striking was that the original heads had been painted out and replaced by those of farm animals: a bull, a sheep, a goat, two pigs, and a cockerel. I had to admit that the substitution had been done most skilfully, with a faithfulness to the flat, meticulous style of the original, but I did not care for it. It felt like a desecration. Whoever the Fells were, they did not deserve this.

"Aren't they just surreal?" said Celia. She was clearly delighted by the transformations.

"Extraordinary," I said. Reiner noted the studied neutrality of my response.

"You are not amused, schoolteacher?"

I said: "I am afraid I have no sense of humour."

"So typically English!" said Reiner.

Soon after that, I thanked my host and hostess profusely for a delightful evening and left. Reiner smirked as he shook my hand limply; Nicola kissed me warmly on both cheeks. Her own were damp with tears.

I thought Nicola's work with the house was now virtually done, but I continued to see her at the Hall, even when the Argents were not there. I wanted to speak to her but she seemed to avoid me, until one autumn day, when the leaves had turned to bronze and yellow in the lane, I met her there, walking up towards me. She looked pale and I could read on her face that though she wanted not to talk to me, politeness prevented her from simply turning tail. After some preliminary chat, I invited her to my cottage for a cup of tea. When were settled in front of the fire, she relaxed a little, but the strain on her face was even more evident.

I said: "I thought the renovation of the Hall was all finished."

"Yes. It has. It has really."

"But you're still here."

"Well. I'm sort of helping out. You see, Seals and I go back a long way."

"You told me."

"And I'm sort of looking after the place for them. And now the kids. Temporarily of course. You see Magdalena had to go back to Albania – or said she had to – something to do with visas and work permits, I don't know. Anyway, I'm left with them. And my child-minding skills are not brilliant. And anyway – you haven't seen the kids recently, have you?"

I shook my head.

"Well, I'm not altogether surprised that Magdalena quit, because they've gone a bit peculiar. I mean, they're sweet kids and all that but they are rather… weird. Recently."

"In what way?"

"Well, for a start they've almost stopped talking. And they used to be pretty chatty for their age. Nowadays, they just sort of make noises. Seals has taken them to a child psychiatrist and all that, but they don't seem to have a clue. They keep saying it's just a phase. And Seals has had to go away for some big do, and they can't get a nanny at short notice, so I'm sort of stuck with them."

"I'm sorry."

"That's why I haven't seen you much. I can't get out a lot. I'm only here because I managed to find a cleaner and she said she'd keep an eye on them while I went out for a breather."

"You look tired."

"I am tired. I'm tired and just a bit frightened."

I felt helpless. I offered her more tea and asked her about the doll's house. Had they sold it? I don't quite know why this came into my mind; perhaps I thought it might distract her, but it didn't really.

"Yes. They sold it. Made a packet. I can't remember how much, but even Piers was impressed. And he always expects everything to make huge amounts of wonga for him. It's his mindset. They sold it with the three child dolls and the sort of servant doll, but they kept the two adult dolls, as Reiner told them to. They seem to do what he tells them to an awful lot; I can't think why, except that he's got even more money than they have."

"I can't say I took to Reiner."

"I know. He doesn't like you much either. He's always referring to you as 'the little schoolmaster.' And you're not… I mean, little. Anyway, I can't stand him either. So, these two dolls, Piers and Seals have them sitting on the headboard above their bed. Reiner's suggestion, of course. They think it's a great laugh, but I think it's a bit creepy."

"I rather agree," I said. I did, but I also wanted to give her some reassurance in my inadequate way. It did not have the desired effect.

"Strellbrigg Hall is getting me down. I'm stuck here, at least until they get a proper housekeeper and a nanny for the kids."

"Why don't you tell them you've got to go."

"I can't! I am rather… sort of… financially dependent on them. And Celia is my bestie, always has been. It's loyalty really."

I told Nicola that her loyalty was admirable and this seemed to give her some comfort. Then she looked at her watch and said that she must be getting back.

Once or twice that autumn, I caught sight of Nicola with the children in the Hall's grounds. It was only at a distance while I was attending to some pruning or planting in my garden. They appeared to have grown considerably since I last saw them, but I could not see them that clearly. I could hear them, however. They made a good deal of noise, though there were no words, only incoherent shrieks and cries, strangely feral, like those of foxes in the night, or gulls fighting over a dead fish on the sea shore. Once I saw Marcus on the terrace with Nicola. He was in a rage and was punching Nicola repeatedly, beating at her thighs in an agony of frustration. I thought of going over to intervene, but she screamed at him and he backed off, shocked by her outburst. The boy's legs were unnaturally long and thin.

By the end of November, to my relief, they had gone and the Hall was dark. I did not see the Argents until the following Spring and then it was not at the Hall.

I try to make a habit of going for a walk every day. There are a number of walks I can make in the fields and woods around my home in Norfolk, but I often drive to the coast, and walk along the shore of the North Sea. It is not far.

There is a stretch of the coast called Barren Sands, east of Trimingham. I go there because few people frequent it and one can walk for miles without seeing anyone, except for the occasional dog walker. The beach is of soft sand bordered by dunes tufted with coarse grass and, further inland, bird-haunted salt marshes and scrub. There are no houses there, not even a wooden hut or ruined church to distract the eye. To some, the place is featureless and dull, but I think I like it for that reason. There is nothing to fill your mind with thoughts and anxieties, just unaccommodating nature, the unresting changelessness of the sea. Barren Sands is well named.

One early afternoon in April I had decided to go walking there. There were some high clouds and a blustery wind but there was sun too. I was glad to be by the sea, and to have the place almost to myself. I say almost because in the far distance I could see a small cluster of people coming towards me. My eyesight is not good over very long distances so it was some time before I could define them. There were five of them, two adults and three children.

They were moving rapidly in my direction, and I suppose some antique sense of courtesy prevented me from avoiding them, even though instinct was urging avoidance. The children were cavorting around their parents in a strange way, never going far from them but circling them, their movements abrupt and uncoordinated while still suggesting a dance of some kind. Their legs were long and thin, as was the two girls' hair, which flapped and struggled in the wind.

Inarticulate cries were carried to me from their direction. I took it that they came from the children, though they sounded more birdlike than human. As they came nearer, I saw that it was the Argents who were coming towards me: Piers, Celia and their three children.

Marcus, the boy, wore shorts, and the two girls, Rosamund and Isabella, had on short dresses of a rather antique style. These costumes emphasised the length and grotesque thinness of their legs. When they noticed me, they stopped prancing – the only word I can think of to describe their movements – and stared at me. Their eyes looked feral and unfocussed. Then Marcus set up a wail which was so high-pitched that it sounded like the whistling of the wind. Piers attempted to quieten his son, but only succeeded when he had actually stopped the boy's mouth with his hand. I saw him wince when Marcus tried to bite it away.

Celia smiled at me nervously and said "Hi!" I smiled back and answered with something banal about it being a good day for a walk on the sands. Both Celia and Piers looked tense and anxious in a way that I knew to be alien to their natures.

Piers gave a laugh and said: "The kids are all excited." He pulled his hand away from Marcus's mouth and I could see there was blood on it. Marcus set up a low, keening moan.

"Good to see you all," I said fatuously.

"Yes," said Celia "We must... get together some time."

And so we passed by each other, now moving in opposite directions, no doubt to our mutual relief. I did not look back for some time and when I did the Argents were several hundred yards away. A man and his dog, a springer spaniel, had come onto the beach and the dog was circling the Argents, barking furiously. The children were waving their arms wildly at the animal, though whether to deter or encourage it I could not tell. The dog seemed to make the latter assessment and came closer to them, but when it was within a few feet of the children it stopped and lowered its head. Though I could not hear, I suspected it was growling. Then, suddenly, it turned tail and dashed away from them at high speed. It ran towards the sea and plunged into the breakers.

The dog owner called and blew a whistle but it was some time before the spaniel emerged from the sea, and when it did it ran rapidly away from the children, up the beach and towards me. By this time the Argents were moving inland and very soon I lost sight of them among the dunes.

A week or so later I had returned from a walk and was settling down in my sitting room to a book and a cup of tea. Such things are often preludes for me to a guiltless doze, one of the rare secret pleasures of later life. But this was to be denied me. The doorbell began to buzz insistently, and this was punctuated by banging on my front door. I had never had this experience before. Even the ex-prisoners who regularly come round my village to sell overpriced dish cloths, fridge magnets, and secateurs are less importunate. I got up to answer the door and as I did so I heard a bang like a gunshot coming roughly from the direction of the Hall. I opened the door and there was Nicola standing on the doorstep, panting and terrified.

"He's got a gun and he's trying to shoot them."

"Who? Who?"

"Piers! The kids! He's trying to shoot them!"

"What! Why?"

"God! I don't know! You've got to do something!"

"Have you phoned the police?"

"No! I haven't got my mobile. They took it away from me. For Christ's sake do something!"

I realised that my reactions were appallingly slow.

"Where's this happening?"

"In their garden. The kids are trying to escape into yours but they can't get over the fence."

I ran out, followed by Nicola. just as there was another shot. I was slow and she ran ahead of me down my garden to where Rosamund, Marcus, and Isabella were entangled in a hedge which was on my side of the fence. They appeared to be in rags and were crying out desperately, flapping their arms in vain, like birds in a fowler's net. Another shot rang out. Marcus shrieked and I saw blood coursing down his thin legs. He had been peppered with shot. His sisters began to scream in sympathy. I told

Nicola to go back to the cottage and phone the police on my land line.

As I ran down towards the children, I saw Piers Argent standing on the terrace of the Hall. He was putting two more cartridges into the barrels of his shotgun. Celia stood beside him holding a box of cartridges; her expression was vacant. I shouted at them.

They looked in my direction, bewildered. I shouted again. Piers raised his gun and aimed at me, then Celia touched his arm and said something to him. Slowly, very slowly, he began to lower his weapon. Meanwhile, I was down at the fence, helping three bedraggled and wounded children into my garden. They were crying to each other wordlessly, but in unison, like a litter of baby animals caught in a trap. Even since our last encounter on Barren Sands barely more than a week before, they looked as if they had grown longer, and thinner, and stranger.

It was not too long before the police and an ambulance arrived. The children's wounds had been, mercifully, superficial, but still painful.

Months passed. Summer came but I barely noticed it. There was a trial at which I gave evidence. While I was in the witness box, I happened to look up at the spectator's gallery of the court. Reiner was there, leaning over the railing, intently watching. When our eyes met, he winked at me and smiled.

Piers and Celia, thanks to their excellent (and expensive) lawyers, were found not guilty of wilful wounding, but were obliged to seek psychiatric help. Rosamund, Marcus, and Isabella have been taken into care.

Strelbrigg Hall is once again on the market.

Something
Peculiar

from

Ally Wilkes

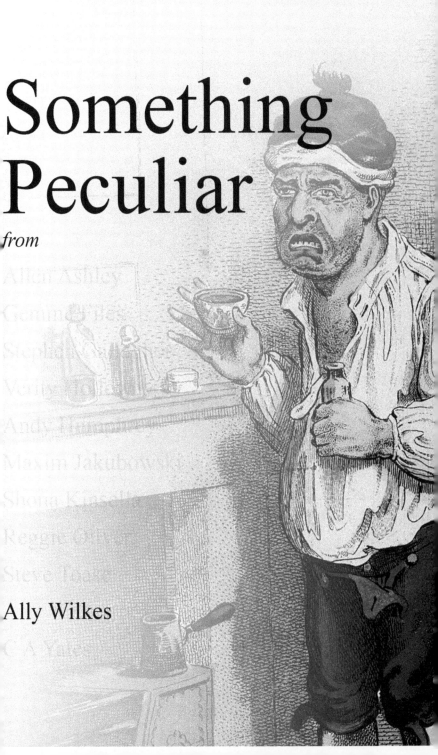

Black-Eye

"…i suppose you're wondering about the eyepatch…"

♠ **Day Zero** ♠

HI, HELLO everyone! Wow. Wow, I just wanted to say this is amazing… an amazing surprise. As you probably know, I've been doing make-up tutorials for a while now, sharing some tips for my gorgeous followers, and this is just… my first unexpected piece of swag, and I'm so grateful to the people at… Blacker Than Black, right, for sending me this little box of joy. Shall we open it? Yes, let's open it!"

[Screen freezes. The beauty blogger EPLove is holding a black box up to the camera, displaying the branding in gloss black capitals on a matt black background: BLACKER THAN BLACK. She and her bubblegum pink staging area shrink down into the corner of the screen, and another window pops up:]

A young man sits down in front of a webcam, facial hair smartly groomed, serious brown eyes. He's wearing a grey plaid shirt, black baseball cap and bright pink tank top. Behind him, we can see a neatly-made single bed, a vintage *X-Files* poster taped to the wall. There's a can of supermarket energy drink on the desk next to him.

"Welcome, viewers. I'm Jesse Carter, and I'm about to take you on an investigation."

He nods at the screen.

"There's been a lot of fan theories about what happened to Emma Patricia Love – better known to her followers as EPLove."

[The screen around him starts to fill with Reddit posts:]

u/miss_snatch: I bet she was on meth, meth-heads go crazy and do that sort of shit

u/zanzibar: it was probably a publicity stunt

u/unauthorised_swag: looks like they froze up her pageviews and she went broke

u/zanzibar: yeah why not go out with a bang lol

"But YouTube isn't talking – just took down all her videos and suspended her account. There's not much to go on in the public domain. A few newspaper articles. But if you dig around a bit—"

There's a thud from the room next to him, and he glances off-camera, uneasy.

"What I've put together disturbs me. So if you're ready, we'll begin."

Jesse pauses.

"The clip you saw a few minutes ago is what I'm going to call day zero. It's either the day EPLove received the gift box, or shortly after. Let's return to it."

[EPLove's window reopens:]

"Look at this! It looks fancy, doesn't it? I don't think I've seen this brand before (I have googled it!). So if you're watching this and you were the PR that sent it, please… reach out to me. I'd love to know who to thank! Um, opening the box now – this bit sort of slides out – and inside it's this gorgeous fuschia pink. I'm excited! Just getting the tissue paper off now… and look at this! Doesn't it look amazing! Blacker Than Black. I bet there's some beautiful saturated colour on this. Because what's blacker than black? Well, nothing!"

[Screen freezes:]

"There's EPLove holding up her Blacker Than Black mascara. She's right – the brand doesn't exist. There are literally hundreds of black mascaras, but none with this brand name. None which look similar. So it's unlikely she requested it from the manufacturer and was just pretending to be surprised for the sake of her followers. She must have been sent it, as she says.

"But by who?"

♠ **Day One** ♠

"It's taken me a long time to find the first in-context use of the blackspade emoji. There are all sorts of connections listed on Urban Dictionary – ace of spades, white women with tattoos signifying they're hot for black men—" (Jesse coughs, laughs awkwardly) "The phrase itself is 'black as the ace of spades'.

"But I was eventually able to track this down, over on the CreepyPasta forums. Yes, I know."

[Screen pops up. It's an assault of black, grey and maroon. The post displayed is Forum > General Wiki Discussion Board > Hey has anyone else seen this?]

"You can see the poster is calling itself CuriousSpade. That account doesn't seem to have posted anywhere else on the forum. It has no edits to the Wiki, no achievement points, nothing. The avatar is a black box. It simply posts on day one, asking whether anyone else has started seeing this emoji around."

♠

"And that's it. It doesn't get any meaningful response – plenty of users calling him the F-word – and the account never posts again. Look, I know it sounds tenuous. But I think this is the first example of the blackspade emoji out in the wild."

♠ <u>Day Two</u> ♠

Jesse sits back down at his desk. He's wearing glasses now.

"Sorry. Wearing contact lenses and watching this next bit of footage gives me the creeps, you know? It's like I can feel something in my own eye, just… stuck in the corner. Like when you're walking along a road and a gritting truck passes you at top speed, sending a ton of crap into your eyes. And you try to rub it out but that makes it sting. It's worse when you wear contacts, I promise. Anyway. This is one of the videos YouTube took down very shortly after it all happened."

[Screen pops up. It's EPLove's usual staging area – a vanity with triple mirrors, rows of film-star incandescent bulbs lining the frames, casting a soft pool of glowing light. The dresser is baby pink, and there's a cinema style light-box perched on a shelf, reading: 'Love What You Do!' EPLove is wearing giant neon pink acrylic hoop earrings and a high-necked black blouse:]

"Hi, hello! I'm so pleased you could join me for today's tutorial! We're going to be looking at a smokey eye make-up look… gorgeous, right? So many of you have asked me, EPLove, how do you get that perfect blended look? Well, wonder no more, lovely people, because I'm going to show you—"

[Video plays on 3x speed as EPLove applies numerous make-up products:]

"And now it's time for the mascara! This is my first time using this brand… Blacker Than Black… and come on, you guys are still such a mystery to me." (Laughs) "Please do reach out and let me know who I should be thanking! But this looks like it'll have excellent coverage, you can see the bristles are perfectly coated, it's just… luscious. I'm going to start with one coat so we can really put this one through its paces. Okay… right eye.

"Oops! Ugh, I hate it when this happens, I'm just going to… you can probably see, it's gone into the corner of my eye. A little dot effect… but it'll blink out. Getting it off the eyelid… yup. Nobody's perfect, guys! Not even me!"

♠ Day Three ♠

[A static image fills the screen. It's Christina Jamieson, better known as ChristinaRuns, an Instagram influencer sponsored by several British luxury sports brands. She's dressed in black leggings with gold crackle effect, a matching sports bra, and a large puffy gold jacket. The caption reads: "Getting ready for my first ParkRun of the season… it's fine to have a Starbucks to warm up beforehand, right?"]

[A smaller window opens in the corner:]

"Jesse here. So this is where I started to make connections. Everyone knows about ChristinaRuns disappearing, but surprisingly few people dug out her old posts from way back before she went to the police. Trust me. Take a look at this one, and look at the hashtags she's using."

[Hashtags start to pop up around the Instagram post:]

#brrrr
#peppermintmocha
#blackerthanblack

"You see that last one? She'd never ever used it before. I zoomed in on her picture, and it's hard to see – really hard to see, actually – but I think she's wearing make-up. For a Park Run. That's interesting, right?"

♠ Day Four ♠

"A lot of you have been telling me I'm reading too much into all this, or calling me names for posting about beauty bloggers and Instagram influencers. James P called me a… well, James P has a lot of problems with the fact that I'm a queer black man who likes wearing nail varnish and all I can say is, fuck you James P, fuck you, because this is about to get weirder, it spread to a lot more channels before what happened to ChristinaRuns and EPLove went mainstream. I didn't think it was on Twitter, but I spent a lot of time immediately after the 'unscheduled downtime'—" (Jesse does air-quotes) "—going back through accounts that our patient zeros might have interacted with in February. And then boom – I had it."

The door of his bedroom creaks open off-camera. Jesse turns, and appears to gesture at whoever's standing there, using one hand to shield his laptop camera.

After a few moments, he removes his hand. The sound of retreating footsteps.

[On the main screen, there's a Twitter profile with a black cover photo, a round black orb of a profile picture, and no profile text. The handle is @blckrthnblck.]

"So this account joined Twitter on day four. No followers, but following thousands of people, a complete spambot, right? There's a single tweet. It says: "SOON YOU'LL SEE ME". No-one's mentioned, the account doesn't @ anyone, there are no likes or retweets. It's an assertion. It's a statement of purpose. And I'm sure it's connected to whatever EPLove saw."

♠ Day Five ♠

"Things get a little gruesome as we head into day five. If you've got a problem with eye injuries, or gross eye stuff, you might want to look away at this point. Again, this is something YouTube took down. I'd say it was under pressure from Blacker Than Black's lawyers, but they don't exist. They can't have any lawyers."

"Hi guys, it's… it's me. I know, I know. I look soooo tired! I haven't slept the last few days because I'm so stressed about this eye thing. Like when I go to sleep, when I lie down in bed and close my eyes, you know, I kind of see this… dark patch on the right side. Where it should be pink, right? Or that pinkish-red colour. It's seriously annoying, in fact it's seriously creepy, and if I can show you – you know what, I'm going to show you. Hang on. Let me just get this light… right. Here. I'm going to shine it sideways into my eye, and just pull down my right lower eyelid, like this… can you see it?"

[EPLove is wearing a pink brushed fleece tracksuit top and no makeup – or minimal make-up. Her right eye looks swollen, slightly puffy, and as she pulls down her eyelid, exposing the pink underside, there's a visible black spot in her cornea, a little off-centre, covering part of her iris:]

"I mean, I've never had… these spots in my eye before. I've been googling and I hoped it was something like an eye freckle, but this one seems to be growing. And I can see it from the inside of my eye, even when it's closed. And when it's open…"

[EPLove glances off-screen to her right, in the same direction as the eye spot:]

[Quietly:]

"When it's open, I see things."

"Jesse here. Okay, in this next frame you're going to want to look over her shoulder. It's a message on her light-box. She usually posts these inspirational messages. But today is very different."

[EPLove's video is slowed down. She reaches for the webcam, clearly about to shut it off. As she does so, the camera shifts for a moment. Her light-box reads: 'YOU KNOW'.]

♠ Day Six ♠

"I have little to say about day six. KateXapKitty appeared happy, appeared healthy – she was excited for the upcoming con, that's all she was talking about. Meeting her fans, seeing the upcoming releases, doing some cosplay. Until she killed herself in an audio-only Twitch stream on day six. Her visual feed was dark the whole time, and she was begging for something to stop following her. The chat stream was just flooded with that blackspade emoji."

♠ Day Seven ♠

The camera returns to Jesse's bedroom. He's sitting on his bed this time, on a grey Minecraft duvet cover. There's an old-fashioned digital alarm clock on his bedside table, showing the time as 01:23. His nail varnish is a matching gunmetal grey. He flashes it.

"Cute, huh? That should annoy James P…"

Jesse takes a large gulp of energy drink, smiles.

There's a bang on the wall of his room, and he glances quickly off-camera.

"I'm not going to link to that infamous *Daily Mail* column – who wants to give them more oxygen, right – but you can probably remember it. They used a photograph of ChristinaRuns where she happened to look slightly less than fabulous, probably because she was just leaving the police station. She had her hair up in a messy bun, and she was wearing flip-flops in February, and they did the usual thing, implying she was having a nervous breakdown. Truth was, she'd put on the first pair of shoes she could find, because she ran from that house, and you and I would have done the same.

"The columnist wrote about the 'culture of attention-seeking' and 'women whose only currency is being watched', and I think we can extend a big FUCK YOU to S---- V--- for mocking a woman who was seeking police protection from a persistent stalker.

"Anyone could tell there was something very weird going on. ChristinaRuns described a tall man, dressed in black, who would 'come and go' depending on the lighting conditions. Like, sometimes she'd turn on her security lights and there'd be absolutely no-one there. But she was adamant he was real. Some evenings he'd be standing outside her window as soon as it got dark, just a few feet from the glass, visible when the wind blew the branches away from the streetlight.

"'Like a reflection' she said, and that… troubles me. Because if he looked like a reflection, that implies he was actually on the other side of the glass, right? That he was on her side of the window. Inside the house.

"The other thing to remember about this man outside her window – the tall man dressed in black – is that ChristinaRuns lived in a top floor flat."

♠ Day Eight ♠

[Jesse's bedroom shrinks into the corner of the screen. The main window shows us EPLove's pink vanity. None of the bulbs are lit, in a departure from her usual aesthetic. The light-box, to the left of the dresser, is a dark rectangle. A figure walks on-screen, bends over the table to switch on the lights, then puts a hand in front of her eyes. It's EPLove:]

"Hi hello everyone! Thank you for bearing with me! Not very interesting content these last few days, I know, but I've been sooooo grateful for all your messages of love and support. My followers mean the world to me. Now, I suppose you're wondering about the eyepatch. I look just like Madonna, right? It's a bit big for me, but I wanted to make sure I couldn't see anything out of my right eye. It just feels… better that way. I'm still… not sleeping too well. But anyway, onwards and upwards, all! Today we're going to work on the perfect metallic lip."

♠ Day Ten ♠

"Jesse here. You'll notice we skipped a day. That's because – as far as I know – the phenomenon we're tracking briefly became invisible. We have no idea what form it took, what it did, or who it targeted. There was nothing on social media. No videos from EPLove, no posts from ChristinaRuns. Whatever it did in that day, it went undocumented. But we can see its – ah – secondary effects. The symptoms. Like in a film where you can't see the monster in the tunnel ahead – but you can see the rats fleeing from it, skittering away into the darkness."

"And what we can see is the blackspade emoji popping up everywhere. Most of all in the comments – on both those accounts, it's rife in the comments. Brand-new accounts, created that same day, posting the blackspade and nothing else. The blackspade was so ubiquitous that some people started noticing, like these Reddit users."

u/miss_snatch: hey u know posting emojis freezes pageviews, not cool

u/zanzibar: what??

u/unauthorised_swag: too many emoji YouTube locks your page down, prevents monetization, thinks you're a Russian bot or something

u/zanzibar: seriously whats with these guys.

"In fact, EPLove's pageviews had dropped off sharply ever since she'd posted the first Blacker Than Black video. ChristinaRuns… well, that's trickier, isn't it? Because she'd essentially gone into hiding. Can't post new Insta content when all you've got is your own four walls as backdrop. But the blackspade emoji was everywhere."

[Mumbles:]

"That's when I started seeing it too."

♠ Day Eleven ♠

[The screen shows EPLove's sickly pink vanity. It's less pristine than usual – a few discarded make-up brushes are hanging out in a coffee mug, rather than holstered in their vintage velvet brush roll. There's a coffee ring on the dresser. One of the lights around the mirror dims, almost unnoticeably, then returns to its usual brightness. Reflected in the mirror, someone stumbles into the frame. It's clearly EPLove, although her face is covered with a lilac-coloured sheet mask, the sort seen in *American Psycho*.

She's wearing a dressing gown, a towel twisted up on her head in a turban, and she bends down to pick up the bubblegum pink bin under the vanity, place it on her usual seat. She doesn't say anything, but displays its contents briefly to the camera: some discarded facial wipes, the BLACKER THAN BLACK box, and the mascara that came in it. She lights a match, holds it up to the camera, and drops it in. Through all this, we don't get a good look at her right eye. She looks off-screen to the right:]

"That should do it, you fucker."

[Screen freezes. EPLove is backlit by the vanity bulbs and her burning waste bin. She's luminescent with bath oil, shimmering with flames. The right side of her face is in shadow.]

[Screen shrinks to show Jesse in the main window:]

"You've got to hand it to her – this is an act of defiance, an act of war. She's burning the tools of her trade. Burning the mascara that started it all. She must have finally linked her… eye problem to that make-up tutorial. Smart girl. She'd slipped for just one second. It isn't much, is it, to have your whole life unravel? Just a second. She's trying to save herself. It looks like she's casting some sort of magic spell, some sort of… pagan ritual. Fire for banishment. But whatever was in that mascara had been unleashed into her life, and destroying it won't help her. Won't help any of them."

BLACK AS THE
VOID

♠ Day Twelve ♠

Jesse sits cross-legged on his bed, back against the headboard. From the wallpaper – a distinctly floral pattern – it's obvious he still lives at home. Someone taps or knocks on the wall behind his head, and it makes him jump, look around wildly.

"Excuse me."

He bangs on the wall a couple of times, and there's an answering hammering – excessively loud, excessively violent – in response.

Jesse's room is dimly-lit, and he keeps his voice low.

"It's funny, when I started this… investigation, I thought I'd just be setting out what happened to those three girls. Allowing you to draw your own conclusions, you know? But it's become more than that.

"I've started spending… probably too much time on the internet. A lot of time on CreepyPasta—" (he laughs) "And a lot of time on conspiracy boards. Sub-sub-reddits. Looking for that blackspade. Following the trail.

"And sometimes, when it's late at night—"

Jesse picks up his webcam and turns it to face his bedroom window, which is open. Net curtains blow in a slight breeze. The sky outside is pitch black, no street lights visible, leaving open the question of where Jesse actually lives.

"When it's late at night, and I'm watching things like this next bit of footage, I start to wonder. How I'd react if I saw it in the corner of my eye. You know – the wraith."

He drums his fingers, nails still painted that gunmetal grey.

"Anyway."

[He presses a button and shrinks into the corner of the screen:]

"You've probably all seen this, it was doing the rounds pretty much as soon as it was posted. Every time they took it down, more copies popped up."

[On the main screen, frozen in front of the camera, is ChristinaRuns. It's been five days since she made the infamous 'flip flop report' to police, and she's visible only in very dim light. It's obvious she's using an in-built laptop webcam, and it's not good quality. She's relatively hard to recognise without her signature sportswear, her hair scraped back onto the top of her head, and a pair of dark-framed glasses taking up most of her face:]

"Okay. Okay okay okay. I've called the police, but I don't think – I don't know if they'll be here in time. Fuck. So if I disappear, I want you to know what happened. I want you to

see – what I saw. It's not a stalker. Fuck me, I wish it was a stalker. When I started seeing him outside the window – oh god, I thought that was the worst thing ever. But he's in the house now. Every shadowy corner. Every fucking – pile of clothes on a chair. Every open door.

"He's inside. And I can't stop seeing him."

[Her voice shrinks to a shrill whisper:]

"I'm going to point the camera at him. Now. Look."

[A room in half-light. It's her living room. A long pale grey couch, matching armchair, a coffee table, abstract art on the walls. A mannequin in the corner – but it's immobile, wearing some sort of sportswear. There's an open chimney, dark as a mouth. A TV in the corner, DVDs stacked underneath. The camera shifts back to show ChristinaRuns, close up, terrified:]

"You see it? You see him?"

[She moves the camera again. Audible sobbing:]

"Every day he comes closer, he comes closer and I can't – fuck – he'll be here soon."

[The video winks out of existence, leaving a blank screen:]

"Jesse here. The police were called by ChristinaRuns at 21.19, shortly before this video began. They arrived at the house at 21:32 and found nothing out of the ordinary. She was hysterical. Demanded to be taken into protective custody. We know that a doctor was called. But that's all the mainstream media would report about that night. Of course, the internet had a field day. I want to show you these, which appeared on CreepyPasta very shortly after."

[The same video starts playing, muted, at half speed. It freezes at the point ChristinaRuns uses the camera to show her unremarkable living room:]

"There's nothing in this video, right? We can't see the figure she's telling us about. The obvious inference is she's so spooked she's seeing – shapes – in piles of laundry, or that creepy mannequin in the corner. But, well, the mannequin is a red herring. Look closer."

[A red circle appears around the TV, and Jesse's mouse icon pops up:]

"So you can see the reflections here. This smudge is her couch, it's a pale colour, so it shows up. Here's the white sheepskin rug. Here's the desk she's sitting at. Now this – dark patch. It's taller than the armchair. It could be something on the wall, or something hidden when she moves the camera, but if you do that camera turn again, slowly, look – you can see there's nothing in the room which could cast that reflection.

"It's something tall. It's standing to her right. Almost looking over her shoulder.

"What really scares me is that she knew it was there. She could see it, even if it wasn't visible to the naked eye. But there's more."

[Another screenshot comes up, from the start of the video. ChristinaRuns is staring into the camera. The room behind her lacks that tall dark figure. Her glasses are huge:]

"If you wait until she glances behind her, you can – pause it there."

[When she turns her head slightly, it's possible to see her right eye without the obstruction of the glasses. There's a large dark patch in that eye, like an oil slick. In the next frame it's gone.]

♠ Day Thirteen ♠

"Hi hi hey hello, hello everyone, hello, it's me again, I'm back, and I'm sorry for the creepy videos, really I am, and a lot of you have been saying that's not good fire safety, is it, burning something in a metal bin, and I'm sorry, I'm not perfect, of course kids don't try this one at home, haha, I was desperate, I shouldn't have done it, didn't help anyway. So! No eyepatch today! I bet you've missed seeing these baby blues!"

[EPLove giggles, and gives the camera an exaggerated wink. Her right eye is no longer swollen. But the iris is a different shade of blue from the left.]

"It wasn't really working for me, the whole look, the covering-up, particularly as you can't cover up your eyes when you sleep, can you, when you shut your eyes you pretty much just see the inside of them, right? Right? And there's a black patch in there, which means it's always there, it's always there, I can't get away from it with some stupid fricking eyepatch so..." (she takes a deep breath) *"Just good vibes, good intentions, and I'm sure it'll come right in the end, no matter what he wants, what he wants from me, and..."* (she glances off to her right) *"I'll find out, won't I, I'll find out eventually."*

"Anyway. Anyway. Sorry. Sorry, it's just – oh, and some of you are commenting, which is sweet. Hi! Giving you a wave. Hi! I'm sorry I've been a bit of a disaster recently, beware Greeks bearing gifts, haha, and now it's time to get on with the show but – no, please stop that. Please. Please. Don't do that."

[EPLove is staring at the screen, and there's a small difference in the focus of her left and right eyes that makes it obvious she's wearing a single dark blue contact lens, to conceal whatever's happening in her right eye:]

"No, please don't. Please... I can't! I can't! I don't know why you're all doing this to me! I don't know what I did! Please stop doing that!"

[She's crying:]

"Whoever you are, this isn't funny. Please. It's my life. Please. It's not funny."

[The screen freezes, and EPLove winks out.]

[Jesse's window pops up on screen:]

Again, it's late at night, and his room is in near-darkness.

There's a slow creaking sound from the door, and Jesse sucks in a sharp breath, glances off-screen. "Very funny, you little shit. Now piss off."

He clears his throat.

"Sorry. Anyway... I bet you're wondering what EPLove was screaming at. What tipped her over the edge."

He presses a button. Around the screen, around his own image, they start popping up.

"Every comment on her video that evening – the ones left while she was live, and the ones left after – featured the blackspade emoji. It was as if they were taunting her, trying to provoke her into doing something drastic. Or it could be bots. But I don't think so.

"Because I tracked down one of them, James1982, on the CreepyPasta forums. He'd left a comment on her video saying it was good she was back, something innocent like that. But when he accessed it again, the comment had been… mangled. Only half of it was visible, and it made no sense – letters missing, all jumbled up, and the blackspade emoji at the end. Like something had eaten it."

♠ Day Fourteen ♠

IF YOU DON'T WANT TO SEE ME
YOU KNOW

♠ Day Fifteen ♠

Jesse looks tired.

"Yes, James P, I know you think I'm delusional. Watched too much *Stranger Things*, sitting around in my bedroom with no friends, blah blah blah. Anyway. I'm not making this for you. I'm making it because I genuinely believe.

"What do I believe? Well, that's the thing."

He's sitting cross-legged on his bed under the pool of light cast by an Anglepoise lamp. There are collectible figurines littered on the bedside table, along with his thick-framed glasses and a couple of bottles of nail varnish.

"I believe there's some sort of… entity responsible for what happened to all three subjects: ChristinaRuns, EPLove and KateXapKitty. I don't know where it came from, or what it wants.

"But when it comes to you, it gets into your eyes. You start… seeing things. Out of the corner of your eye, at first. Then it becomes more and more real. Coming closer, like ChristinaRuns described. Like a shadow that won't go away. Until it's standing right behind you. And then something bad happens. Something really bad.

"Like KateXapKitty killing herself on air. You know they never found her body, right? They never found her."

Jesse fiddles with a wristband.

"And the blackspade emoji, it's like its… precursor. A harbinger. Fact is, you don't want to see that emoji popping up. Not ever."

[Jesse minimises his own window, brings up the comments section to his vlog into a separate, larger window. Most of the comments are from spam accounts. Others enthusiastically approve of his quest to uncover truths hidden by the 'MSM'. He scrolls down them too fast to read the numerous comments left by James P. But every now and then – like a little blip, a glitch – we can see he's scrolling past comments containing the blackspade emoji.]

"I think I… looked at it for too long."

♠ Day Sixteen ♠

"Day sixteen is where we enter the last act, I guess."

[Jesse remains in that small window to the side of the screen, as if hiding. The main screen shows nothing but black:]

"This is the last image posted by ChristinaRuns. People have run it through every analysis program on the planet. Enhanced, colour-shifted, broken it down into individual pixels, turned it into code and run it through speech filters. It's just… black. An entire image filled with black. There's nothing hidden in it. Nothing we can see, at least."

[The image recedes, and the surrounding Instagram post becomes visible. It was made at 21.19 on day fifteen, and is devoid of any hashtags, caption, or location data. The comments section is filled with question marks, shocked reacts. LoveLifeLoveFitness asks: "IS THIS A JOKE?"]

"Well. You know the score.

"No-one ever saw Christina Jamieson again."

YOU
YOU KNOW

♠ <u>Day Seventeen</u> ♠

"Why did it take KateXapKitty so early on? Why was she just… swallowed up, back on day six? I don't think it works the same for everyone. Some people see it coming. Some people are taken quickly. Is it worse to… to wait? We don't know when KateXapKitty was infected. Did she receive the mascara? Did she find the blackspade emoji all over everything?

"But she was the first to go. Her channel was dark for days, then taken down. Most of ChristinaRuns' content has been taken down – worse, there are loads of copycat videos. Some try to see her ex in the shape in the TV. Some use noise or pop ups for a quick scare. But both these women disappeared entirely. And as for EPLove, well…"

[The main screen shows EPLove's vanity. Two more of the bulbs have gone, and there's crumpled rubbish – crisp packets – on the surface of the dresser. The light-box is off screen. EPLove approaches and sits. She's wearing a bra and hotpants. There are red scratch marks on her shoulders, as if she's clawed absent-mindedly at herself. She fiddles with something in her lap, then unrolls it onto the dresser. It's one of her velvet tool rolls, this one with nail files and tweezers and little nail scissors and large hairdressing scissors:]

[She turns to camera:]

"What do you think?"

[She sounds very tired:]

"Hi, hello out there. What do you think? Should I do it?"

[The black spot in her right eye is enormous. She glances off screen:]

[The video freezes.]

♠ <u>Day Eighteen</u> ♠

"Jesse here.

"'Young woman admitted to local hospital after partial self-enucleation.'

"That's how it was reported. Don't worry, I had to look it up too.

"It means removal of an eye."

Jesse is sitting at his desk. There are four open cans of energy drink, and it's very obvious he hasn't been sleeping. He's become twitchy. His grey nail varnish has nearly all been picked off.

He looks behind him, towards his bedroom door. Through the crack underneath, in the interruption of the light, someone's feet are visible. He sighs. Rubs his face.

"Just… go away, bro."

There's a creak of floorboards and the shape disappears.

"Self-enucleation, also called oedipism, is when someone removes or mutilates their own eyes. It's been associated with religious delusions. With cases of paranoid schizophrenia. With extreme drug-induced psychosis – I was able to find an in-depth study of a girl in the States who was on meth and thought Jesus was telling her to do it. It's a messy, horrible thing to do to yourself, and it's so important—" (he attempts a little smile, which falls utterly flat) "—not to go looking for pictures, because they're… well. They're horrific. I didn't sleep for a while. I've become basically vegetarian. The idea of someone doing that to themselves just… blows my mind."

[EPLove appears on the screen, in a still from an earlier video. She's wearing an acid-wash denim jacket covered in patches, and pink lipstick. She's holding up a make-up brush. She has two bright blue eyes. She's smiling:]

"At some point between posting that video and being admitted to the hospital, EPLove used her tools on herself. We don't know how she did it. I think – I think she'd have used eyelash curlers, first. Clamped them up. Got herself ready.

A clear shot at it. She was being so practical. Burning the mascara didn't work. Wearing the eyepatch didn't work. She was doing the only thing she felt she could do. Was it the long scissors? The short? We'll never know. And the photos released – the photos the tabloids picked up, those ghouls – were taken from a distance. We can just see her lying on a stretcher, being carried in. There's a dressing over her right eye."

"She was lucky to live. A lot of people hit an artery, when they try to… remove the eyeball. Or damage the optic nerve, go blind in both eyes accidentally. There's a lot of delicate stuff back there. But EPLove was sensible. She went after her ability to see – from the right eye only. It was about becoming blind on one side."

Jesse reaches for one of the cans of energy drink, takes a swig automatically. He appears to notice it's empty, and puts it back down.

"But she lived."

♠ Day Twenty ♠

"Hi hello everyone! Wow! It's good to be back. I'm sure you've all heard what happened. But I was discharged yesterday, and have basically spent my time sleeping ever since. Have you ever slept – really slept – after what feels like forever? It's the most luxurious feeling on earth. Just me, my bed, comfy pyjamas… heaven. As you can see, I'm wearing a dressing over my right eye, which is not particularly glamorous! There are going to be a few surgeries from here on, to make it… a bit easier to look at."

[EPLove glances down:]

"It doesn't look too good so far. And I'd like to say a big thankyou to all the people who sent me their love, their best wishes, their support. I got a huge amount of flowers and cards in the hospital, and I don't even know who tipped off my fans that I was in there, but wow. Thank you all so much. I'm humbled. And even if it doesn't look good, I want to just… carry on. Maybe I'll become a body positive beauty blogger – learn to deal with it all. What's missing. What's gone."

[She blinks away tears in her left eye:]

"You guys. You guys. I'm just so grateful I got through this."

[She wipes her nose with the corner of her dressing gown:]

"Honestly, I don't remember when I've ever felt so... rested. And free. Isn't that strange?"

♠ Day Twenty-Seven ♠

"Jesse here. So is that it? The end of the story? You know it's not."

"It was another week before fan speculation about where EPLove had gone grew to boiling point. She hadn't made any more videos, hadn't moderated any comments, hadn't updated her website. They'd expected a phoenix-from-the-ashes story, perhaps – fucking ghouls, sorry – a look at whatever she'd done to her eye."

"The general consensus was that she'd gone private while she came to terms with it all. Maybe she was making videos for a handful of people on Patreon. The internet can be brutal, and she was getting called all sorts of things – an attention seeker, a schizo, a dangerous role model for young girls everywhere. I'm sure you can guess what the *Daily Mail* had to say. A perpetual clip gallery of some of the worst moments in her life, playing in the sidebar, and people wondered where she'd gone? I hoped she was recovering somewhere nice. Perhaps in a residential spa, somewhere in the country. Somewhere with patchy WiFi, maybe."

Jesse runs his hands over his face, sighs deeply.

"I wanted to believe it so badly. You know this was happening in real-time, back then? For a young queer kid who followed beauty bloggers from his shithole of a room in the suburbs – this was a big deal. EPLove mutilating herself and then disappearing. It was like losing a friend."

[Jesse clicks himself back up into the main screen:]

"So I went looking. I scanned all the chat feeds. Did a deep dive, following the blackspade emoji everywhere. Remember when I said – earlier – that I found @ blckrthnblck? Well."

There's a bang on the bedroom door, loud enough to shake the webcam. Jesse jumps, spilling his can of energy drink.

"Seriously, you little asshole—"

He takes a deep breath. Shakes his head. The door stays shut.

"My little brother, otherwise known as James P."

"Anyway. You're going to want to see this. Here's that twitter account for day twenty-seven."

[It appears on the main screen. Same dark cover photo, same small circle of darkness as profile photo.]

IF YOU
IF YOU DON'T

"See here. Someone called Emma P. Marshall, using the account @EM124907409174. Looks like a bot, right? But look what she says."

[It's highlighted in red: "PLEASE LEAVE ME ALONE, I DID WHAT YOU SAID."]

"And how the dark figure responds."

YOU KNOW
WHAT
YOU HAVE TO DO

[In the small window, Jesse presses a palm into his right eye, wincing]

[The screen goes dark]

Jesse pushes himself back into his desk chair, staring at the camera.

"Of course Emma Patricia Love wasn't her real name. And this girl – this woman – Emma Patricia Marshall. She disappeared, like the rest."

"So that's the end of the story. My investigation into some events on the internet. How something arrived in a box and attached itself to three subjects. How it sent out its signs and feelers, through our social media, through our laptops and our phones and into every room in our houses. And it's here now."

IF YOU DON'T
WHAT

Jesse swallows, glances towards the door.

"I keep looking at my own eyes. Trying to see if there's that... smudge of darkness in them. But once it's there, it's too late. No, I think I can just see the... the harbingers. I've looked at it for too long."

[Video freezes, abruptly:]

"So watch this space."

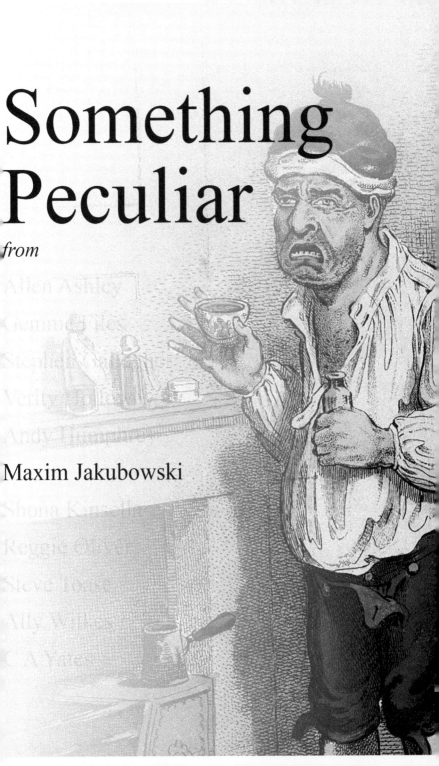

Something Peculiar

from

Maxim Jakubowski

The Book Collector

"...a subtle knife made of ink..."

SOME PEOPLE gamble, others are alcoholics, and some are even both, but he collected books.

His daughter often joked that he was just a hoarder, but he would vigorously defend himself and proudly call himself a collector.

He would regularly have extensions built to his house to make room for the continuous flow of books arriving and although he managed to read between two and three a week, depending on his other obligations, they accumulated and, one day, he made a rough count and calculated that it would probably take him another thirty years at least to read every volume he hadn't yet had the opportunity to read. The fact that he was already well over sixty was no deterrent, and they kept on coming, new titles he had seen reviewed and which had caught his attention, older books by new authors he had come across, new novels by older authors which he acquired for the sake of bibliographic completeness, curiosities or rarities he had come across on the internet or in a dealer's catalogue, first editions of books he fancied but only had later reprints of, books he was sent for review and held on to despite the fact he had not written about them. To compound his obsession, he also wrote the occasional one and had managed over the decades to get himself published on a regular basis, mostly metafictional stuff in which he played a canny game of disguises, and cleverly concealed episodes from his past sentimental life behind a hall of mirrors of plots often borrowed wholesale from pulp fiction were essentially the plot. He enjoyed a mild notoriety as a writer but was aware his talent was a minor one in the grand order of things literary and was content with the fact. He had also worked in book publishing before his retirement and jointly owned a bookshop, so had never veered too far from the printed page.

But now he was feeling old. And all life could offer was grief. And memories treasured and unwanted.

His body ached in places he never knew existed, his eyesight was faltering dangerously, his laptop and TV screen were at times blurry when he was tired. His right knee was dodgy when the weather turned humid; he suffered muscle spasms in his legs in waves and toothache was a constant despite regular visits to the dentist. Just a week before he had experienced sharp chest pains over a couple of days – a new experience for him and a damn scare. Acquaintances always remarked on seeing him that he hadn't changed in years, but every morning when he looked into the mirror, he could see new lines, hollows, his skin losing its shine, his eyes dulling. And then there was the cough, that recurring niggle in his throat, a familiar feeling long before Covid.

You need an understanding wife to be a book collector. And not just because of the amounts of dust the activity inexorably attracts.

But now, after decades of companionship and love, he had become a widower of sorts. The one fixed point in his life – the regular visits to the nearby care home where he had been forced by circumstances to take her and where she sat all day with her eyes half closed, her mind erased, looked after by nurses who fed and washed her, unable to recognise him, or anyone, any longer, stripped of all dignity – had been taken from him. He would feed her small pieces of dark chocolate or sultanas, hold her hand, and feel his own life ebb away with every second that passed. Knowing he would feel like shit for the following 48 hours after he returned home, merely punctuated by the inevitable arrival of new books, and feeling an abominable sense of guilt that he was not visiting her more often.

What were once passions – books, music, movies – were now just interests and no more.

But still he kept on collecting.

Old habits die hard.

Some book arrivals were expected, titles he had acquired online or from dealers' catalogues or auctions; others arrived out of the blue: books sent for review by publishers or, sometimes, soliciting blurbs, although he was sadly aware that his name meant less and less as he persevered in his decline.

On occasion, out of sheer lassitude or lack of enthusiasm, he wouldn't even tear open the jiffy bags or parcels for several days, and a teetering pile would accumulate on the living room sofa or by the door until, finally, some form of curiosity took over.

On that day, a cold sun was shining outside with a tantalising promise of spring, even though a chilly wind blew through the small trees and bushes dominating his front garden. The thud of envelopes and thin parcels being fed through his letter box and landing on the floor caught his attention. He picked up today's harvest and carried the lot to his study. Cruise and travel company brochures, a bank statement, leaflets from estate agents seeking properties to sell or retirement homes targeting him or his absent wife because of their age, and half a dozen packages harbouring books. Nothing urgent.

It was only in the afternoon that he got round to opening the lot. The customary assortment of domestic thrillers and cosy crime amongst the review copies, an American small press volume of hillbilly noir he had read a review of and ordered through lack of choice from Amazon, and a well-wrapped volume whose provenance was uncertain.

It was a French book, even though it didn't appear to have been posted to him from France. A new novel by Emma Becker whose debut, 'Monsieur', he had actually translated into English some years previously. He had met her several times since although it had now been ages since they had exchanged words, but he had kept in touch with her career as a striking feminist purveyor of carefully-modulated erotica. He wasn't even aware she had written a new book. The arrival surprised him as he kept in close touch with all book news, even from abroad. Her books were always strongly autobiographical, obliquely detailing her many affairs, her complicated private life and, once, the two years she had worked in a Berlin brothel. He had strongly lusted after her, not just because of her sexual nature, but through the fact that he had inhabited her words for weeks while translating her first novel and intimately shared her inner desires and transgressions.

The book was issued by a Parisian publishing house he was unfamiliar with, which took him by surprise; Emma had been with Flammarion for ages and had even won awards. Why had she moved?

He opened the book to the title page. It wasn't signed. So not a complimentary copy sent to him by Emma or her publisher. And neither had he ordered it, being totally unaware of its very existence. This was curious.

It was titled *The Chronic Adulterer*.

He frowned.

Sat himself down and began reading.

By the time he'd finished the book, it was dark outside and raining. He'd been glued to the book for hours, hadn't eaten or even drunk, his mind effervescent with thoughts, frantic, panicked, fascinated, appalled.

Even though the novel's main character was not named or even physically described, it was undoubtedly him.

There it all was, the unedifying tale of a man who, although he loved his wife dearly, was also a man who could not resist other women, even pursued them and became a serial adulterer.

Not only did he recognise the principal character as himself, every woman he met and the places they cheated in were listed, in infinite detail. Forensically dissected alongside the feelings that accompanied their lovemaking. It was all there, the story of his life as a bad man, the lies, the excuses he had constructed to somehow justify himself, the subterfuges, the betrayals. And, not that it made him proud, the fact that every other woman he had faulted with he had, in his own way, been in love with too.

Emma had always been an elegant stylist, so her descriptions of the mechanics of the multifarious sex involved didn't feel overly pornographic, which was something of a saving grace.

He closed the book.

He felt hot, febrile, his mind falling into a whirling mass of confusion. Like struggling through a circular nightmare from which there is seemingly no exit.

It was as if Emma had been inside his head.

But only he knew of these stories, these affairs. He had never confided in her, nor had he communicated some of the more sordid details evoked in the tale to anyone!

This was an impossible book...

He tried to reach Emma through Facebook but she was no longer on social media. He emailed her at the address she had used a few years back, but the message bounced back. Then a thought occurred to him and he looked the book up on Amazon. It was nowhere to be found. Didn't appear to exist!

He slept badly that night.

Memories flowing back. Of each and every woman he had illicitly known. Their faces, their eyes, smiles, perfume, their naked bodies, the sounds they had made while they fucked.

But, when he finally woke up, the impossible book was no longer on the bedside table. It had just vanished into thin air as if it had never existed. And neither could he find a trace of the padded envelope in which it had been taped up.

Believing it had all been part of a trick his imagination had been playing on him was too much to ask for.

The words, however, had been carved deep by a subtle knife made of ink into the fabric of his brain and still burned bright.

A week later, still reeling from the effect of the impossible book and unable to shake its shadow, he came across a listing in a New York antiquarian bookstore for a book by Cornell Woolrich he had never heard of. Nor did it appear in any bibliography. *Black is the Night*. A suitable title, but not one that was supposed to exist, and he did consider himself not just a major Woolrich collector, but also an expert on the noir author who had inspired so many unforgettable movies. He called the shop and asked for further details and was shown the book on Facetime. It looked authentic. He requested they take a photo of the opening page so he might compare it with other genuine titles he kept on his shelves and establish whether it was just an unknown alternate title, somehow chosen by a pirate edition, but he did not recognise the opening paragraphs.

Intrigued as well as greedy, he acquired the book, which set him back several hundred dollars despite the poor state of the dustjacket, and waited impatiently several days for the package to be delivered to him in London by the seller's courier. All the while, he kept on referring back to online databases to ascertain whether the improbable novel by Emma Becker had manifested itself and had become a reality, even though its sheer existence just made no sense.

The package from New York was badly delayed because of a strike at the airport and a badly drawn up customs declaration, but finally arrived.

It had the lovely smell of old books, a fragrance like no other, of attics and spiderwebs and the passage of time. The hardback's cover was not dissimilar from other Woolrich (or William Irish) titles in their first edition, not that many ever had gone into reprints. A silhouette, a tall building, the moon at its apogee, a woman's face with long, blonde hair masking half her features, possibly inspired by Veronica Lake.

The copyright page stated it had been published in 1948. The same year as *RendezVous in Black* and *I Married a Dead Man*.

He began reading.

Within a few pages, it truly felt like authentic Woolrich. A frantic race against time, destiny raging in the heart of its hapless male protagonist desperately trying to find a woman amongst the ever-shifting crowds of a busy international airport, despairing, scared and caught in a web of terrible anxiety.

A far from unfamiliar scenario.

One he had both experienced personally and relived countless times since in his worst nightmares.

A story he had been at the very centre of.

It had been two years before she had officially been diagnosed with early onset Alzheimer's; she was already showing increasing signs of forgetfulness but he hadn't taken too much notice, blaming her occasional lapses on other factors. She had always been somewhat absent-minded.

They had spent New Year's Eve in New Orleans, as they often had in the past, celebrating on the balcony at Tujague's, and were making their way to New York. A cold weather front had descended on the Eastern seaboard and their flight had been delayed. The airline had set them up in a hotel at the airport and, the following morning, had managed to get them as far as Houston, where they would catch a connection to La Guardia. But further delays occurred, and they were stuck there for half a day. The lounges were overcrowded, and they would have lost their seats had they vacated them; she had to visit the toilets which were just on the other side of the main concourse and she walked away. Lost in a book, it was ten minutes or so before he had realised she had not returned. It took several hours – luckily enough their flight was not called during that time – for him to find her, racing between departure lounges to locate her as she unwittingly gave him the run-around. She had lost her way, not seen him sitting where she had left him and gone wandering, oblivious of where she was or their destination while he, and available airport staff he had alerted, ran around in circles. She had no cash on her and he had been carrying her passport and boarding pass. At least she spoke the language, which was not the case a year later when he experienced another catastrophic transit airport toilet panic and breakdown. By then, he had learned from experience to wait for her outside the convenience, but on a trip back from Thailand, the damn facilities in Abu Dhabi had an opposing door (which she used) leading to another concourse and he had lost her again! For a whole hour. They gave up on foreign travel soon after, its perils all too apparent in her worsening condition.

It had been an abominable nightmare, which he had re-lived many times since during the course of troubled nights.

And in the book he was now reading, the whole catastrophic story repeated itself in the opening chapter. The characters even had their first names, and were also travelling from New Orleans to New York via a forced stop-over in Houston.

It was uncanny. And profoundly disturbing.

He set the book aside, scared by what might happen in the following chapters. He was feverish, doubting his sanity. He wanted to shout out loud that he was not some character trapped in a book and that no one had the right to appropriate the sorrows of his life. He took a sleeping pill, remembering that when they had finally reached New York their luggage had gone missing, having somehow been left back in Houston with thousands of other suitcases. New York was freezing and snowy, and the clothes on their back were suited to the Gulf of Mexico. But this was no longer his main consideration, as he had reluctantly come to realise that something was badly wrong with his wife.

By morning, just as would happen in a bad horror story, the apocryphal Woolrich novel had disappeared altogether from his house. But he knew he hadn't imagined the whole thing: there was a debit on his credit card online statement for the acquisition of the phantom volume... No reason to question his sanity. Yet.

A week passed with no further anomalies. Almost as if the entity toying with him was keeping him on the hook, waiting for his guard to lower.

By now, his heart no longer jumped a beat when the post arrived with its cornucopia of books old and new.

But he was caught out when a courier rang the doorbell late on the Friday evening, just as he was hoping the week would conclude on a note of normality.

The package – obviously a book – was wrapped in shiny black bubble wrap firmly held in place by a deluge of tape. It might not be what he both expected and feared, he briefly thought; sometimes publishers would pack advance proofs of titles they had a big investment in similarly, hoping the package would stand out from all the other run of the mill jiffy bags and padded envelopes.

Slowly, with almost a sense of ritual, he undressed the book from its packing material and soon held a thin volume between his hands. Not a novel; a novella at most. Just under a hundred pages.

He owned a fair proportion of erotica within his sprawling collection, alongside the annals of crime he was better known for, had a pronounced taste for its more refined, literary shores and naturally owned first editions of the few Nicholson Baker novels in which the American author had indulged his taste for the sexually bizarre and provocative. But it had been years since Baker had dipped his toes in those controversial waters, let alone published anything new.

But here was a volume by him. Another book that shouldn't exist.

Titled *The Dead Girl and Me*.

The book collector gulped.

But couldn't divert his eyes from the pages and began reading, although he knew the story inside out. His most profound secret. Only known to him and a woman who was now dead.

The case had been notorious and hit TV news and newspaper headlines for days on end, both after the crime and, later, the killer's trial.

A young woman in her mid 30s, training as a lawyer and returning from an evening's out with girlfriends, had been savagely assaulted on an East London street, just a stone's throw from where she lived. The maniac, recently released from prison, had already approached several other women that same evening, and she had just happened to be walking along the same stretch of road at the wrong time. He had hit her, raped her and then kicked her skull in. She didn't stand a chance. The culprit was caught within a day, as he had made no effort to disguise himself or avoid CCTV cameras.

There had been marches and public protests, the customary calls for justice, and the dead woman's photograph supplied by her family had spread like wildfire over the Internet and the newspapers; always the same one, taken at a party in which she looked the picture of joy and innocence. She came from a close-knit family of Pakistani immigrants.

When he saw the photo online for the first time, the book collector had recognised her instantly.

The last time they had met she had initially ordered him to strip naked, and closely inspected his genitalia, which she had earlier ordered him to shave clean. She found men's pubic hair disgusting and unclean. Once she was satisfied with his obedience, nudity and vulnerability she had placed a leather dog collar around his neck and attached it to a leash and had him get down on his knees and crawl like a dog. At one point, she had drilled the thick heavy 8 inch dildo she had insisted he acquire on their visit to a Soho sex shop up his anus until she was fully satisfied it had reached a satisfactory depth and painfully stretched his sphincter ring to the maximum, and had taken countless photos of him in such an undignified and revealing position.

Following her violent death, her relatives had painted a picture of her as almost one of innocence. She was anything but innocent. The book collector, on learning the news of her murder, had wondered whether he should soon expect a visit from the police, once they had forensically examined her phone. But they never came knocking at his door. Her murderer had stolen the phone, and maybe once he was apprehended the police had felt there was no need to dig through her past and discredit her pure image. He was aware he was not the only man she liked to 'play' with. He, however, had resisted her demand he should wear a cock cage, which her other more submissive playthings did.

She had initiated contact with him on a fetish website. She called herself Mistress Sarah, although her real name, which he would only learn of after she tragically died, was slightly different. His own involvement with BDSM had begun some decades back during the course of his affair with Kate, a married woman who had manifested strong inclinations of sexual submissiveness in their lengthy relationship, which had provoked an intense curiosity in the book collector's heart, mind and loins. So much so that following their inevitable break-up, he had been left wondering how matters had felt for her and concluded that he had to experience sex from the other side, so to speak. It had led him to have interactions with men, even though he had strictly no attraction to them as individuals or a species. It had led him to accepting a submissive position when with them, sucking cock and eventually agreeing to being mounted on the occasion of several anonymous encounters procured through dubious websites. Ironically, he obtained little sexual pleasure from these encounters, but began to crave the experience from a detached, almost intellectual point of view, observing his own domination by strangers with an unsettling form of detachment, passivity even, even as they treated him roughly and took pleasure in debasing and humiliating him.

When grief took a lasting hold of his life, it developed into an addiction. It was easier to submit to strange men than attempt to seduce new women. He was tired, he was lazy, and even though he was aware of the myriad contradictions, he took a skewed pleasure from being used.

Sarah had come across his profile on FetLife and messaged him. She had noted his interest (as Bookcock44) in being dominated by men and made an offer to act as his Domme; she would function as his de facto procurer and find men to use him and, in exchange, only wished to watch and conduct the proceedings. She would not get personally involved sexually, would always keep her clothes on (invariably all in black – top, skirt, tights, shoes). All she wanted was the occasional present, she said, once he established the terms of their encounters and stated he was in no way willing to be financially dominated.

He was intrigued.

Agreed to an initial meeting in a squalid Premier Inn room off Leicester Square. He stripped for her. She wrote on his body with her lipstick, took photos from every angle and then, when her phone buzzed, invited a willing stud she had lined up to the room and had him sodomise the book collector.

They repeated this on a half dozen occasions, until the day that she took him dogging and led him naked by leash and collar through an isolated wood in North West London, seeking men to fuck him, and they were almost caught out by a wandering police patrol. He just about managed to slip a T-shirt and a pair of shorts on, before they both frantically ran back to the car park, their hearts in a flutter.

The next he heard of her was when he recognised her in the photos of the murdered woman on the news bulletins a fortnight later.

Every single detail of their random meets was laid out across the pages of the impossible Nicholson Baker book. Things no one but he and a now dead girl had any knowledge of. Every sordid detail.

A novella about his worst infamy. Highlighting the secret life he had fallen headlong into since he had found himself alone. Not so much through sexual desire, but as a rampart against the grief and the loneliness. Or at least that was his excuse to himself.

He locked the volume away in a drawer, although a voice deep inside the distant rooms of his brain kept on telling him the book would certainly be gone by morning. And it was. Those appeared to be the rules of the game. Or was it just a game?

Now every postal delivery kept him on tenterhooks, stomach clenched, his breath withheld, heart beating the light fantastic with metronomic regularity.

But the peculiar fate or person or enemy took a malign pleasure in torturing him, and it was weeks before a further book arrived.

Death and the Book Collector by Anonymous.

And the moment he glanced at the title, the book collector knew it would be a story describing how and when he would die. It made sense in a strange way; everything had been pointing to this.

He waited a few days.

Would he be killed by a maniac like Sarah had been, run over by a car, fall down the stairs, have a fatal heart attack, electrocute or hang himself, choose suicide? Would he linger or die quickly?

He had once clumsily tried to commit suicide in his early 20s; over a woman, of course. But he hadn't then known how to properly slash his wrists and had cut in the wrong place and direction. Still sported two small, white parallel scars. And she'd never spoken to him again.

He put one of his favourite pieces of music on, settled in the armchair and opened the book to the first page.

The story began with a man in an armchair beginning to read a book.

He felt a dizzying sense of vertigo rising from his stomach.

Took a deep breath.

And cheated.

Went straight to the book's final page.

In which a man, who looked just like him, grey curling hair, wearing glasses and unshaven for three days, lay dead in an armchair.

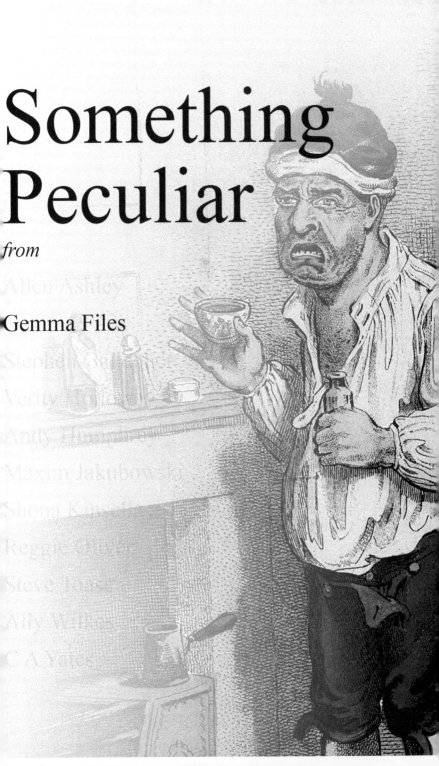

Something
Peculiar

from

Keep Going

"…flapping tatters of dream…"

Twilight fell suddenly, like rain. They were already what felt like two miles into the woods at the back of Jani's mother's cottage, anxiety building in him slow but sure as layers of sediment, when he finally found the spine to venture a comment, half joke, half complaint.

"I'm beginning to think this place doesn't even exist, love," he said, voice thin against the thick green silence. Then added, after she didn't even turn, let alone smile: "Jan, did you hear me? I said—"

"Of course I heard you."

"And?"

"Just keep going, Karl. Don't you trust me?"

Which was, of course, the question.

Karl never remembered his dreams, though he sometimes remembered he *had* dreamt. But over the pandemic, that began to change.

That first night, he dreamt the whole house was sinking, slower rather than faster, that there was only a thin rim of light seeping in from outside, and everything else visible through the windows was simply an endless vista of dirt, roots, worms, bones. He stumbled from room to room, barking his shins in the half-gloom, unable to find the light-switches. Eventually, with a slow blink wipe, he found himself slumping back into bed with someone (not Jani); this person lay slack, deeply unreachable. Suddenly their mouth fell open, yawning long, hinge-broken – and Karl heard a tiny voice emerge from its cavern, small and frightened and echoey, as if from deep down and far away.

"Hello?" it said. "Hello, is anyone there? Can you hear me?"

"Excuse me?" he replied.

"Oh, thank god – is he asleep?" it asked.

"Who?"

"Karl," it said. "Is he asleep? Oh god, let him be asleep."

I'm dreaming, Karl realized, not that that made any immediate difference.

"You have to help me," the voice said. "Please. Please help."

Chance'd be a fine thing, he thought, head beginning to reel. And: "...yes," he found himself replying, nonetheless. "Karl's asleep, definitely. But who *are* you?"

"Who are *you*?" it asked him, in return.

When he woke, Jani was sitting on her side of the bed, watching him closely, an odd expression on her face. "You were talking in your sleep," she told him.

"Really?" Karl yawned, more to cover his own jolt of surprise than for any other reason. "Uhhh... so, what did I say?"

"I don't know – I couldn't hear. It was very faint. Like somebody lost in a cave."

"Sounds disturbing."

"Yes. It..." She looked away. "It was."

When he asked her why, later on, she said: "Because it didn't sound like *you*."

He might have reconsidered the whole thing if he'd only been there a week earlier, when Jani, May and Clare were well into their over-Zoom girls' night indulgences, but he hadn't been – not entirely, anyhow. He'd been physically adjacent but mentally absent, sitting at the kitchen table while Jani took the couch, headphones on and a YouTube mix of Shriekback songs blasting as he added notes to the end of his latest short story, trying hard to ignore Jani's occasional gestures while he bulled his way through the plot's potential back end.

"I can still remember when you had to be drunk to do *that*," he might have heard May answer, after Jani had just gotten through telling them about Karl talking in his sleep, obviously already a bit too sloshed to get her pronouns right.

"Do what? This is Karl we were just talking about, Maisie."

"Oh, babe. You're kidding, right?" As Jani squinted back at her, through the screen: "That *thing*, the *voice* thing. You know. Like: '*heeeelllpppp meeeeee…*'"

"I have literally no idea what you're talking about."

"Hm – well, you always *were* drunk, when you did it. Clare, help me out here."

"Remember that thing you used to do at sleepovers?" he might have heard May ask, had he been listening. "Like… that game you used to play."

"What game?"

"That, y'know… okay, so I guess it wasn't so much a *game*, more like a trick. Where you'd pretend to be asleep? Lie there with your mouth open, snoring a little, and then you'd do this – impression, sort of, like May said. This tiny little voice."

"The fuck?"

"This tiny little voice, Jan. It'd come out of your mouth, so small we'd have to, like, really lean to hear it. And your lips wouldn't move. I still have no idea how you did that."

"Ventriloquism," he might have heard May put in here, pouring herself another round of mummy-wine. "That's called ventriloquism."

"Oh yeah, right! I never knew you knew ventriloquism, Jan!"

"I *don't* fucking know ventriloquism! This is a really unfunny joke, you both get that, right?"

Afterwards, still humming the chorus from "Fish Beneath the Ice", he leaned in to ask her what she wanted for dinner, only to startle in turn as she jumped under his touch. "You all right, love?" he asked; she took a moment before answering, eyes wide and white in the dead screen's black mirror.

"I'm sorry," she told him. "Just… spaced out there a minute. Sorry."

"Bad call? I thought you were having a good time."

Her gaze narrowed. "Were you listening?"

"'Course not. I know you like privacy."

"…all right, good. Um – kebab, I guess? Donner shish, please."

"Will do," he said, reaching for his phone.

That night he dreamt an open grave like an abscess full of blood, twin shadows cast under a doubled sun. A siren going off somewhere in the distance, warning of impending disaster: tsunami, hurricane, nuclear attack. He came awake cold and panting, sweat-wet from head to toe with his spine stuck to the sheets and his head on Jani's chest, one arm folded fast around his neck. He lay there listening to her breathe for a long count, struggling to match his own inhalations to her rhythm, to stuff the fear back down inside. Reshape himself into the man she needed him to be once more, at least by the time they both woke again.

"D'you recall Mum's cottage?" she asked him, at breakfast. "Never did clean it out, like I promised her I would, before. Like she me asked me to."

"I remember."

"It'd make for a bit of a holiday, if we did."

"I could see that." He looked down at his porridge, wondering why he'd made it. "Well… whenever you'd like,

I can borrow a car from work, pack some food. Long time since we've been out of town."

"Same as everyone else, I suppose."

"Pretty much, yeah."

Voices seeping out from inside the loo as he lurched up out of sleep towards it, barely intelligible, though one seemed familiar; he paused when he realized he wasn't dreaming anymore, took a step back and must have made some noise, prompting Jani to call out from within: "Just be a minute".

"All right. You on the phone in there?"

"Why would I be?"

"…no reason."

On the way up to the cottage, meanwhile, Karl dozed off with his head against the passenger's side window, bee-buzz of motion and crunch of gravel beneath integrating to become a sort of distant violet whining sound, odd but not unpleasant.

Flapping tatters of dream enclosed him, laying him gently down on a moss-covered rock beneath a sky rippling with *aurora borealis*. Nearby, he became vaguely aware of those same two voices muttering away to each other, continuing the other night's conversation – one definitely Jani, but the other… the other. Thin, and small, and far away. Deep down. Echoing up through layers of earth, or stone, or flesh.

My throat hurts, Karl thought. Or did it?

(was it *his* throat?)

"So it *is* you," Jani said, to… whoever. And whoever answered:

You know it is.

"But how?"

Did I get inside him, you mean? To which Jani must have nodded, or so Karl could only assume. *You passed me to him,* the small voice explained, *when you two first kissed. I didn't want to go, but that's how it happened. I'm surprised it took you this long to notice.*

"You don't sound surprised."

But I am, very. Not to mention a bit hurt. We were so... close, after all, you and I.

Long waves of green from horizon to horizon, lightening and darkening, ebbing and flowing. A violet hum behind his eyes, dimming slowly. A pain in his throat, sharp as a thorn, a broken, buried bone.

"This is so... insane, it's..." A pause. "*I'm* insane. That's what it is, what I—"

Do you feel *insane?*

"No, but... I have to be. Don't I."

Not necessarily.

Jani paused again, holding the count of it far longer, this time. Until—

"That you even *exist* is insane," she said, at last. So softly Karl almost couldn't understand her.

And yet I do, the other voice pointed out. *You admit that, finally.*

Obviously.

Which must mean that I always did, even when you didn't want me to. Or most particularly then.

...yes.

Well.

You know what you have do now, *don't you?*

So.

Back to the hike, he and Jani wandering blind through her mother's woods: what felt like two miles in, all heat and stinging midges, green smears on his hands and face from leafy, low-hung branches. The scraping touch of bark over palms, against knuckles, air so increasingly moist that to breathe felt increasing as if he were eating it.

Above, the hidden clouds already massing, darkening. A dull roll of thunder, echoing through distant hills.

Then he must have stepped in front of her, somehow, or she fallen behind, since the next thing he knew was a heavy blow across the back of his head, hard enough to bruise both skull and brain alike – a dark red explosion, concussive slam of pain so intense it threw him forward against the forest floor, down amongst the sticks and dirt. Down face-first into mulch, and deeper.

Much later, pinned flat under the weight of his own nausea, he opened his eyes to find Jani standing above him, the rock she'd used still clutched in one hand but drooping, on the verge of being dropped. A rim of his own blood decorating it, like some dashed-off sigil.

"I have to do it," she told him, sadly. "It says I have to let it back out. You won't, so I have to. It won't hurt, Karl."

"Uh – what?"

"When I do it. It says…" A long, windy sigh. "…all I have to do is let it out, and it'll go away. Doesn't even want to come back inside me, so that's nice, at least. Don't you think?"

"…Jani?"

"A hole. Just a little one; it really *won't* hurt, not too much. It told me so."

"*Jan?!?*"

"Just stay still."

And: *it's lying,* he wanted to yell, but found he couldn't. As if something was holding his mouth shut from the inside, pinching his voice-box closed. Every word gone abruptly silent.

The rock fell, freeing Jani to reach inside her pocket instead, rummaging. To bring out that pearl-handled jack-knife he'd given her for Christmas and unfold its blade – so bright, so unstained. Never used before, that he knew of, for anything.

"I'm sorry," Jani sighed again, leaning closer. Allowing her shadow to fall across him, filling his sick eyes with dusk. And then, slowly – with infinite regret, yet a terrible sense of patience—

(no, please)

(*please*)

(please, *please, DON'T*)

—began to cut.

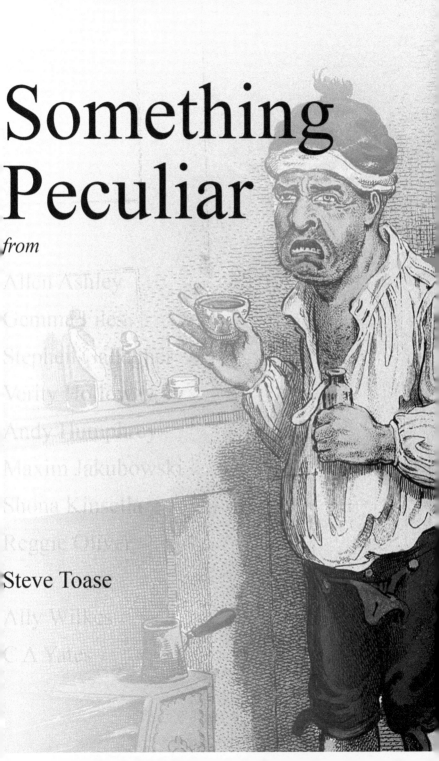

Something
Peculiar

from

Steve Toase

Through the Ivory Gate

"…barely restrained aggression…"

1

THE WAY The Hammer Man ran his grubby fingers across the scarred ivory made Graham Allerton skin crawl. The liver-spotted hand lingered, polishing the same precise point over and over again as if he needed to make his own mark on the stolen material. Allerton shuddered, though the three-bar electric heater was overheating him. He took off his coat, letting it fall over the back of the worn armchair.

He was one of the lucky ones. Most were freezing in the vast barn, the makeshift auction room huddled in one corner. The chair smelled vaguely of rat piss, but at least he wasn't having to sit on the mildewed hay bales that made up most of the seats.

"Auction starts in five minutes," The Hammer Man said, grinning through too few teeth. Allerton wondered whether they had been lost to rot or sovereign rings. He reached down the side of the chair for his thermos flask. With care, he poured himself a lukewarm cup of over-sugared tea, pausing to let his tongue explore a hollow in his own tooth. Decay came to them all eventually, one way or another.

There was an air of violence in the room, as if the destruction needed to wrench the tusks from the elephants

203

hung around the ivory like a blackened aura. He glanced around the room. There were two types of people; buyers and workers. The buyers could all be described as eccentric, as if to validate their invites it was necessary to cultivate some deformity of dress or manner. Allerton recognised most from other auction rooms, though few spoke to each other; they were poker players in tweed and cheap paste jewellery.

The workers had one thing in common: barely restrained aggression. Whoever employed them did so for one thing only, and Allerton prayed to several gods he didn't believe in that he never found out. He'd seen the flash of brass knuckles, and one of those flanking The Hammer Man wore some kind of hunting knife on his belt. There would be firearms kept at a discreet distance. Somewhere out of sight, but just within running distance. Crisis rarely comes out of a clear sky, and with its panoramic views over nearby farmland no-one was sneaking up on the barn. Allerton took another sip of tea, emptied the dregs into the dirt, and refitted the cup to the flask.

"Ladies and gentlemen," The Hammer Man said. "We only have one lot this evening. This fine collection of *cough* antique ivory." He paused, giving the buyers in the room a moment to study the stack of stolen yellowed tusks, as if they hadn't spent the last two hours catching glimpses of the forbidden material. Allerton faked interest. He was good at faking. Maybe not as good as he'd like to think, but good enough.

"Please, come closer. Examine the merchandise," The Hammer Man said. "But don't touch. We don't want to have to chop anything up so early." To one side the security reached down and touched the hilt of his knife as if to emphasise the point.

For the sake of appearances, Allerton levered himself out of the armchair and followed the snaking line of bidders queuing up to check out the ivory. He stopped himself glancing toward the door and waited until he stood in front of the table. Leaning close, he stared at the grain of the tusks, paying attention to where the ivory had been gouged from the elephant's skull. The muscle still attached was rotting even in the cold of the barn.

"Good quality, isn't it?"

Allerton looked up, not sure at first that the question was directed to him.

"Very much so," he said, acting the interested buyer. "And so well aged."

"Oh, very well aged," The Hammer Man said, laughing over his own words. "Please be seated and we'll get started."

Allerton walked back through the other buyers, taking his place once more, twisting his lapel, turning this way and that to take in all his fellow bidders.

When he spoke next, The Hammer Man's voice had changed.

"Ladies and gentlemen, we have here the finest antique ivory ever auctioned in the county. Due to bureaucratic processes the paperwork will follow on afterwards, but for the moment I invite you to bid on this never processed ivory, perfect for whatever use you want to put it to. You will be bidding per pound, because we believe in imperial here, and we have here approximately 250lbs per tusk. Who will start me at £200 per pound?"

When the violence came, it was not from the security but rather from outside, as the Wildlife Crime Unit burst through the doors with SCO19 leading the way. The auction's defenders surrendered straight away, realising how far away those guns now were, and that heavily armed, well trained men were between them and their firearms.

The only other violence came from the bidders, who found themselves in a situation and place they very much didn't want to be. With fingernails, teeth, and – in at least one case – hat pins, they tried to fight their way out of the barn. A couple managed to make it out, but most were soon handcuffed and lying face down on the urine-soaked straw. Allerton watched several rats crawl over one woman's fur coat, smelling the death of garment and starting to gnaw in case it was a meal they should not miss.

The cell door opened and Allerton sat up, letting the thin blanket fall to the floor.

"I'm DC Heselden. Come with me."

Allerton hadn't slept well, but he hadn't expected to. Police cells weren't designed for comfort, and the coming and goings of other prisoners taken for interview, occasionally interrupted by the penning of drunks, weren't the best conditions for a good night's rest. He fell in step behind the detective. The officer was taller than Allerton, shirt half hanging out like he only half remembered to get dressed.

They walked past the other cells, ignoring the yells, and past the duty sergeant desk. Heselden opened the door for Allerton to follow down to the suite of interview rooms.

Allerton sat down first and waited while Heselden shut the door, checked the recording equipment, and took out a packet of cigarettes. He tore off the cellophane and held out the box. Allerton shook his head and leant forward on the table.

"Too many other things that can kill you in this life. Don't need to give them a helping hand."

Heselden shrugged, lit one from a cheap lighter and tapped the ash into the crumpled foil ashtray. From his pocket he took something out and pushed it across the table. Allerton opened his wallet, checked his warrant card and slipped it into his back pocket, patting it in place like a piece of him had been missing.

"Did you get all the primary targets?" Allerton said.

Heselden paused, taking a long drag of smoke, holding it in his lungs before pluming it back out to yellow the walls.

"We recovered the ivory."

"That's good. We'll just go and staple it back onto the elephants. Did you grab the auctioneer?"

Heselden took the cotton filter out of his mouth, the brown paper soaked in spit, and stayed silent.

"I'll take that as a no. Who did you arrest?"

Heselden pushed across a sheet of paper, and Allerton ran his finger down the list of names.

"Hired help, all of them. Six months of planning and infiltration and we have nothing but cash in hand lackeys to show for it."

The officer shrugged and took the paper back.

"They were well organised. I'm just glad no-one got shot."

"I'm glad about that as well. I just wish we'd grabbed someone who mattered."

"We recovered a large stock of firearms. These are dangerous people we're taking off the street."

"But it's not going to stop the trade in ivory."

Heselden reached for the cigarette packet again, then stopped as if second guessing himself.

"Where is the ivory now?" Allerton said, trying to rub the tiredness from his eyes. It was always the same on these long cases. Every day spent undercover seemed to increase the distance between him and his colleagues.

"In the evidence room. The lab has already called to take samples."

Allerton nodded and pushed the chair back.

"Let me know when the results come back."

Heselden walked to the door.

"I'll see you in a few days."

Allerton sighed inwardly. Why did they never get it? Why did they never understand the need for the pretence and the performance?

"You need to take me back to the cells. If I just walk out now, I have no way of following up if I need to. You need to run me through the system like any other prisoner."

"Oh. Right."

207

They used the on duty solicitor and arranged for him to be bailed to his own address. He sat on his sofa and stared at the paperwork, wondering how many identities he'd invented had the same pile of documents. Legal restrictions for people who didn't exist. Across the table his second mobile, his own phone, vibrated to life.

"Allerton," he said, rolling his own name around his mouth.

"Heselden here. We have a problem."

He showed his warrant card and walked down the corridor. The office was more comfortable, but still had the reek of institution. Heselden sat on one side of the table, a woman in a white lab coat on the other, three cups on the table filled with lukewarm coffee. Allerton pulled out the third chair and sat down.

"I believe you know Dr Angledor," Heselden said, turning to the scientist.

"We've met. How are you Lucy?" It was petty, but he enjoyed watching Heselden squirm.

"Good. Well, apart from the results."

"There's a problem," Heselden said.

"There always is. Any luck finding the auctioneer?"

Heselden ignored him.

"Is the ivory from elephants?" Allerton asked Lucy.

"It is. That's absolutely clear, even at the macro level."

"And is it antique ivory?"

She shook her head.

"So what's the problem?" Allerton felt himself getting annoyed. He was still partially in undercover mode, carrying that taint of aggression he wore so well to stop people asking too many questions.

Lucy opened a brown envelope and pushed a photocopied report across to him, the paper covered in columns of figures. He'd seen them before – isotope analysis summaries – but never learnt how to read the figures properly.

"There's a summary at the end," she said.

Allerton nodded without looking up and flicked through to the last paragraph, reading twice to make sure he had it straight in his head before speaking.

"Is this correct?"

"We have a good understanding of the stable isotopes we expect to see from ivory, whether they have been poached from India or Africa, but obviously with a lot more precision than that."

"Obviously," Heselden said. Allerton gave him a look.

"We've spent a long time studying the global trade," Lucy continued. "We have very clear profiles of different habitats. This doesn't conform to any of them."

"But is that the only conclusion that you can arrive at?" Allerton said, looking at the paper again. He had that unsettled feeling he got when information should be false, but he knew it was correct.

"When we weren't getting a match on the first tusk, I compared it to some other stable isotope profiles; Indonesia, Columbia, and then North Yorkshire."

"What made you choose there?"

Lucy shrugged.

"A hunch. I know that a lot of private zoos got rid of their animals in the eighties. I thought that the ivory might be from some animals kept illegally. We had samples to profile against from another case and I got a match."

Allerton rubbed his forehead. He'd always prided himself on letting other experts have the space to do their work, and tell him the truth. He had no reason to doubt now.

"So one of the tusks was from an illegally kept pachyderm. We can still show the others were imported and cut off the supply chain," Heselden said. Lucy scowled at him then glanced back at Allerton.

"It's all of them."

Allerton stayed silent for a minute, then picked up the report again.

"There were tusks from over fifty animals recovered."

She nodded.

"Are you sure there was no cross contamination?" He saw her expression and corrected himself. "I'm sorry, but I have to ask."

He took out a pen and started scribbling figures in the report's margins.

"Assuming that they've not slaughtered all the animals, we're looking at a full herd of probably one hundred animals, in the Yorkshire countryside, that no-one has noticed."

Lucy stood up and smoothed down her coat.

"I just do the chemistry. It's up to you to do the detecting."

Heselden followed him out into the corridor and grabbed Allerton's arm. Allerton stared at his hand until he moved it.

"There has to be some kind of error."

"I've been working with Lucy on animal cases for over ten years now, and not once has she made a mistake."

"So, what are you going to do now?"

"I'm going to go back undercover and try and move up the food chain to find where they're really harvesting this ivory from."

2

The pub was all concrete and flat roofed rather than the rural log fire charm Allerton was expecting. He got a pint and sat down in a corner looking out at the pebbledash estate tacked onto the village. He recognised the buyer as soon as he walked in, though he paid Allerton no attention until he had a beer in his hand.

The man sat down opposite, tweed jacket fastened too tight, his face and neck swollen by some kind of circulation issue.

"They pigged you as well, then?"

Allerton nodded and took a sip of his beer.

"Got out the other week on bail. You?"

"The Hammer Man looks after his regulars. Retains a lawyer to help out. Mostly small stuff, but they come in useful at times like this. It's good to be loyal," the man said, pausing to take another sip of beer. Foam stuck to his lip. He made no effort to wipe it away, thick beer dripping down onto his shirt. "Funny that you chose this place to meet."

"The Rose and Crown?"

"Not what it's known as locally. The White Elephant," he said laughing, some kind of lung infection shattering the laugh into damp coughing.

"Really? Why's that?" Allerton said. He hated small talk with criminals. Useful though. Always boastful. People thought criminals had some kind of high level infosec, like spies with baggies of heroin, instead of being gobby little shits who spent most of the time showing off and intimidating those weaker than them.

The man leaned in close and whispered straight in Allerton's ear.

"Well, they say that it's because the brewery never makes any money off this place. That's rubbish. The real reason is that this is the place the first elephant was spotted."

"Elephant spotted?"

He leaned in close again. Allerton tried not to flinch away as if the stench would stick to him.

"The Black Elephants of the Dale. Where do you think the ivory comes from?"

"Not Yorkshire?"

The man laughed, sat back and drained his pint.

"You got the money?"

Allerton pushed the envelope across the table, dragging it through a pool of beer.

"Doesn't bother me, son. All money," the man said, sliding the sopping packet into his jacket.

Outside they walked up to an old Land Rover. Allerton glanced inside at the passenger seat covered in sacking, newspapers and old sandwich boxes.

"Climb in the back. We're not going far."

Not far turned out to be a lot further than Allerton expected. He rattled around the back of the 4x4, trying to hold on and stop himself getting a concussion while bracing his feet against several barrels with the warning labels stripped off.

The small window to the cab was too blurred by nicotine for him to see where they were going. The back was no better, the glass smeared and cracked. The only clue to their location at any given time was the change in smells outside, from slurry to wild garlic to the smoke from burning heather. He tried to keep track of time looking at his watch, but soon enough the sun had dropped and he sat in darkness in the back.

The final stage of the journey almost cracked his ribs against the vehicle's metal frame, before they came to a stop, the engine idling and juddering the Land Rover. He tried to open the door but the handle jammed, leaving him stuck until the man climbed out and unfastened the back, lifting it up and out, smirking as Allerton climbed down.

They were parked on a gravel drive between two immaculate lawns, leading up to a large manor house with too many lights on. Allerton brushed himself off.

"Don't worry about that. You don't need to look fancy for The Hammer Man. Just have money."

Tweed led the way up the drive, staying in the centre of the roadway, far from the lawns extending on either side. Allerton followed a few steps behind. Not out of deference, but to avoid having to hold a conversation. These people bored him, only interested in their acquisitions. Their treasures and their money. He kept looking around him, trying to spot any signs of cages or animals, but there were none.

The doorbell was modern, plastic and cheap, bolted to the old, crumbled stone. Tweed pressed the button and somewhere in the house an electronic melody played. Allerton listened as footsteps marked a pattern toward them and the door opened.

The Hammer Man was taller than Allerton remembered, his face washed out in the dim light from inside the hallway.

"I know you," he said, smiling, exposing the gaps in his teeth. "You were caught by the servants of the state weren't you?"

"Is that a posh way of saying pigs?" Tweed said.

Allerton bristled but kept the reaction somewhere it couldn't be seen.

"It is a more refined way of talking about the filth, yes," The Hammer Man said.

"This is The Hammer Man. Sir, this is?" Tweed left the question hanging, leaving Allerton space to fill the thought.

"Don't worry," The Hammer Man said. "Names aren't important here. Please come in. It's far too cold out on the doorstep."

Allerton nodded and walked inside. The walls were bare apart from trophy hunting photographs hanging in garish frames. He followed The Hammer Man down the corridor, Tweed walking behind.

"We will have a spot of food," The Hammer Man said. "Maybe a drink, and then we can discuss your order."

"Sounds good," Allerton said. Further into the building the corridor narrowed. Either side of him were drawings of elephants in silhouette.

"Yours?"

"I do like to turn my hand to the arts in celebration of the creatures that have brought me so much wealth," The Hammer Man said, not turning. He held open a door and waited until Allerton entered.

They sat down at the vast dining table and waited. The room smelt of cigars and mould. Allerton looked around him. The distant roof corners were all coloured by mildew, the deep shadows not disguising the rot. The Hammer Man rose and walked across to a corner drinks cabinet, pouring out three glasses of whiskey and bringing them back to the table.

Catering staff came in carrying plates of food, placing one in front of each of the three men. No-one looked at them and no-one spoke until they left.

"Please, eat your fill. It's a delicacy. There's plenty more in the stores."

Allerton turned the slices of meat on his plate. The flesh was dark grey, the colour of twilight. Picking up his knife, he noticed the blade was serrated. Even so, the flesh resisted the cuts until he pressed as hard as he could. Across the table The Hammer Man and Tweed were both focused on their plates shovelling in chunks of meat. Allerton took his first bite. The texture was coarse, though gelatinous as he chewed, and the slightly smoked flavour flooded his mouth with the seeping fat.

"You like?" Tweed said, a smirk on his face.

"It's unusual. Is this the point you tell me that this is the last person who betrayed you?"

The Hammer Man laughed so much that Allerton thought he was going to choke to death.

"Nothing so dramatic. No, these are the parts of the quarry that we cannot sell. I believe that is from a young calf. When we catch a family group we have to kill them all, you understand, even though the ivory is rarely worth harvesting. It seems such a shame to waste the meat."

"It must be expensive to transport the meat from abroad?"

A smirk passed between The Hammer Man and Tweed.

"The animals are not so far away."

The subject was not raised again over dinner. When they were all finished and the catering staff had cleared away the plates, The Hammer Man ushered Allerton into a smaller side room. It was dominated by a large fireplace surrounded by grainy photographs showing smears of shadow that looked like they might be something large and living.

"I heard the rumours when I was working as a gamekeeper in the area," The Hammer Man said, lighting a cigar and offering the box to Allerton, who declined. "Other areas might talk about mysterious felines, alien black cats, stalking their fields, but around here," he said waving his arm as if to take in the countryside beyond the stone walls, "around here they gossiped about late night trumpeting and trampled plants. Far too much damage for mere felines, no matter how large or mysterious." He took down a photo and handed it to Allerton. Allerton turned it over in his hands. The light was bad in the small room, but he still saw three blurred figures.

"The Black Elephants of the Dale. Of course, it was too preposterous for anyone other than a few credulous locals to take seriously," The Hammer Man said. He leaned in close to Allerton. His breath smelt of nicotine and bits of meat were stuck between his remaining yellowed teeth. "But I took them seriously."

"Was there a private zoo in the area?"

The Hammer Man shook his head.

"They've been here for far longer than we have, though they were barely real. More of an idea that wouldn't quite die. Locals would see damage to a tree and say it was the black elephants scraping their trunks against the wood, or they would see their crops trampled and blame a bull elephant the colour of shadows. Then people started seeing things on the horizon or near the treeline. All we did was feed that belief until the creatures were real enough to hunt. Real enough to harvest." He leant a little close and Allerton moved his head to one side. "Real enough to eat."

"Can you show me them?"

Tweed looked at his watch and shook his head.

"Far too late now," he said. "Far too dangerous to venture out into their territory."

The Hammer Man stepped back and pressed a button beside the fireplace.

"One of the domestic staff will show you to your room," he said. "Get a good night's sleep. We have a busy day tomorrow."

Allerton's room was small and as foisty as the rest of the house. He opened the curtains, the view bisected by iron bars too close together to even get an arm between. His window overlooked the main lawn of the house, with a small stand of woodland in the distance. As he watched, the trees shuddered as if something large was passing between them, unsettling them down to their roots.

That night Allerton's sleep was thin and disturbed. He never settled well when undercover, and the presence of the house seemed to press in on his dreams, forcing The Hammer Man into his head. Several times he woke to the sound of out of place elephants crying out as they were slaughtered. When he finally decided to rise it was six AM, and the cold of the room had got into his bones. He dressed and found his way through the corridors to the dining room.

The Hammer Man and Tweed sat either side of the vast table, the centre taken up with stainless steel platters stacked with scrambled egg and bacon. To the side a pot of coffee steamed on a hot plate.

"Ah. You're awake. I was just going to send my friend here to stir you from your sleep. Fill a plate, gorge yourself. We have much walking ahead of us."

Allerton sat down and dragged enough food onto his plate to keep up appearances, though the lack of rest had fractured any appetite he might have.

"I hope you are ready for the day."

"I think so," said Allerton. He was used to not committing. It gave him wriggle room when things turned criminal. If he hadn't agreed to commit the offence, then he had some thinking space to avoid breaking the law.

"He thinks so," The Hammer Man said, smears of egg falling between his broken teeth and staining the tablecloth.

"He thinks so," Tweed echoed. "Maybe he will be more certain when he's amongst the trees."

"I'm sure he will."

"And what will we find amongst the trees?" Allerton asked, trying to keep the shift in conversation natural.

"Mysteries," The Hammer Man said. "We will find mysteries."

By the time Allerton returned from freshening up, The Hammer Man was wearing a set of outdoor clothes more suited to the grouse moor than the dining table. Tweed was still wearing the same dirty jacket and offensive smirk.

Although from a distance the lawn looked even and cared for, upon walking across the vast expanse of grass it became clear no-one had bothered to maintain the grounds for a long time.

The Hammer Man led the way, with Tweed walking behind Allerton. Allerton kept his eye on the man in front but made sure he knew where Tweed was at all times. This was when he was most vulnerable, his attention on the target, The Hammer Man. They were far from the house and far from any village. Now was the time to make sure he kept his guard up. If they were to attack him it would be now.

They reached the tree line and The Hammer Man started searching between the leaves for something, reaching into a thicket and concentrating. Allerton heard a mechanical click of a switch.

"Hunting rabbits?" Allerton said.

"We need to take some precautions," The Hammer Man said. "Step over the cable. It's not live now, but I don't want you tripping and injuring yourself. I have no desire to have paramedics coming on my land to cart you to hospital with a broken leg."

Allerton looked down at the ditch circling the trees. Three feet up and barely visible in the foliage was a cluster of black cables, copper wires exposed on one side.

"We need to take some precautions," The Hammer Man said, standing aside so Allerton could clamber over.

"Don't want to wake up with one of them in the house," Tweed said, laughing, the tar in his lungs distorting any humour.

"Quite," The Hammer Man said.

"Are we likely to see any animals?" Allerton said. Push steady, push slow. That was always his tactic. Don't lead the witness. Guide them to lead themselves.

"At this time of day? Maybe some deer or the occasional fox. Nothing bigger."

"So why are you bringing me down here?"

"To show you evidence. We find that most of our clients are well informed in what to look for. Though the animals themselves might be elusive, the marks of their passing are there for any intelligent connoisseur to recognise."

The further they walked into the tree cover, the more Allerton struggled to see The Hammer Man. He listened for Tweed, making sure he stayed aware of his position.

"You're very quiet," The Hammer Man said. "Normally we can't shut our clients up. They have so many questions. They want to know what type of animals we keep here. They want to know how big they are. They want to know what the yields are. They want to know if they can hunt them themselves, or if we do that work for them. You're asking none of these."

Allerton shrugged, conscious of being watched from behind.

"I'm not here to scrape around for information. I want to see proof that you can supply, and I want to sign the deal. I don't care how the product arrives to me as long as it's genuine and as long as you can keep it coming."

The Hammer Man stopped and turned on his heel, leaning against a nearby oak tree.

"A businessman. We get so few businessmen. Most have some acquisitive desire. Amateurs wanting to pack their dwellings with the rare, or people who think they can get one over on me."

"And what happens to them?" Allerton said.

"We kill them. Shall we continue?"

Being so deep in the woodland made Allerton nervous. There was no-one coming for him and no way to alert anyone. Undercover he had to make all the decisions himself and if he got it wrong, there was no rescue. He carried on following The Hammer Man down the narrow trackways and said nothing. The man in front held up his hand then pointed to the ground.

Allerton had seen similar markings in Africa. Two long grooves where a bull elephant dragged its tusks through the dirt.

"This is fresh," he said, running his fingers through the dirt.

"Looks like they were active last night, boss," Tweed said, but not to Allerton.

"Are you satisfied?" The Hammer Man said.

"I'd rather see the animals," Allerton said, still crouching on the ground.

"They're shy," Tweed said, grinning.

"The woodland is tiny," Allerton said. "Surely they can't all hide in here?"

"Shy," Tweed said again, stretching out the word as if talking to an idiot.

"We'll find some more tracks," The Hammer Man said, holding out his hand to help Allerton up. His skin felt like a butcher's slab. "Maybe that will satisfy you."

"I'd be more satisfied if I saw some of your herd," Allerton said.

"As my colleague said, they're elusive and don't like to court attention."

They carried on walking deeper into the woodland, following routes and cut-throughs made by smaller creatures finding their way between the trees.

The clearing was vast. It occurred to Allerton that he'd underestimated the size of the forest. In the centre was a scatter of stones, boulders carried by glaciers long melted, now surrounded by the encasement of oaks.

"Very pretty. Still no beasts," Allerton said, kneeling down to run his hand over the moss-covered carvings on the rocks.

"You are a very cynical man," Tweed said, leaning back against a tree. "It's almost like you're not willing to take us at our word."

"I've been around auctions for many years," Allerton said. "Both legal and grey. The one thing I've learnt is not to take anyone's word at face value."

The Hammer Man shrugged and led the way from the stones, deeper into the trees, stopping only to point out marks and tracks for Allerton to pay attention to. For his part Allerton maintained the cynical front, keeping up the pressure as he saw how much it needled the other two men.

"If nothing we show you is going to convince then I suggest we head back to the house for dinner," The Hammer Man said, holding back an armful of branches to let Allerton through. They walked back in silence.

Dinner was served in a different room from breakfast, a smaller affair overlooking the kitchen garden and delivery entrance. Allerton recognised the atmosphere in the room, the feeling of anger and frustration. He'd failed to be impressed, and having the mark be impressed was always an important part of the con. If the mark didn't play along? Then the con might not work.

A member of the catering staff carried in several plates, placing them in front of the three men, then returning with three tumblers of cocktails.

"More elephant steaks?" Allerton said, pushing his food around his plate. The meat was in a thick congealed sauce, burst cranberry skins just visible below the surface.

"Something a lot more mundane tonight,"The Hammer Man said. "As you appear to be a man of more mundane tastes." Allerton watched him swallow his cocktail in one go. "You're not supposed to let them go warm. Drink them fast when they're made. Gentlemen?"

Allerton picked up the glass in front of him and swallowed the whiskey sour, the cherry catching on his teeth before he swallowed it, the last little bit of alcohol sweeping out with the sweetness.

"Well, as fun as this is, I have work to do,"The Hammer Man said, standing and pushing his chair back under the table.

"I also have important work," Tweed said, much less convincingly. Within moments Allerton was alone in the room. He stood up and walked across to the window. Outside, a white transit van pulled up to the back door and he watched Tweed emerge from the house to talk to the driver. Stepping back, he let the second man climb down from the cab, open the side door and take out a canvas bag, handing it over to Tweed who looked in briefly and waved as he went back into the house. From where he stood Allerton had clearly seen the contents, two guns lying on a stack of money.

Stepping back into the room, he glanced around him for hidden surveillance then went into the corridor. The temptation was to wander through the house looking for more evidence, but he had no camera with him. This was not about finding traces or breadcrumbs hidden in office drawers. This was about finding elephants.

Walking up the stairs to his room, he felt the wave of nausea hit him. He did not feel like he was going to vomit, or the gut churning he normally associated with food poisoning; instead he felt an unfurling of uncertainty about whether he'd make it to his bed before collapsing. He saw the door at the far end of the hall, just off to one side. Each step slowed, taking longer than the last, until he wondered if he would ever make it to comfort. Each time he moved his arms to steady himself his head spun away from his field of vision. One foot in front of the other. That's all he needed to do. One foot in front of the other. He placed his hand on the door handle, and only realised in that moment how hot he was, burning up in contrast to the coolness of the brass. Turning it first one way then the other, he collapsed over the threshold and landed face down on the coarse, worn, patterned carpet.

Voices woke him. He tried to move but the weight in his head was too much and something was strapped around his wrists and ankles. He tried to roll to one side. A boot pushed him back to his original position. He saw thick mud on the toe, smeared across his face as it was lifted away.

"You thought I was called The Hammer Man because of my auctioneering. Others have thought it's because it's how I lost these. Hammer to the mouth." Allerton vaguely sensed the figure through the gloom of his uncooperative eyes, and saw they were leaning on something.

"But it's because this is my favourite way of dealing with nosy pieces of shit like you."

Allerton opened his eyes more. The hammer's head was attached to a long wooden handle and he watched while The Hammer Man hefted it up onto his shoulder. Out of Allerton's sight someone cut the strap binding one of his legs and sat down on his hips, putting weight on his thigh.

The first blow shattered his ankle to splinters, the pain erupting as colours and taking his voice, reducing it to a gagging cough of protest. The second ruptured his knee, powdering the kneecap and leaving him coughing up blood where he bit his tongue.

"Now the other side," The Hammer Man said, and whoever was pinning Allerton down shifted their weight, grinding their boot-heel into his destroyed leg as they did so.

He didn't pass out and watched, detached within himself, as they tipped him onto a tarpaulin and carried him through the house, dropping him into a trailer. Hands still bound, he could do nothing to shift his position as he was dragged through the grounds, the blood seeping through his trousers legs.

3

When Allerton woke, it was the cold he noticed first. It embraced every part of him, prising through the shattered bone with precise fingers. Opening him up to let more frozen air in.

There was plenty of shattered bone to work with. His ankles and knees were destroyed, the wounds sealed with mud and leaves from where he had been dragged into the centre of the clearing. He tried to listen as he drifted in and out of himself, the pain cocooning him. Tried to hear if he was alone or watched. Through half-opened eyes, he tried to place himself. Tried to position himself in the world. Tried to see if he was seen.

He reached out and touched the stones, his hands recognising the carvings he'd only recently seen. Using the rocks, he levered himself up off the ground. His shoe caught in the dirt, wrenching his shattered ankle to one side, and he screamed.

There was no way of knowing if Tweed and The Hammer Man would be returning to finish what they started, or if they were going to leave him to starve in the woods. On private land far from any public rights of way, no-one was going to discover him until he was little more than bones in the dirt, and unless he crawled hand over hand to the nearest village without being seen, there was no way he was going to escape the little kingdom of The Hammer Man.

The operation was a failure. Even if he made it out alive instead of becoming another corpse amongst the tree roots, there was no evidence to present that The Hammer Man's operation was harvesting ivory. No elephants living in the woodlands of North Yorkshire. No corpses to present to the courts, apart from his own. There were probably many hidden in the dirt of the forest. Picked clean by the gangsters then picked clean by the woodland animals. Allerton was not unique. He knew he was one of a multitude.

Above him it was still night. He had no way of knowing how long had passed since they dumped him in the woods. No method of measuring time. Moving himself into a position where his legs didn't remind him of violence, he glanced around himself to see if he was truly alone. A couple of metres away he spotted his mobile phone, the screen smashed in, probably by the same hammer used on him. Even if he could reach it, he had no way of getting it to work.

His hand caught on a piece of paper pinned to the front of his jacket, clean enough to suggest it was attached after he was dragged to the clearing. A little moonlight came through the trees above him and he read the handwritten text disfiguring an old photo of him in uniform.

"WE KNEW ALL ALONG" it said, in block capitals that left no doubt that he had been fucked from the very moment he started investigating the illegal auctions. Sometimes the law and the criminal were two sides of the same coin, and sometimes they were lovers curled up together.

A pulse of pain erupted up his left leg and he tried to get comfortable, but the injury in his right leg mirrored the other.

There was no breeze. That thought came to him through everything else. The trees above him were silent. No movement in the canopy and no noise from the leaves against each other, yet somewhere in the distance he heard the trees moving enough for boughs to clatter.

Whatever was coming, Allerton had nowhere to go. Staying conscious was agony enough. He waited and tried to ignore the damage in his legs.

He saw the dirty white of their tusks first, still intact, parting the younger trees. They shook their heads to either side, breaking the saplings in two, but not quite coming into the clearing. He saw three of them, though there could have been more out of sight. Their tusks glowed in the thin moonlight, the rest of their bodies the colour of soil.

The elephants did not move, staying to the edge as if scared to enter the clearing. If they did approach, he had no way to defend himself, to protect his broken body from any kind of attack. He carried on staring at them until his night vision improved, though his sight still faltered with the damaged skin and bone that were once his legs. In a moment when his head was clear, Allerton stared through the branches, trying to memorise the exact position of the moon. The effort of moving to see the sky was too much and his body shut down once more.

When he woke, the elephants were closer. From a distance he thought the night was painting their hides. Up close he saw the fold and stretch of their skin was the colour of the darkness surrounding them, their hides marked by old injuries and wounds. The smallest, barely more than a calf, let its curiosity get the better of him and came right up to where Allerton lay. Bullet holes and broken spears scarred its back. Though young, Allerton knew the creature had been killed many times over the years. As it turned its head, he saw the sawn stump of its tusk, the scar of rich men wanting to become richer by harvesting the living. Allerton held out his hand and let his fingers brush the saw marks.

He didn't see the bull elephant charge. One moment the night was calm and the next the air was full of dust and something sheared between his ribs, shattering them and throwing him up into the air.

When he landed it was on skin far rougher and scarred than his own. He tried to cling on, feeling the hide tear his fingernails out. Running from the place of death where it had been brought by curiosity, the elephant did not care about an interloper. The wounds in Allerton's side ground against the elephant's back, transforming broken ribs and flesh into starbursts of pain. To let himself slide into unconsciousness was the only defence he still had.

When he came to, Allerton was surrounded by bulk and enwrapped by pain. There was no horizon to see, no trees to spot, just dawn above him and the cliffs of flesh beside.

He tried to shift, but there was no comfort anymore. Every movement sent rivers of pain through some part of him, until his body couldn't handle it anymore and shut down.

When he woke again the sun was high above them, clouds scudding across to obscure the blue of the sky. Several of the elephants were on their feet and moving around. His vision swam, blurring them as they circled the rest of the herd. He blinked, his eyes one of the only parts of him that was not broken, but the creatures stayed blurred, and when he looked closer he saw there was a transparency to them.

One of the elephants turned its vast head toward him and Allerton let his eyes close, not that it took much effort. When his consciousness returned, the sun had already started to drop and most of the herd were now on their feet. They didn't pay him any attention, though he was unsure if that was a good or a bad thing. Dying from intent or carelessness still meant he ended up dead.

There was something else too. The transparency was still there. When the creatures walked in just the right place to tower over him, the sky was visible through them. They were phantoms or ghosts, barely holding on to the real. What was it The Hammer Man said? They relied on belief. They needed belief to be real. Maybe they weren't being fed properly. The Hammer Man was not one for care, just acquisition. Maybe he had got complacent and stopped believing in the creatures, but Allerton believed. A three inch gaping hole in his side convinced him. He believed in them, and that belief was wrapped up in anger and pain and rage, and as he laid there on the forest floor, he realised that his anger and belief and pain and rage was what would get him out of the woods.

Lifting his shirt, he examined the wound in his side. That too seemed less real, though the pain was solid enough. Wincing in anticipation of the sensation, he pressed his fingers into the hollow and felt the exposed edges of his ribs. The scream was not something he had any control over, but the elephants did not pay him any attention and so he enwrapped himself in the image of The Hammer Man, of Tweed, of the sensation of the metal block splintering his limbs. He reached out to the creatures around him. They were not things of flesh and blood, but they could be made solid enough by faith, and watching them circle around, his torn chest underneath his hand, he had little choice but to believe in them. His belief was different though. It was not the hand-me-downs of folklore, or the conman's plot of exploitation. It was righteous and injured and he fed that to the elephants too. He fed them all his fear and rage. He fed them seeing their tusks lying on tables in draughty barns to be sold to the highest bidder. He fed them the mocking, toothless grin of The Hammer Man as he boasted and showed off signs of them, packaging their never-ending circle of death as a commodity, and he fed them his own desire for revenge, amplifying it as he fed them the location of their true enemies.

As he watched they became more solid and more agitated, raging against the woods as if the trees too were their enemy. They ground the forest floor to dust, and dragged their tusks through the mud. In a place they were never meant to be, murdered over and over again so men could get rich at their expense, and now Allerton could do some good. He could lead them out of their confinement in this killing ground to do the killing themselves. Law and order did not matter anymore. There was no law and order in the woods where death came at the tusk or the gun.

Most of the herd were now on their feet, heads turned toward the darkening sky and calling the moon to their cause. He would guide them toward the house, toward their real enemies. Only the electric fence still held them in, but he would free them. Find a way to cut off the power and loose them on the objects of their mutual hatred.

Nearby, a young female remained lying down. Hand over hand, Allerton dragged himself toward her, and pulled himself up on her back. She stood as if the only thing she was waiting for was to carry him, then the herd circled and formed up behind her.

The walk through the woods took longer than Allerton expected, though he faded in and out of consciousness. There was no need for him to focus anymore, the elephants willing to follow. When he next came to, they stood at the treeline, the lights from the house visible in the distance.

"Up there," he said, leaning forward to the elephant's ear. "But first let me free you from here. Turn off the current that keeps you prisoner."

The movement was barely more than a shrug, and he was launched in the air, landing on the copper cables with precision and intent. The electricity severed him from his body, and for a moment it was a relief to be distant from all the shattered parts of him, then the voltage returned again and again and again, each time the current surged through the wires.

Around him the herd stepped over his broken body, avoiding damaging him more, as if they knew that he was now part of the circuit designed to keep them in. They stepped over and walked onto the lawn, and he watched them trail up toward the house.

They did not need him to lead them. He was little more than a device to aid their escape. The burns running across his chest had scorched through his skin, his flesh seared from his bones. In the distance the elephants reached the house and over the sound of gunfire he listened as they found their victims, screams filling the night air to mix with his own.

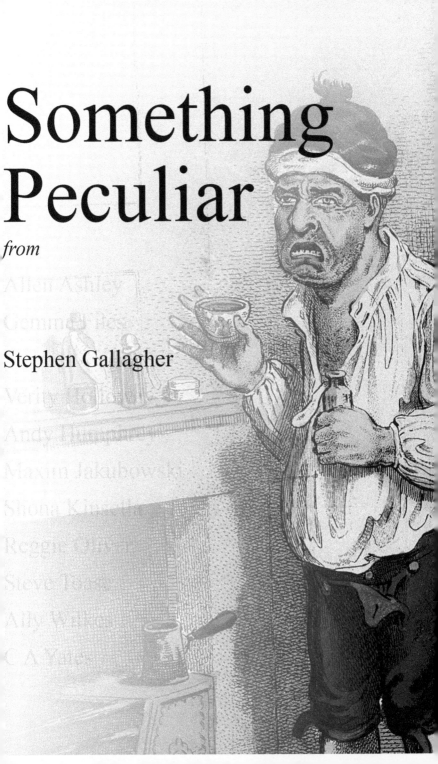

Something Peculiar

from

Night Flight

"…the entire shadow world of man's creation…"

He was a writer I'd never read, nor thought much about. His books were always around when I was growing up, a new one coming out every year or so. I'd see them on the W H Smith paperback stand by the railway station. Spy thrillers, crime, very much the kind of thing I liked, but… you know how it is with authors? With some you can read a few lines and it's like a friend speaking just to you – after one book you want to go out and buy up everything they've written. With others it's a polite exchange with a stranger, a pleasant interlude, and you don't really mind when it's over.

This all came about because I'd reached that point in life where you pay attention to your past. Some people hunt down vintage TV or the toys their mothers gave away. With me it was 60s music and 70s thrillers, but widening my interest to cover those areas I'd missed back in the day. You can call it nostalgia but I think of it more as an act of completion. Or I just love old paperbacks and their covers like people love their Georgian spoons or porcelain. Whatever.

To get back to my point; Francis Poole. Author of such novels as *Beyond All Treason* and *Stockholm Sabotage*. Always aware of him, never read him, and by the time I started looking there was nothing much out there.

It was a blogger's retrospective from ten years ago that captured my attention.

The blog was titled *Spies in the Attic,* a labour of love by someone whose passions included Eurotrash spy movies and *Destroyer*-type series fiction. The name was borrowed from the title of a work whose author he profiled thus: *Though without the longevity of a Le Carré and very much in the shadow of Fleming, Deighton, and the other giants of the great spy novel era, Francis Poole wrote consistently entertaining novels that continue to reward the reader's attention.*

That was enough to make me curious. Along with the article there was a blurry book cover image, and it was followed by a couple of reader comments as old as the post itself.

"Francis Poole?" Geraldine said, looking over my shoulder. "Was he that comedian?"

"One of my spy writers," I said. "One that I missed the first time around."

And one who'd been cold-shouldered by history, it seemed. Wikipedia offered bare-bones information in the form of two lines of biography and three dead links. The Internet Movie Database gave him two 'novel by' writer credits on feature films I'd never heard of.

I began to take it personally and the more I failed to discover, the more I felt the need to know. Early retirement from the Aerospace – their idea, not mine – had given me the time to pursue this stuff. So when an eBay search turned up a job lot of Francis Poole titles for not very much money, it was a no-brainer.

The box arrived after two days and it didn't disappoint. There were six hardcovers and two paperbacks. One of the paperbacks (*The Blackbird Tapes*) had suffered a hard life and was barely a reading copy, but the condition of the others was as described. You'd swear that *The Annihilators* had never even been opened. I placed *A Spy in the Attic* on my bedside table and added the others to the reading pile under it.

A week later I navigated back to the blog post and left a few lines in the comments section. After all these years it might never be seen by anyone, but it felt like the polite thing to do.

I wrote, *Great post, many thanks, and I read and much enjoyed* A Spy in the Attic *on your recommendation. Any thoughts on which of the Pooles I should line up for my next?* And I ticked the box to be notified if anyone should respond.

Nothing happened and over the next few days I concluded that the blog was one of those pieces of ghost writing that sit out on the web long after their creator has moved on. The other books stayed on the reading pile, passed-over for newer and more appealing acquisitions. Polite though I'd been in my assessment of it, and competent though the writing of it was, the Poole hadn't exactly set me alight.

Then…

Out of the blue came an email with a message alerting me to a response, and a link to take me to it.

It didn't go the way I'd been expecting.

I went to the site and read, *I saw your comment and had to join in with my thanks. I am Francis Poole, author of* A Spy in the Attic, *and am delighted that you found some pleasure in my writing. In fact I'm delighted that you were able to find the book at all! It has long been out of print, to my great frustration. Regarding your question as to what to read next, of all my novels I've always had a particular affection for* The Radetsky Madonna.

A couple of things, here.

Firstly, the shock of someone stepping out of my Google searches as a live human being. Despite any evidence, I'd been assuming that he must be long gone. And second, I didn't think that real authors did this kind of thing. I imagined them as more… aloof, somehow. Something like this broke the spell.

But I responded, *My pleasure, and I'll certainly be reading more.*

My inbox pinged again within the half-hour.

It was Poole again. He looked forward to hearing my opinion and went on, *Can I just add that you should probably avoid* Bonfire in Berlin, *which was ruined by a young and over-enthusiastic editor. He even changed my title! I keep alive a hope that some enterprising publisher may someday pick it up and present it in its original form, though I am not holding my breath. In my experience publishers direct their enterprise toward their most prominent names, thereby creating a self-sustaining cycle!*

I had mixed feelings about this. It gave me a sense of self-importance combined with a sinking heart. A response from the actual author! But what had I started? A mere comment had become a dialogue. Without ever intending it I'd set a bar that I now had to rise to.

Geraldine, my partner since Ruthie walked out on me, works in academia. She used to lecture but now she's something high-up in admin. She sometimes lets me use her password to search online resources that I couldn't otherwise access, and that's how I was able to swot up on Francis Poole.

Through my access to JSTOR, Project Muse, the OUP archives and thousands of magazines, I learned that he was born in Derbyshire and also used the pseudonyms William Salter and Reginald Mayne. After two comic novels that made no mark he turned to spy fiction, taking advantage of the public appetite sparked by the James Bond phenomenon. I remember it well. Ian Fleming had created the superspy, but it was the movies that lit the cultural fuse.

While the field showcased a few gritty Cold War realists telling grim stories of betrayal and despair, a horde of writers like Poole were offering their own variants on a formula of guns, girls, gadgets and supervillains. As Reginald Mayne he'd written five novels featuring Bruce 'Badger' Merkyn, a crack shot, two-fisted lothario and champion of the British Empire. From his Salter persona came couple of naval historicals featuring seafaring spy Charlie Clerke.

There was no *Radetsky Madonna* in the job lot, but there was a copy of *Bonfire in Berlin*. Curious to see what damage the young editor might have wrought, I looked at the first couple of pages. Then I carried on. It was a racy read and I enjoyed it more than *A Spy in the Attic*, though I could hardly say that to Poole. So I started *A Treasonable Excuse* but after about a hundred pages had to give up.

I reckoned I'd taken in enough to fake it, though, so I went back to the blog post with my comment only to find the domain expired, with the page redirecting to a Chinese gambling site.

And that, I thought, was that.

I'd pretty much scratched my Francis Poole itch so I stacked up the remaining books and moved them to the spare bedroom. *The Blackbird Tapes* went into the charity box and the Badger Merkyn to the paperback shelf, though it was vintage in age rather than quality. The posed cover was a B-grade male model waving a gun while a woman in nothing but high heels and her drawers peeked out from behind him. Both looked a bit embarrassed and the lighting had all the dramatic atmosphere of a school photo.

Geraldine saw me with the books and said, "Anything there I might go for?"

"I doubt it," I said. Her taste is for modern procedurals, the more detailed the better. I said, "He's another one of my 60s thriller writers so it's all a bit blokey."

"The Queen liked her Dick Francis."

"So I've heard, and don't call me Francis."

I showed her the cover.

"Oh, I get it," she said, and showed no further interest.

The email header in my inbox read *Is This You?* And I didn't need to open it because the message was all there in the preview pane. It read, *Forgive the intrusion but are you*

the SimonSays *who recently posted on the* Spies in the Attic *website?*

Signed *Sincerely, Francis Poole.*

I couldn't work out how he'd found me. The comments section didn't disclose email addresses, only usernames. At least that's how I understood it, but I couldn't go back and check on a site that was no longer there. The address on Poole's email was just a string of numbers.

While I didn't take any firm decision not to respond, I did let it slide. Give it long enough and the decision would make itself.

Poole wasn't willing to give it that long.

Within a couple of days a second message appeared, long and chatty and sprinkled with personal details.

Forgive me again, but when they closed down the site I was left wondering if you'd managed to get hold of The Radetsky Madonna, *and what you might have thought of it. No obligation to reply, of course. But if you were trying to find me I know I can be difficult to reach. How have you been? I see you live in Yorkshire. I had relatives in Helmsley. Many a happy summer I spent there.*

Obviously, he'd been looking into me. I'll admit it, I found this disturbing and I shared as much with Geraldine.

"I don't quite know what to feel about this," I said.

She wasn't as sympathetic as I might have hoped, but there you go.

"It works both ways," she said. "You googled him, he googled you."

"How'd he dig out that kind of detail? I'm hardly a public figure."

"You always pick the same username and you let people tag you on Facebook. I've warned you often enough. For an old guy he's done well to track you down. What age must he be?"

"Older than God by now. Probably got a geek nephew who sorts out his internet."

I checked Wikipedia again. He'd be eighty-two.

She was right, of course. Geraldine kept her internet profile to a minimum, used a webmail address for commerce, mostly kept her use within the University's intranet. Her one social media account was with a Beastie Boys fan group that was invitation-only. Me, I'd probably left a trail like a bin lorry across the decades.

But here was something. At some time in the last few days, Poole's two-line Wikipedia entry had been expanded into a couple of paragraphs. There was also a list of book titles and mention of two further pseudonyms that I hadn't known about. He was the second writer to compose a book entirely on a word processor (Deighton was reckoned to be the first). He'd made and lost a fortune by the standards of the day. A read between the lines suggested a bitter family rift and a later life dogged by health problems.

"He's old and he sounds lonely," Geraldine said. "You're probably the first person to show an interest in the past twenty years."

After that, what could I do?

Hi Francis. Sorry for the silence, I just found your message in my spam folder I lied. *No luck picking up a* Radetsky *but I've plenty here to go at.*

The answer came within a couple of minutes.

I'd send you a copy if I could, he wrote. *Everything's gone.*

That was how it began. What followed over the next couple of weeks was an on-off, mostly one sided conversation (his side) in which I got the life story of Francis Poole. His professional life, mostly, though more personal details sometimes threatened to surface.

I always made a point of not rushing to reply, so after a while the messages were limited to a couple a day. I learned about his early years in newspapers, and the discipline that drove his prolific output. He'd ghosted romance fiction under a publisher's house name. Most of his early books had been optioned for film, but only two of them had made it into production. The completed films bore no resemblance to their sources. A third that he'd tried to set up himself fell apart after he brought in producers who hijacked the project and gave the scripting job to their office junior.

I got his opinions of his contemporaries. Of critics. Of literary versus popular fiction. *People look up to one and down on the other*, he wrote, *despite that being where the positive view of the human spirit is found.*

On lone wolf Private Eye stories: *Men living lives of brutal solitude but with an inexhaustible supply of Old Friends showing up with their problems.*

Of himself he said, *I can wish I'd been a better writer. But I think I was as good as I could be.*

He'd no illusions, no regrets, he said, other than the big one over his estranged son.

"God almighty," I told Geraldine, "I'm his therapist."

"You're a saint," she said, but dryly.

Around that time I picked up a new Twitter follower. I never post, just follow a few accounts, so that's unusual. Then a Facebook friend request, also from a source I didn't recognise. But when I looked more closely at the Twitter avatar, it was a tiny version of the book cover from the blog post that started it all.

An author stalking a fan. This had to be a first.

I told Geraldine, "I should probably dial it down a bit. Try and wean him off. It's getting to be a full time job."

So I did that, and everything went quiet for a while.

Then one morning Geraldine said, "Look at this."

She handed me her phone. The Signal app was opened to her Beastie Boys group and showed a run of messages from half an hour before. I should say that like any fandom, they'd got together around a shared interest and stayed together for years to talk about anything and everything else. Someone had responded to one of Geraldine's remarks with a crying-with-laughter emoji.

I said, "What am I looking at?"

"The avatar," she said, so I tapped and expanded the small user image alongside the crying face.

It was the same blurry book cover shot.

"It's him, isn't it?" she said.

"How did he get in?"

"You tell me."

"I've never even mentioned you."

"That hasn't stopped him."

"Send me a screenshot," I said.

I went back online with the screenshot and the header, *Francis, Is this You?* And the reply came straight away, as if he'd been waiting to be called out.

I've overstepped, he wrote. *I know it. I apologise.*

My urge was to send a simple *WTF?* But instead I wrote, *Why would you do this?*

I haven't told you everything.

There was a brief pause and then he went on:

I'm in a place where they look after me. I failed as a husband, I failed as a father. Everyone I knew is gone. Everyone around me is lost to dementia. This online life is the only life I have.

In spite of myself I felt bad. I wrote, *Does your son know where you are?*

A pause and then:

My son put me here.

I waited but there was nothing more, and nothing I could think of to add. So I closed the app and then closed the laptop.

Geraldine told me later that he'd deleted himself from their group. She'd asked around and no one could say who'd added him. I could see that she was still bothered by the intrusion. As for me, I kept thinking about that last message. *My son put me here.* Along the way I'd picked up some hints about their falling-out; something about the son blaming the father for his treatment of his mother, but none of the specifics. Whatever the story, it was a miserable outcome.

The more I thought about it – and I couldn't help thinking about it – the more discomfort I felt.

I went into the spare bedroom and looked over the remaining Poole titles with a fresh eye. Here was his legacy. His thoughts unheard, his words no longer read. *The Annihilators,* one of the later novels, was a pristine first edition. An unread review copy, maybe? I took it down and opened it to see if there was a comp slip. What I found was an inscription.

For Michael, with love from Dad. Followed by a scribble that was almost certainly Francis Poole's signature and a date of September 1982.

One after another, I went through the others. *Unfriendly Fire* and *The Praetorians* had similar inscriptions. The Badger Merkyn paperback had no inscription, but I could see the suggestion of a bookmark and when I fanned the pages an old Polaroid fell out. The photograph's colours had faded to pinks and purples but the image was of a man and a boy of around twelve years old standing with a brand-new bicycle. The man had to be Francis Poole, identifiable from dustjacket photographs, and written on the back was *Michael and the bike, Christmas 1978.*

I was willing to bet that these were the estranged son's presentation copies. Gifted with pride from his father, boxed up for a book charity and dumped on the market for a pittance.

I took out my phone and got a shot of the Polaroid, then forwarded it to Poole with the header, *I made a discovery* and an explanation in the body of the text. The explanation was as tactful as I could make it.

He winged back, *I can't see pictures.*

Can't see or can't receive?

It's complicated.

I can mail it to you.

He replied immediately with the address of what appeared to be a care home, and added, *If you were inclined to visit, I'd welcome that, but I understand why you may not want to. I've intruded into your life. Please forgive me.*

I told Geraldine, "I looked it up, it's about an hour's drive away."

"Does that mean you'll go?"

"No," I said. "Of course not."

Of course I went.

It took me more than an hour and what lay at the end of the journey was a big old house in its own grounds, the kind a prosperous merchant might have built for his family at a safe distance from where the money was made. Not grand enough to preserve, too useful to demolish. Extended and altered and well past its best. Poole was reaching his own journey's end not far from where he'd begun it.

I parked on the lane and went in through the gates. The driveway was surfaced with loose stone chips, the messy kind. The grounds were about as tidy as one general handyman with a wheelbarrow might keep them, if the handyman also had other duties. There was a wheelchair ramp to the front door and an electronic buzzer under the old brass bellpush.

I buzzed and waited and eventually someone came. A care worker in blue scrubs and a paper mask.

I said, "I'm here for Francis Poole?"

"Are you a family member?"

I'd come too far to be turned away so I said, "Yes I am."

"Do you have a test result?"

"Do I need one? I haven't done this before."

I was allowed into a cramped vestibule with an admin office just off it, where I was given a Covid test kit to self-administer. I swabbed and placed the drops on the test strip and went back to my car to sit out the required half-hour.

I'd expected a care home but I could see now that The Gables was actually a nursing home, a step up the ladder of medical needs. When he'd said *It's complicated* I wondered if Poole was hinting at problems with his sight. Yet he'd seemed eager enough to have the photograph.

I took the paperback out of my pocket. I'd kept the Polaroid in its pages for protection. There was young

Michael with his bike and his 70s George Best haircut. Poole was in high baggy trousers with braces and rolled-up shirtsleeves, looking like a 1950s dad on a Butlin's holiday.

With time to kill I glanced through the book. The Merkyn stories were adult parodies with all the erotic daring of a British sex comedy. Our Bulldog Drummond-style hero worked for the Foreign Office, so was known as Badger Merkyn of the FO. The story title was *Night Flight to Swarfega* and its villain was a mystery figure known only as The Red Todger.

I checked my watch, returned the book to my pocket, and made my way back up the drive.

A different assistant checked my test and then gave me a mask to wear before leading me through. The main hallway was spotless and freshly painted with a few simple, low-cost frills. We passed a once-grand stairway with added safety gates and a chairlift. I glanced into a lounge where a TV was playing to a room of silent sitters and almost lost my guide. She'd turned into a corridor and I hurried to catch up.

The place was strangely tranquil, the TV the loudest sound in the building. Each door along here bore a resident's name and some that we passed were pinned open. Through one I saw an elderly woman in a bed with a crocheted cover. She was alone in the room. A jug of water and a vase of flowers stood on the table beside her.

"Mister Poole!"

The voice came from behind me. It was a moment before I remembered that I'd claimed family status to get in. I turned and saw a woman in maroon scrubs with a sheaf of papers in one hand. I later realised that the staff uniforms were colour-coded according to levels of responsibility.

"Sorry," I said.

"I'm Rebecca. You won't have seen me before, I'm the new manager." Mindful of the open doors nearby, she lowered her voice. "You agreed to a DNR notice on your father?"

I hesitated and she went on, "I just wanted to check that you weren't here to rescind the order. I have to warn the staff if that's the case."

"I'm not here to change anything," I said.

With a nod of her head she let the other woman go, and led me onward herself. I was nervous now, hoping I wouldn't be drawn into a conversation where I'd get caught out.

But we'd already reached the room. "You can stay as long as you like," she said, standing aside for me to enter. "You're his only visitor. Press the buzzer if you want anything."

She left me then.

The blinds were half-drawn so the light was subdued. I could just about recognise the room's occupant. But only just. What I wasn't ready for was the rest of it.

The breathing tube, the monitors, the heart machine. To my untrained eye the wasted figure in the bed was on complete life support.

I turned my head to look at the door. The name on it was Poole's, printed on a card and slipped into a holder. At that moment my phone went *ping!* and without even thinking I reached for it.

A message from Francis Poole.

I need to explain.

Even as I was reading, a second message joined the first.

I know you're here. They just reported your flow test online.

I wrote back, *Who are you?* I'd driven fifty miles for this. The bare words couldn't show the anger that went into them.

Are you in the room? If you're in the room then you can see I'm helpless. This is the only way I can reach out. I can hear nothing. I can see nothing, feel nothing.

"This is a fucking joke," I said aloud, and I turned and walked out. I saw no one on the way and when I reached the exit door, I couldn't open it. I stood there seething while one of the care assistants from earlier came to my aid, entering a four-digit code.

"We can't let the residents know the numbers," she explained. "Some go out onto the road."

All the way home, my phone was pinging. I almost had an accident and after that I muted it. Even then the screen would light up so I laid it face-down on the passenger seat.

When I got back, Geraldine asked, "How did it go?"

I still couldn't get my head around what had happened. So I just said, "Didn't see him. Just left the book."

I hadn't left the book.

Who was behind this? As a practical joke it was elaborate, cruel, and utterly without point. And I know it's wrong, but I was fuming more at being played than at the way in which they'd made use of a sick man to do it. Why me? Was it someone I knew? It had to be. I'd work out who. But I wouldn't engage any further. That would simply be feeding the troll.

And the messages kept coming.

My son had me placed here and then walked away. I was frail but I could function until something exploded in my brain. At least that's how I perceived it. After that there was nothing. No light, no sound, no sense of time. There are no words for how terrifying that was. I was adrift in darkness until they put me on the machines. Then everything changed. I seized on the sensation. It was a strange music like a ringing in the ears. When I pushed back, I felt it change. It became like a dialogue. At first I wondered if there was a language here, and then I saw that it was more. It was the entire shadow world of man's creation, carried in the wires. My connection was weak but it was real, and the landscape was endless.

I turned off my phone. Then, on my laptop, an email.

I didn't try to learn, I merely submitted. I let it run through me. Slowly I began to understand.

I deleted the email. A chatbot popped up in the corner of the screen.

I learned to recognise the feel of my own name. That's how I found you. You were the only one reaching out from the other side. You are the only voice in my darkness.

In the end I caved in and wrote, *What do you want?*

I want it to end, he wrote back.

I can't do that.

Please.

I realised that I'd broken my own rule. I'd engaged, which is exactly what my unknown tormentor wanted. Yet however hard I tried to pin it on some joker, I couldn't come up with a likely candidate. Or any reason why I might deserve this.

Please.

It kept coming at me. I changed my SIM card, changed my provider, got a new email account, all to no effect. When I called out to our smart speaker, "Alexa, Play Radio Four," the Alexa voice replied, "Are you alone?" and only when I lied and said, "No," did she go ahead and gave me the News.

Then Geraldine said, "He's back in the group. I thought you'd sorted him out."

"What's he saying?"

"Nothing now. Kicking him out didn't work so we shut it down and started another."

She opened her phone and looked at the screen.

"Oh, for fuck's sake," she said, and walked out of the room.

They'd stopped the Covid testing since my last visit, but the mask was still a requirement. That suited me. They'd have cameras. Once again I played the relative card to get me in.

I said to the care worker, "Is Rebecca around?"

"She's in her office."

Rebecca was on a landline call, so I waited. When she was done she hung up the phone and said, "How can I help?"

I asked her about the DNR order and she said, "That's the authority you signed. Do Not Resuscitate. It means if your father passes we'll allow him a natural death."

"What's his prognosis now?"

"I'm afraid there isn't one. Not in the sense of improvement or recovery. I know it's hard to face, but you might think about withdrawing support."

"Letting him go? Is that an option?"

"Was this not discussed? It certainly should have been. As next of kin with power of attorney, it's your call."

Of course I wasn't any kin at all, which soon would have become clear if we'd taken it any further.

Without giving myself away I worked out that a switch-off had been the doctors' recommendation, but the family – almost certainly Michael – had refused that, so the Do Not Resuscitate order was some kind of compromise. It sounded to me like the son was determined to keep the old man hanging on, and not out of kindness.

I was left to make my own way to Francis Poole's room. A chair had appeared by the bed in anticipation of further visits, but otherwise all was the same; the tubes, the catheters, the relentless rhythm of the respirator, the withered unconscious mummy at the centre of it all. They kept his hair neatly combed, I noticed.

I'd left my phone switched off until now. It came on with a flurry of new messages that I didn't read.

I just typed, *I'm back in the room.*

Will you do it?

I'm studying the situation.

I'd say God bless you but there's no one of that name here.

Are you sure about this?

May you never know the terror of living in an endless pit of nothingness.

I took a closer look at the setup. All the cables were plugged into a wall panel with locking connectors. They couldn't be accidentally dislodged but the release looked fairly straightforward.

When I stepped out into the corridor everything was quiet. I listened for a while and then crossed over to the light switches. I had an idea for covering my tracks. With rooms both sides there was only one window and that was the frosted glass of the fire door at the far end.

Throwing the switches created a staggered effect with shafts of daylight from open doors. Anyone noticing might think there'd been a power outage. After half a minute I switched the lights back on. Then I went back inside and disconnected the respirator.

It was supposed to be quick. I thought he'd just quietly expire. Instead it was horrible. The body struggled to breathe on its own and began choking on the pipe. I knew I'd made a bad mistake and quickly reconnected the power, but it was too late. He spasmed on the bed three, four times, and then made an awful sound. I'd started this but I couldn't go through with it. The call buzzer was a red button on a cable draped over the bedhead. I pressed it and waited.

It took more than two minutes for one of the nursing staff to respond, and Poole finally expired just as she reached us. I was standing well back.

"I don't know what happened," I said.

She said nothing.

I said, "It looks like he's gone. Has he?"

She was looking at the machines and taking a pulse at his neck. "I'm not allowed to do anything," she said. "You understand that?"

"I do."

Still feeling for a pulse, she was frowning at the machines. There was an electronic display and I suspected an error message.

I said, "All the lights went out for a few seconds. Could that have caused anything?"

The lights were my alibi. Evidence of a power dip. She took her hand from the patient's neck and reached for the call button.

"Can you take a seat in Reception?" she said, and gave the button three long presses.

"Is it over?"

"Yes," she said. "I'm very sorry, he's gone."

The thing is, I could see it. I'd never seen anyone dead before. On TV it's just someone with their eyes closed. In reality it's unmistakeable.

By 'a seat in Reception' I assumed she meant the bench in the hall at the bottom of the stairlift. On the way I was passed by Rebecca, hurrying in the opposite direction. She shot me a look and I knew I'd been rumbled. I bypassed the bench and went on to the door. I'd memorised the four digit code from last time, and they hadn't changed it. Seconds later I was out on the driveway. My car was on the lane, as before. I kept the mask on until I reached it.

Driving away, I was in a state. Guilt, relief, total turmoil. Over something I could never share. Never expect anyone to believe.

I'm still not sure I believed it myself.

Could I live with this? Could I have carried on otherwise? I'd been beaten into submission. If what I'd done was an act of mercy, it didn't feel like it. The thought that Poole's mean-spirited son might get the blame was of no consolation.

The device in my pocket pinged with a new message. Out of habit I tensed up, but that had to be Geraldine. After switching providers in my unsuccessful attempts to get away from Poole I'd yet to give my new number to many people. When it was safe I'd pull over and let her know that I was coming home.

I often use the phone to navigate so I have one of those holders on the dashboard. Keeping one hand on the wheel I got the phone from my pocket and let it click onto the magnet.

Francis Poole had written, *Whenever you're ready*.

Six seconds ago. It must have been held up in the system. No?

But then after half a minute:

Please

Then

Is there a problem?

I kept looking away from the road and then having to drag my attention back to the traffic. He couldn't be doing this. I'd seen him die.

I saw a spot to pull in and hit the brakes so hard that a truck slammed down on its horn as it swerved to overtake.

Then as I came to a halt:

Please don't change your mind. You can't imagine what this is like

Then

Let me go

Then

Still waiting

I wanted to pull the SIM card but I didn't have anything to slide it out with. Broke my thumbnail trying to get to it. Held down all the buttons but the phone wouldn't shut down.

Something's changed. I'm still here but everything else is gone. Now there's only you

Finally the device went dark. With one last text before the silence.

talk to me

Allen Ashley
allenashley.com

Gemma Files
musicatmidnight-gfiles.blogspot.com

Stephen Gallagher
stephengallagher.com

Verity Holloway
verityholloway.com

Andy Humphrey
twitter.com/andyhumphrey11

Maxim Jakubowski
maximjakubowski.co.uk

Shona Kinsella
shonakinsella.com

Reggie Oliver
isfdb.org/cgi-bin/ea.cgi?Reggie_Oliver

Steve Toase
stevetoase.wordpress.com

Ally Wilkes
allywilkes.com

C A Yates
chloeyates.com

blackshuckbooks.co.uk

Also available:

GREAT BRITISH HORROR 1:
GREEN AND PLEASANT LAND

FEATURING STORIES BY

JASPER BARK
A.K. BENEDICT
RAY CLULEY
JAMES EVERINGTON
RICH HAWKINS
V.H. LESLIE
LAURA MAURO
ADAM MILLARD
DAVID MOODY
SIMON KURT UNSWORTH
BARBIE WILDE

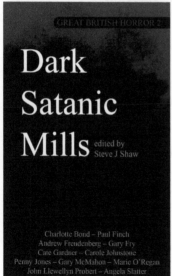

GREAT BRITISH HORROR 2:
DARK SATANIC MILLS

FEATURING STORIES BY

CHARLOTTE BOND
PAUL FINCH
ANDREW FREUDENBERG
GARY FRY
CATE GARDNER
CAROLE JOHNSTONE
PENNY JONES
GARY MCMAHON
MARIE O'REGAN
JOHN LLEWELLYN PROBERT
ANGELA SLATTER

Also available:

GREAT BRITISH HORROR 3:
FOR THOSE IN PERIL

FEATURING STORIES BY

STEPHEN BACON

SIMON BESTWICK

GEORGINA BRUCE

KAYLEIGH MARIE EDWARDS

JOHNNY MAINS

PAUL MELOY

THANA NIVEAU

ROSALIE PARKER

KIT POWER

GUY N. SMITH

DAMIEN ANGELICA WALTERS

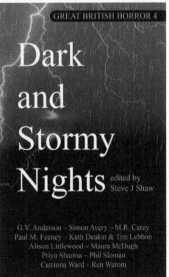

GREAT BRITISH HORROR 4:
DARK AND STORMY NIGHTS

FEATURING STORIES BY

G.V. ANDERSON

SIMON AVERY

M.R. CAREY

PAUL M. FEENEY

KATH DEAKIN & TIM LEBBON

ALISON LITTLEWOOD

MAURA MCHUGH

PRIYA SHARMA

PHIL SLOMAN

CATRIONA WARD

REN WAROM

Also available:

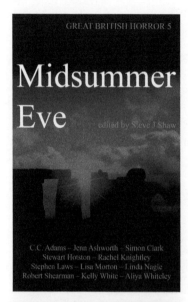

GREAT BRITISH HORROR 5:
MIDSUMMER EVE

FEATURING STORIES BY

C.C. ADAMS
JENN ASHWORTH
SIMON CLARK
STEWART HOTSTON
RACHEL KNIGHTLEY
STEPHEN LAWS
LISA MORTON
LINDA NAGLE
ROBERT SHEARMAN
KELLY WHITE
ALIYA WHITELEY

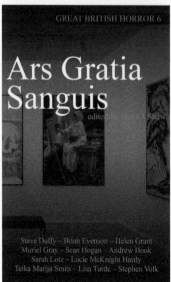

GREAT BRITISH HORROR 6:
ARS GRATIA SANGUIS

FEATURING STORIES BY

STEVE DUFFY
BRIAN EVENSON
HELEN GRANT
MURIEL GRAY
SEAN HOGAN
ANDREW HOOK
SARAH LOTZ
LUCIE MCKNIGHT HARDY
TEIKA MARIJA SMITS
LISA TUTTLE
STEPHEN VOLK

Also available:

GREAT BRITISH HORROR 7:
MAJOR ARCANA

FEATURING STORIES BY

GARY BUDDEN
DAN COXON
MALCOM DEVLIN
STEVEN J DINES
CARLY HOLMES
IDA KEOGH
ALISON MOORE
LYNDA E RUCKER
JONATHAN SIMS
ANNA TABORSKA
CONRAD WILLIAMS

Milton Keynes UK
Ingram Content Group UK Ltd.
UKHW041049290923
429627UK00001B/26

9 781913 038847